Sun, Sea and Secrets

by May J. Panayi

First book in the 'Sun' series

Chapter One

She arrived like a thief in the night. The air was hot, thick and balmy as the taxi driver hauled her cases out of the boot of the cab. She said "efharisto polee" (thank you very much), and handed him a large tip. He gave her a semi-toothless grin, and replied "parakalo" (you're welcome), before climbing back into the cab and driving away, leaving her alone in the night.

The hotel foyer was deserted, and lit only with dim nightlights. She waited a moment or two to see if anyone emerged, and then called out hesitantly, "Yassas." (Hello.)

A stocky, dark haired, bearded man emerged from a door somewhere behind reception, looking like he had been awake for at least a week. His eyes were droopy with fatigue, but kind of wired as if caffeine was the only thing keeping him standing, which it probably was. "Yassas Kireeah" (Hello Miss,) he said, trying to sound as welcoming as someone could at four in the morning when all they wanted to do was sleep.

"Melenee Ella Hudson." (My name is Ella Hudson.)

"Ah, you are English," said the man, immediately changing language as soon as he realized.

"Miss Hudson, yes we are expecting you, we have your reservation. Could we have your passport please?"

Ella handed her passport to the man who put it away in a desk drawer.

"You are in room 36, at the end of the corridor on the third floor," he said handing her a key on a key fob which was a brightly painted ceramic representation of the Greek flag. "I will come round and carry your cases up for you."

"There is no need, thank you. They are light, and I can manage just fine," Ella replied.

"Okay no problem; just call me if you want anything. The bar is open all night."

"Endaksi, efharisto," (OK, thanks,) answered Ella, heading off to the staircase to find her room.

Ella unpacked quickly, getting an unpleasant job out of the way sooner rather than later, so as to more quickly feel settled in and relaxed.

She peeled off her travel weary clothes, and threw them over the back of a chair, pulling a thin cotton slip over her head from the drawer, and collapsing on top of the bed, falling asleep instantly.

She was awoken by the sound of children playing in the pool three floors below. She opened the sliding patio door and stepped out onto the balcony. It was like stepping out into an oven, after the air conditioned room, though once she grew accustomed to the temperature, there was the soothing presence of a nice sea breeze that made the whole oven sensation more pleasant.

She looked down at the pool area.

A few children were playing in the shallow end with pool inflatables. A Nordic looking chap was swimming lengths determinedly, as if in training for the Olympics. A young couple were pressed together very intimately against the side of the pool at the deep end, kissing enthusiastically, without the apparent need to stop for air.

Several people lay on towels on sun beds around the pool, reading or just sunbathing.

In the distance, beyond the pool and hotel grounds, the shape of the village could be seen. Mainly just blocks of square whitewashed houses with uniformly red tiled roofs. But the church tower with its lonely bell stood out above the rest of the buildings, painted with pale blue to accent the white of its walls.

Looking left from her balcony, Ella could see the sea, flat, calm and the deepest blue. To the right were volcanic hills, dotted with shrubs and wild herbs. As she gazed at the hills, which were not really big enough to be called mountains, she saw the shape of a lizard amongst the rocks. Greek volcanic mountains and hills were like that, you could always see shapes in them if you looked at them for any length of time. It was like looking at the shapes in clouds, only more permanent because you could come back to the rock shapes again and again, once you knew they were there. It was very meditative. She knew that she would sit and drink tea and look at the lizard shape so often, it would become like an old friend before she left. She turned the balcony chair to face the rocks; she knew that would be her favourite view, though most people would sit the opposite way round looking at the sea.

She picked out some clothes, had a quick wash and hurried down to the restaurant for a light breakfast. She had grabbed her purse and a bag for supplies, and was going to head right out for a walk to the village, to get some bread rolls, tea and coffee for her room, maybe a couple of local delicacies, and most importantly a walking map of the island.

Ella had a light breakfast of Greek bread and honey with fresh coffee in the hotel restaurant, and then set out along the road that joined the hotel to the village. Really it was more of a track than a road. It had no pavements, but then most of the main roads in Greece had no pavements either. One just moved over to the edge if any traffic came along. What made this one more of a track was, that it was really only wide enough for a car and a motorbike, so cars coming from opposite directions would have to squeeze past each other in slightly wider passing places, and also that there was practically no traffic on it. A somewhat larger road that could be described as a main road ran parallel to the track, connecting the village to other villages and ultimately to the town and capital. Most traffic used this road. The only traffic using the track, were people who lived on the track, as houses were dotted along it every hundred yards or so, and people visiting those houses, either walking or in vehicles. Most tourists hired a car and left the hotel via the main road, so the result was, the track was very still and peaceful.

Low stone walls defined the boundaries of the houses that edged the track, and Ella walked slowly, watching the lizards sunning themselves on the stones. As she drew level, most would scurry off between the gaps to hide in the stone wall, but some were bolder and ignored her and carried on sunning themselves.

In some places, the rocks were already so hot that the lizards were alternately holding one foot in the air away from the heat, rather than moving into the shade. The ones that did scurry away were very fast, their reptilian bodies heated to turbo speed.

Along the track, plants grew abundantly. Palms, pomegranate trees, and everywhere olive and lemon trees, not seeming to be on anyone's land, just growing in sheer joy of proliferation. Food was ripening everywhere Ella looked. It was like the garden of Eden. She thought it would be hard to starve to death in a land like this.

Although it was still quite early in the day, only mid morning, the sun was already quite hot. Ella felt like one of the lizards, soaking the warmth into her skin, feeling it energise and rejuvenate her.

Outside some of the houses, old women dressed in black, despite the heat, sat on the front porches, facing the track. Ella nodded and said 'Kalimera' (Good morning,) to them as she passed, and they mostly either just nodded, or grinned broadly, and often toothlessly, and said 'kalimera' back.

After a time, the track curved round towards the village, and it could be seen clearly in the distance. More houses, packed closely together with almost no gardens, sheltered the church in the village square as if they were forming a protective huddle around it. But before that all started, here on the outskirts, was a little tourist gift shop. Thinking they may well have a walking map of the island, Ella pushed open the door, accompanied by a little tinkle of bells, and went inside, to the cool shade of the shop.

The shop appeared to be empty, but Ella knew someone would appear from a back room soon enough. There was no rush for anything in this heat. She looked around at all the ceramic ornaments and porcelain statues of Greek Gods and Goddesses. There were plates with blue and white island scenes and kitchen ware decorated with olives. Salad tossers made of olive wood, and tea towels and aprons with the same olive motive as the bowls and plates. In another section, jewellery hung from racks, and elsewhere, cards and pictures. It was by the cards and pictures that Ella spotted a selection of maps. She looked through a few, discarding the ones in German, to find the most suitable one in English. She selected that, as well as one entirely in Greek; as it was handy when off the beaten track, deep in the countryside, to have a Greek map to ask directions if lost.

Sometime, while Ella had been looking at the maps, a large man had stepped out from the back of the shop and smiled at her from the counter.

'Kalimera' Ella said to him, smiling back.

'Kalimera sas' he replied. (Good morning to you.) She put both the maps on the counter and said 'Aftou, parakalo.' (These, please.)

'Ah, you are English,' he said. Ella wondered how the Greeks always did that, no matter how perfectly you pronounced the words, they always knew. Some trace of accent must give it away. They seemed able to do it with any nationality too, even being able to perceive the difference between Dutch and German by accent alone. She thought it quite a talent.

'Yes,' replied Ella, 'I just got here last night.'

'And so you plan to explore our island?' he pointed at the maps about to be purchased.

'Well, not just that,' she answered, 'I am also on a bit of a hunt. There is someone I am trying to find, but he is a mystery person from the past and I do not even know his name. Nor do I have a picture.'

'Aha, a bright sunny day on a Greek island, and a mystery, that must have a story to go with it. Sit down.' The rotund man pulled out a stool from behind the counter and put it by her. 'My name is Bani, and my wife is Haroula. Haroula, come out here,' he called into the back of the shop.

'My name's Ella,' Ella introduced herself.

From the dark room out back, a short, dark haired and equally corpulent woman waddled. Bani rattled something off to her in Greek very quickly, which Ella did not quite catch, and she disappeared out back again. From under the counter, Bani produced three shot glasses and an unlabelled glass bottle of clear liquid.

Ella sat down as he meticulously poured three shots of the stuff.

'Have a glass of Tsipouro, and tell us your story,' said Bani as Haroula reappeared with a plate full of chocolate bread sticks. Bani and Haroula sat down, picked up their glasses of Tsipouro and looked at her expectantly. Ella picked up her own glass and said 'Yammas.' (Cheers.)

She pulled an old photo out of her purse, depicting a glamorous woman, with dark hair piled on top of her head, in an off the shoulder cream dress, looking like a film star straight out of the sixties.

'This woman lived here on this island for a little while in the sixties. She had a brief encounter with a local man, but I do not know his name. I would like to try and find out about him if I can, so I am asking if anyone remembers her. Her name was Elizabeth.'

Bani and Haroula peered at the photo and at each other. Bani took a sip of his Tsipouro and sighed.

'This is the best Tsipouro I have ever tasted. My friend from the next village makes it himself.'

'It is very good,' agreed Ella, 'very smooth, with a lovely raisiny aftertaste.'

Haroula offered the chocolate breadsticks. Ella took one and tried it. It was delicious, and she told Haroula so.

'I do remember this woman' began Bani, 'She stayed in the village for a few months. She worked at Manolis' bar for most of the summer of '61.'

'Was there anyone she was especially friendly with around then?' asked Ella. 'You know, anyone she was seeing, a boyfriend?'

'Well,' replied Bani, 'she was friends with a few people. I can think of three lads she was friends with, and a local girl.'

'Can you tell me anything about them?' asked Ella.

'Why is it of interest to you?' enquired Bani. 'It was such a long time ago, and just one summer.'

'Elizabeth was my mother,' began Ella. 'She came here back then, but I only know because I found photos with the name of the island and the date written on the back. There was a coaster for Manolis bar too, and some pressed dried flowers. My mother died when I was almost five, in an accident, and I was brought up in a home. I only had one small box of things to remember her by, and I have gradually been working backwards through them, meeting people who knew her, and going to places she went, trying to get an idea of who she was and what her life was like. This is one of the last places I had to visit, so if I can meet anyone who remembers her from back then, it would make me very happy.'

'Paythakee' murmured Haroula.

Ella knew this meant something like my child, or my little lamb chop, something said in sympathy to her situation and kind of mothering, in a very Greek way of showing their love and kindness to strangers.

'She was friends with Heleni, Nikos, Yiorgios, and Panicos. Of course Manolis' bar is still open, but his son runs it now, as he died five years ago. But they do have a lot of photos from the old days on the wall. You should definitely go there.

Heleni married Christos Argyros and they live out in Limonaki now. I'm not sure of the exact address, but there are only six houses in Limonaki, so if you asked everyone would know.' Bani jotted the information down on a piece of paper as he spoke. 'Now Nikos, he went to the capital, Vathy, but he never comes back here, so I don't know where he lives. He was a fisherman back then, so if he is still doing the same thing and living in the same place, it might be worth asking at the harbour. His full name is Nikos

Andreadis. Yiorgos, I'm sorry to say, died of a heart attack about ten years ago. He still has family in the village. If you ask at the bank where his daughter, Nikki Michaelides works, you might be able to find out something maybe. Panicos went away to Athens for a few years, but I heard he came back to the island, like everyone does in the end. Do you remember where he lives now Haroula? Panicos Papadopoulous.'

Haroula frowned and thought for a moment, clearly going through a mental filing system of years of news and gossip. 'I think he lives in Agios Nikalaus now,' she finally decided. 'I think he drives a bus.'

'Thank you so much,' said Ella, as Bani handed her the piece of paper, 'you have been so very helpful. I feel like I at least have somewhere to start now. Could you possibly tell me the way to Manolis' bar please?'

Bani gave her directions, which were pretty straightforward; on down the road into the village then about midway down main street on the right was Manolis Taverna. It had a big sign, he assured her, and she would find it easily.

Ella pulled out another picture, a tatty old photograph. It showed a woman who was recognisably Elizabeth, posing with a man, a little taller than her. He wore sunglasses and a baseball cap, and was kind of hidden by Elizabeth, so it was very difficult to make out what he looked like. She showed it to Bani and Haroula.

'I don't suppose you can see who that is with her in the picture?'

They both looked but after a while, sadly shook their heads- Greeks hate to have to say no to a request. They could not make it out from such a picture, it could have been anyone.

Bani chatted to Ella for a bit longer about his years living in New York. It was fascinating and Ella could have stayed all day, but the tsipouro was giving her a warm buzz, and she was aware that there was a prescribed polite time to this sort of casual socializing, so she bought the maps, thanked them again and left. They of course told her to come back soon and let them know how she was getting on. Outside, the heat of the midday sun hit Ella full body, like walking into an oven. She immediately felt soaked in a thin film of sweat, and felt like gravity had increased and she was about three times heavier. But she felt good, like she was getting somewhere at last. She carried on along the track into the village. She realised she would need to eat some sort of lunch at her next stop, as the tsipouro had made her a little bit light headed and tipsy. She decided that when she got to Manolis' bar, she would check the board outside and see if they served food, and then stay and eat something before making enquiries. Otherwise she would find a taverna and then go back to the bar after lunch. The houses marking the outskirts of the village started to become more frequent, and soon the track had opened out into a regular rural street. Pretty gardens blooming with white scented jasmine flowers and red hibiscus bushes, bordered the pavement that had just begun underfoot. There were big bushes with sticky stems and large yellow flowers that smelt a bit like lemons that Ella did not know the name of. The smell of blossoms in the hot midday air was heady and seemed to engulf her. It was a wonderful sensation of heat and smell, by far overwhelming the smell of exhaust fumes and poor Greek drainage systems. There were now shops in the street; a small greengrocers on her side, and a hairdressers that looked closed, on the other side of the road. Ella realised that the track had become the main street. A bigger road, the busier one she had seen earlier, fed into it from the left. There was nothing much in the way of traffic, though occasionally a small motorbike buzzed past. Ahead on the right, she could see the sign outside the bar reading Manolis. There were a few more shops between her and the bar, on both sides of the street; a little newsagent doubling as a tourist shop selling towels, inflatables, cards and knick knacks, all hanging decoratively around the outside of the shop, a bakery, an ice cream shop- open fronted with a few tables and chairs, a pharmacy and a travel shop selling trips round the island, and to neighbouring islands by boat. Ahead, beyond Manolis' bar, Ella could see a bank, a restaurant- it's many tables sprawling into the street which became a square, a church and a petrol station. She couldn't make out the smaller shops. Manolis' bar was wooden fronted, with steps up to an open air porch type area, containing about half a dozen table and chair sets. Inside the bar continued with the wood theme and was dark. There were menus on each table and sets of olive oil and vinegar, so Ella assumed that the bar did in fact sell food. She seated herself at a table with a view of the comings and goings of the village, and waited for someone to come out. In no time at all, a young woman in her twenties, with dark hair pinned up, but still managing to tumble around her face with curls that had broken free of the pins, came over to her table.

'Yassas' she said.

'Kalimera sas,' replied Ella.

'Tee tha thellettay?' asked the girl. (What would you like?)

Ella had been looking at the menu, but more to check that they had things she wanted than anything else.
'to tzatziki, to psomi, kay ee salata, parakalo.'
(yoghurt dip, bread and salad please.)
'Do you want the country salad with feta?' asked the waitress, having somehow spotted Ella was English.
'Yes please, that would be nice,' replied Ella.
'What would you like to drink with that?' the girl continued, scribbling notes on her little pad.
'A Greek coffee please.'
'How do you take it?' asked the waitress.
'Gleekez,' (sweet) replied Ella.
'polly auraya pillogee,' said the waitress walking away. (good choice.)
Ella sat and watched the sleepy village. There was not much going on. An old woman clad head to toe in black, shuffled along the street carrying a basket, no doubt fetching supplies. Two old men sat outside a coffee shop (a kafaynion) across the street playing backgammon and drinking coffee. A ginger and white cat strolled nonchalantly down the main street, surveying the world as if he owned it, swaggering slightly to accommodate his un-neutered manhood. He occasionally stopped to sniff out various nooks and crannies in search of abandoned food. He sat down for a wash.
The waitress came out with a small cup of steaming coffee and a large glass of iced water. Ella thanked her and the girl disappeared back into the darkness of the bar. She drank some of the crisp, cool water while she waited for the coffee to be cool enough to take a sip. The cat noticed that things were arriving at Ella's table, and crossed the road to sit near her, in case any food became available for which to beg.
Ella sighed with contentment; the sun was hot on her shoulders, and the coffee smelt delicious, with just a

hint of cardamom aroma wafting from it. Soon it was cool enough to take a sip, and it tasted as delicious as it smelt.

Then the waitress brought out the food; a basket of chunky cut Greek bread, coated in sesame seeds, a large bowl of salad with lettuce, cucumber, tomatoes, peppers, olives, onions, and a slab of feta on top of it, and a plate of tzatziki.

Ella dipped a slice of bread in the tzatziki. It was delicious; rich and creamy, flavoured with garlic and mint, the cucumber grated so it melted into the yoghurt. The salad was wonderful too; dressed with olive oil, salt, wine vinegar and thyme, all the vegetables bursting with flavour, and somehow tasting like sunshine. Such a simple meal, yet it felt like sheer luxury on the taste buds.

The cat moved close enough to do a walk past, briefly nuzzling against Ella's leg. She broke off a small piece of feta cheese for it, and it trotted back, purring, and sat contentedly and ate the cheese, without ceasing to purr.

The cat did not leave, as Ella continued to eat her way through the meal, and she rewarded it with a final chunk of feta at the end.

A couple of minutes after she finished eating, the waitress came out to collect the plates, and asked if she would like anything else. Ella replied that she would take an iced peach tea, but would come into the shade of the bar to drink it. The waitress nodded and disappeared indoors with the crockery, and Ella picked up her bag and followed her in.

Inside, the bar was not as dark as it at first appeared. Her eyes soon acclimatised to the indoor light, and the shade of the dark wood décor. All around the side wall were photographs of staff and patrons having fun in the bar; drinking, dancing, singing, posing for the shots, smiling and laughing. Ella moved towards the back of the bar where there were a group of black and white photos on the wall. She peered at them, looking for any depicting her mother, Elizabeth. Soon she spotted her. Elizabeth was sitting at the bar between a young woman with long dark curls and a swarthy young man in a dark shirt with a full moustache.

She had not noticed the man come up alongside her, and gave a slight jump of surprise, accompanied by a very small squeak.

'Signomee,' (sorry) said the man, 'sorry to surprise you.'

Ella turned to look at him. He was tall, with dark curly hair and a little trimmed goatee beard, in the modern style.

'I am Dimitris, the owner of the bar,' he said.

'Ah so you are Manolis' son. My name is Ella. Ella Hudson.'

'Did you know Manolis?' asked Dimitris.

'No,' replied Ella, 'sadly not, but my mother did.' She turned to the photo on the wall and pointed at the woman in the middle; 'that is my mother, Liz Hudson.'

'Ah yes,' Dimitris said as he peered at the old photograph. 'And beside her are Heleni and Yiorgios. Yiorgios died ten years ago now, he was the local bank manager. We do not like to speak ill of the dead, but there was a lot of dark things happening just before he died.'

Ella was about to ask more, but just then the waitress came over with her iced peach tea. She thanked her and took a sip, it was cool, refreshing and sweet, just the thing for a hot day. Ella gave a small appreciative sigh.

Dimitris smiled, 'it is good yes?'

'Very' said Ella.

'So where is your mother now?' asked Dimitris.
'She died when I was very young, and I have only a few pictures and a small box of mementos to remember her by. In that box there was a beer mat from this very bar. I am trying to find out about the short period of time she lived on this island, and meet anyone who knew her back then.'
'She is in another photo here, with Panicos,' said Dimitris, pointing to a photo higher up on the wall. Elizabeth was dancing with a man in a white shirt, with short dark hair, but his face was not as clear as hers.
'My father kept a lot more photographs in an album at home, the ones that didn't go on the wall. Perhaps she is in some of those. I will have a look for them. How long are you staying for?'
'I have booked a room in the Zeus hotel for three weeks, but can extend to four or even five if I need to,' replied Ella.
'I will find the album and bring it in tomorrow,' said Dimitris. 'I will ask my mother if she remembers anything too. She rarely goes out these days as her health is poor, but I will see what she says.'
'Thank you very much,' said Ella, 'you are very kind. I will come back tomorrow afternoon.'
'Now if you will excuse me, I have to get on,' said Dimitris.
'Of course,' replied Ella, 'Efharisstow kai yassas' (thank you and bye.)
Ella finished her peach tea and went to the bar to settle up with the waitress. The whole thing cost twelve Euros, but Ella left fifteen. The food had been good, the staff friendly and she wanted people to think well of her. She needed all the contacts and friends she could make as it looked like finding people from back then might be quite the task.

Outside once more, the afternoon sun felt like walking into an oven in a bakery. Ella took a slow walk back to the hotel, watching the cats and lizards, and sniffing the sweet aroma of the flowers. She noticed a fork off the track that didn't seem to go anywhere, and as she was not busy, she walked along it to see where it went.

The path meandered along getting smaller and less used. Ella began to suspect it was not really a path at all but just a turning or passing point on the original track. The path was now grassy and overgrown and heading into some nearby low hills. Ella was about to turn back when she noticed the edge of a wall up ahead. All around her wild flowers were growing amongst the long grass, and the sounds of the village, few as they were, had completely disappeared. The only sound she could hear was the rhythmic lull of crickets chirping. She felt a deep sense of peace. The wall she had seen became the ruined shell of an old stone cottage, probably once a shepherd's house. Originally, it was not bigger than two small rooms, just somewhere to sleep and build a small fire to cook on. Ella sat on the edge of the wall and let herself imagine what it must have been like to live here. The hot sun was making her feel sleepy and she decided to head back to the hotel before she fell asleep, and ended up with a dose of sunstroke and a fine collection of mosquito bites, or maybe even worse. There could be snakes in this long grass. But she did not feel panicky as she wandered idly back to the track, and the hotel, the air redolent with floral and herbal aromas. In such a tranquil environment, Ella felt very much at peace with her world.

Just as Ella drew level with the hotel Zeus, where she was staying, she remembered she had not bought the supplies she had originally set out for that morning. She noticed that just ahead of her, a further fifty yards down the track, where the track joined the main road, was a small mini supermarket. She made her way up to it and entered the shop, which felt rather like walking into a fridge, as the cool air conditioning enveloped her.

Ella picked up a basket and mooched about collecting supplies; a jar of coffee, some tea bags, milk, bread, olive oil, two cheese pies- impossible to resist, a packet of rusk pieces (like big croutons), a bottle of washing up liquid, a bar of soap and a bottle of shampoo. She couldn't resist some halva from the deli counter, and a little pot of purple kalamata olives. The whole lot came to a few cents under twenty Euros, and she thanked the sales assistant and stepped out once more into the heat of the afternoon. Soon she was back in the shade of the hotel and on the way up the stairs to her room. The maid had pulled the curtains across but left the patio doors open, so there was air movement, and the room was surprisingly cool, considering the air conditioning was off. Ella put the milk, halva, olives and cheese pies in the small fridge, and put the bread, rusks, olive oil, tea and coffee in the cupboard. The washing up liquid she left by the sink, and took the soap and shampoo into the little bathroom.

Ella kicked off her sandals, then peeled off her other clothes which had begun to stick to her in the heat. She pulled the cotton shift back on, and wondered whether to have a nap or a shower first. She sat down on the bed, and that was the decision made, the nap won. She lay back on the cool crisp sheet; the maid had folded the top cover down to the end of the bed, and instantly fell asleep.

It was five o'clock when Ella awoke from her nap, having slept for about an hour and a half. She woke to a gentle breeze blowing the still pulled curtains into the room. She opened the curtains, letting a waft of hot air and bright sunlight flood over her. Ella put the kettle on and made herself a cup of tea. She took it out onto the balcony, along with the pot of halva and a spoon. In the distance the sea was flat and tranquil, bright blue sea, bright blue sky; nothing to see there. The pool was full of the usual tourist activities, so Ella sat and looked at the mountains, looking for shapes in the rocks. A solitary goat picked its way up the craggy lower slopes to a tasty looking bush a bit further on. Ella nibbled at the sweet, sticky halva, as she tracked its progress. Soon the goat was at the bush, having clambered sure-footedly over the rough rocks to claim its tasty prize. Ella smiled and sipped her hot tea.

A little red and black beetle marched across the balcony wall by Ella's arm; she moved her arm to allow it easier passage. Its colour markings were stunning, and she watched it until its journey took it to a plant at the end of the balcony, where it disappeared.

After a time, Ella got up and rinsed her cup, put the remains of her halva in the fridge and went for a shower. After the shower, she brushed her teeth, and then looking at herself in the mirror, combed her long dark hair. She wrapped herself in a light cotton dressing gown and then once again, sat out on the balcony to let her hair dry naturally in the late afternoon sun.

The goat was making its descent now, picking carefully amongst the rocks to rejoin the other goats on the rough grass below.

In no time at all Ella's long thick hair was dry, and she went into the apartment to brush it and put it up. She took a long blue dress from the wardrobe, and slipped on a pair of white sandals. She added a silver pendant of a sun on a chain, and looked in the mirror, pleased with the overall effect. She picked up her bag with her money and keys, and at the last minute, as an afterthought, took a light cardigan out of the drawer. The evening would likely be cool enough on the walk back to warrant it.

Ella went down to the hotel bar.

'Yassas,' she said to the barman, who was the same guy who had greeted her on her arrival in the wee small hours of the morning. He still looked somewhat tired.

'Yassou,' (the informal version of yassas, when you know someone) he replied, letting her know they were now friends. 'How are you today Miss Hudson?'

'Oh please call me Ella,' she replied, 'I'm very well thank you, and you? Do you ever get any time off to sleep?'

The man smiled. 'We all work long hours in tourist season, then we sleep all winter.' He laughed and Ella joined him, politely.

He continued, 'I sleep in the mornings, then work here on bar and reception from evening through the night. Twice a week flights come in late at night and I stay up to greet them, and keep the bar open late too.'

'May I have an ouzo with water please?' asked Ella.

'Of course,' replied the barman, reaching for a glass, 'but have you tried it with lemonade instead of water? It tastes very good and you don't get a hangover, maybe because of the lemon, I don't know.'

'That sounds nice,' replied Ella, 'okay then, I will try it like that.'

The barman grinned, 'You will like it very much, you'll see.'

He put the drink down on a cardboard bar mat in front of her, ice clinking against the glass. He turned around and busied himself getting something from the bar as Ella took a sip.

'You are right, it is delicious,' she said.

The barman put a small bowl of nuts down beside her drink. Greeks do not like to see anyone drinking alcohol without something to eat with it, however small. He also put a shot glass with a till receipt beside the nuts. This was the price of her drink, and she could either pay it, or make a collection of them as she kept drinking, and pay at the end.

'I am Christos, the eldest son of Yiorgos, who owns this hotel,' he said, holding out his hand to shake. Ella shook hands with him saying,

'I'm very pleased to meet you Christos.'

'My grandfather of course, was Christos too,' he continued. Greek custom is to hand the name of the firstborn down skipping a generation. 'My son is Yiorgos. My grandfather built this hotel himself years ago. Everyone in the village helped but it still took him many years. It was really very small at the beginning.'

Ella looked impressed, and continued sipping at her drink.

'Where is a nice restaurant to walk to for dinner?' she asked.

'You must go to Aphrodite's. It is very close to here. Walk out onto the main road and turn towards the village. After about two or three minutes walk, you will see it. My cousin runs it. If you say Christos from Zeus sent you, she will give you a special rate,' replied Christos.

'Thank you, I will do that,' said Ella, eating some of the nuts, and washing them down with the last of her drink. She took the receipt and looked at it. Three Euros for the drink. She dropped four, one euro coins into the glass, and hopped down off the barstool. 'I'm off to have my dinner now,' she said, smiling, 'See you later Christos.'

'Kalee orexi' (enjoy your meal,) called Christos after her, as she left.

'Yassou,' she called back over her shoulder at him. Ella turned out of the hotel, past the little supermarket and onto the main road. She began to walk along the narrow token gesture of a pavement, towards the village. After just a couple of minutes she saw a sign hanging from a post advertising Aphrodite's. Just a small car parking distance from the main road the restaurant was set back. In true Greek tradition, about half the tables were outside on a patio covered by vines. The whole front of the place was open to the night air, and the sides were lined with open windows, to keep those choosing to eat indoors cool. Ella walked inside and sat at a table beside one of the open windows. A small candle flickered in a little red shot glass in the centre of the table.

A waiter came over and said 'Kalee spaira' (good evening.)

Ella replied with the same greeting.

'Pos borrow na sass voytheesoo?' (how may I help you?) asked the waiter.

'tha eethala o catalogos parakalo,' (I'd like the menu please) replied Ella.

'You are English, yes? Where are you staying?' asked the waiter.

'At the hotel Zeus, and Christos told me to come here, and say he sent me.'

'When did you arrive?'

'Late last night,' replied Ella.

'Ah the night flight; is very tiring, yes?'

'Indeed.'

The waiter moved to a central table and got her a menu, then went out the back to the kitchen. After a moment or two a tall woman with dyed blonde hair came out and made her way over to Ella's table, bringing a jug of water and a glass, and a condiment carrier.

'Yassas, I am Carolina, cousin of Christos. I will give you special rate because of Christos,' she smiled.

'Thank you, my name is Ella Hudson, I am staying for a few weeks at least. What is good tonight?'

'Well, of course everything is good, but I made the dolmades (rice stuffed vine leaves) fresh this afternoon, so they are lovely. My brother caught some barbouni (red mullet) this afternoon, and I am cooking it in a lovely herb and lemon sauce. That is what I recommend.'

'Thank you, then that is what I will have; dolmades to start and barbouni for the main course.'

'And to drink?' asked Carolina.

'ena miso litro kokkino krassee parakalo,' (a half litre of red wine please.)

'Amaysus,' (right away) said Carolina, turning back to the kitchen.

Ella drank some water and breathed in the wonderful smells of Greek cooking coming from the kitchen. Traditional Greek music was being piped through to speakers all around the restaurant, it was very peaceful and relaxing. There were two other couples already eating, one outside, and one further indoors nearer the kitchen.

In no time at all Carolina returned with a jug of red wine and a glass. She also had a basket of bread. She poured a little wine into the glass, before going outside to see if the couple sitting out there needed anything.

Ella tasted the wine. It was delicious and fruity, almost more fruit juice than wine, but she knew better than to be deceived, local village wine was always like that, but it had the kick of regular wine, whilst tasting like grapes and sunshine.

Soon Carolina brought out a plate with six dolmades on it. They were served with a small portion of tzatziki, which had a few small wrinkled black olives sitting on top of it. Ella had had the small black olives before. They didn't tend to be exported, they were too delicious to make it out of Greece. Carolina said 'kali orexi,' and disappeared into the kitchen once more.

She ate the dolmades and tzatziki with just one slice of bread. She did not want to be too full to manage the barbouni when it arrived.

The dolmades were indeed scrumptious, stuffed with rice, shallots, pine nuts, thyme and mint and covered in an avgolemono (egg and lemon) sauce.

About five minutes after Ella finished the starter, Carolina came and took her plate away, asking if she'd enjoyed it. Ella replied that they were indeed, the best dolmades she had tasted in a long time. Carolina smiled, and took the plate away. She returned almost immediately with a platter that looked amazing, but Ella wondered how she was going to eat it all.

A large red fish with grill marks on the skin, coated in herbs and a lemon sauce, sat in the middle of the platter. All around it were accompaniments. A small green salad, some chips, a portion of rice with vegetables mixed into it, two wedges of lemon, some more tzatziki, some tomatoes, all dotted about with green olives.

Ella smiled and thanked Carolina, saying it looked and smelled delicious.

Satisfied with her response, Carolina once more left her to it.

Ella ate most of it, sipping the wine as she tackled the full platter. First she stripped one side of the fish off the bones. It was moist and had a lovely flavour, not dwarfed but complimented by the herbs and lemon. It tasted fresh, with a tang of the sea. Caught and eaten the same day; it didn't get much better than that, thought Ella. She had to leave some of the rice and chips, but by the time she had finished, the only other things left on the plate were fish bones and lemon peel. She sat back stuffed, and breathed a deep contented sigh. She was glad she had worn a loose shift dress.

As she digested the meal, Ella finished the jug of wine. Carolina came back out and asked her if it had been good. Ella said that it had been magnificent, 'fantastiko.'

Carolina asked her if she would like anything else, a coffee perhaps, and Ella assented that a frappe (iced coffee) would be nice.

Carolina took the platter and bread basket and wine jug and glass away and returned shortly with a tall glass of frappe, and a small plate of some kind of cake. Ella inwardly groaned. She had forgotten how fond the Greeks were of bringing out extras at the end of a meal, on the house. It would be rude to refuse.

Carolina put the cake down, then sat down at the table with Ella.

'This is ravani (honey cake), I made it this morning. It is very nice with frappe.'

Ella thanked her and tried a piece. She assured Carolina that it was indeed wonderful. She took a sip of the cold frappe to help make some room.

Carolina asked, 'How is your Greek so good? Do you have family here?'

Ella wanted to say, I hope so, but thought that was probably a conversation for another day. So instead she just said, 'I have been to quite a lot of the Greek islands. I work at a travel agent and it is my favourite holiday destination. After the first couple of visits I loved it so much, I started taking evening classes to learn Greek.'

'Well you are very good at it,' said Carolina.

'Thank you,' said Ella, 'and thank you for the wonderful meal, it was truly delicious, and I am very full.'

'You will sleep well tonight,' said Carolina, 'what are you doing tomorrow?'

'Just exploring the village, and I have some people to see.'

'Well if you come back tomorrow night, we will cook you something special again.'

'At this rate I shall have to buy new clothes, because none of mine will fit anymore,' laughed Ella.

'borrow na echo to logareeazmo parakalo?' (can I have the bill please) asked Ella.

'Of course, right away,' replied Carolina, smiling.

The bill arrived shortly afterwards, and Ella looked at it. The fish was nine Euros, the dolmades four Euros, the wine five Euros and the frappe two Euros. The total should have been twenty Euros, but Carolina had only charged her fifteen Euros. Ella left eighteen Euros, because she liked to tip well, but didn't want to insult Carolina by giving all the discount back as a tip.

She said goodnight and left with friendly waves all round. Outside there was a cool breeze now and Ella slipped her cardigan on. It was only a short walk back to the hotel, but there was no point in getting chilled. On the way into the hotel Christos called out 'yassou' to her from the bar, so she went over for a Metaxa (brandy) nightcap.

Christos asked her if she had eaten at Aphrodite's and she replied that she had, and that it had been delicious. The bar was quiet, just one old Greek man from the village down the other end, nursing a tsipouro, so Christos stopped to chat with Ella.

'Do you like what you have seen of our little island?' he asked.

'Very much so,' replied Ella, 'it is very pretty and tranquil, I can see why my mother liked it so much.'

'Ah, your mother came here too? When was that?'

'A long time ago, back in 1961, she was here the whole summer. She came at Easter and didn't leave until the late autumn. I heard she even had a job here at Manolis' bar for a while, I don't know.'

'Didn't she tell you?' asked Christos.

'Sadly she died in 1966, when I was still very small.'

'That is very sad,' said Christos.

Ella pulled her mother's picture out of her purse and showed it to Christos, 'I am asking around, wondering if anyone might remember her. Her name was Elizabeth Hudson, Liz.'

'She was very beautiful, and you have her looks too.' Ella blushed and muttered thanks.

'I will ask my father Yiorgos, if he remembers her. Maybe he will be in tomorrow and you can show him the photo. I will tell him about you. Yiorgos knows everyone that comes to the village, and knows most everything about them too.'

'Thank you, that is very kind of you,' said Ella.

'I will send a message for you in the morning, when he is going to be in.'

Ella was suddenly very tired, and said her goodnight making her way up to her room to put the air conditioning on and get a good night's sleep. She put her mother's picture on the bedside table and instantly fell asleep.

Chapter Two

Ella awoke bright and early. The sun was shining, of course, it always did in Greece, and the birds were singing at full volume. Ella went over to the little kitchenette area and made herself a cup of coffee and took it out onto the balcony to wake up, turning the air conditioning off first, naturally.

It was indeed a lovely day, bright blue sky, and quiet, apart from the birds, as no one else was up yet, and there was no activity in the pool. An elderly Greek man was doing something to the pool; testing the chemicals in the water, or cleaning the filters or something. Ella got her swimsuit out of the drawer in the dresser and pulled it on. She pulled her hair into a hair band and grabbed her towel and room keys, slipping on a pair of flip flops as she went. She loved to swim very early in the morning when no-one was about and she had the pool to herself. It was seven a.m. as she plunged into the pool at the deep end and began swimming lengths. The water was slightly cool, but not enough to be unpleasant, and Ella felt invigorated as she swam up and down. She thought it was a wonderful way to wake up; coffee followed by an open air swim, then dried by the already hot sun. She finished her swim, wrapped her towel around her, and padded back up to her balcony, where she could sit and dry off. There was a washing line across the balcony, and she hung the towel over it to dry. In no time at all Ella was dry. She peeled the swimsuit off and threw it in the bottom of the shower to rinse after breakfast.

Ella made a hearty breakfast- swimming always gave her an appetite- of bread with olive oil, a cheese pie and some kalamata olives. All washed down with a cup of tea.

After breakfast, taken on the balcony, naturally, looking at the lizard shape in the rock, and searching for other shapes, Ella went for a shower. She took her clothes that needed washing in with her and washed them as she showered, in travel wash. She wrung them all out and left them in the sink while she got dry and dressed, and brushed out her hair. Then she took the washing outside to hang on the balcony line. It would be dry in an hour or two at most. She had put on a pair of knee length green culottes, the look of a skirt, with the practicality of shorts, and a yellow smocked top embroidered with green flowers. She put on brown sandals, and left her hair loose, grabbing purse, keys, sunglasses and bag on the way out. She never bothered with sun cream, her natural colour was olive and she never burnt in the sun, just got even browner. All her friends back home were jealous and said she was very lucky.

Ella stopped at the hotel reception desk. A young girl was behind the desk, she seemed shy, but smiled at Ella.

'Kali maira,' said Ella, 'Melenee Ella Hudson.' (Good morning, I'm Ella Hudson.)

'A, Keereah Houdson, Kali maira,' (Miss Hudson, good morning,) said the girl and reached for a piece of paper, handing it to Ella with a smile. Obviously she did not speak English, or not much, or she wasn't confident. Ella said 'Efharisto,' (thanks) and smiled at the girl as she walked outside.

Unfolding the piece of paper she read; My father Yiorgos will come into the hotel at five this afternoon. He will wait for you in reception lounge.

Ella decided to walk along the main road to the village. It was not as pretty a walk as the track, but she liked to see everything, and be aware of her surroundings in daylight, so she could better enjoy strolling at night. She walked past Aphrodite's, which was shut now, the day had not yet commenced for them. There were bus stops on both sides of this road she noted, so she could get a bus from here to the capital, Vathy, and likely to some of the other villages and towns on the island too. She reminded herself to look for a tourist office and ask for a bus timetable, or failing that, ask if they had one at hotel reception, as they often did on the Greek islands. The bus stop was marked only with the village name, Agios Spiridos, and the bus company name KTEL. This was the main bus company in Greece, and Ella knew from previous visits it stood for keena tamea eespraxion leoforion – common fund receipts bus. But they were nothing like English busses, more like National coaches. Mostly they were a very comfortable, and reasonably priced way to travel. In some places you could get right across the island for just one Euro.

Ella passed another restaurant on the other side of the road called Zefiros. Alongside that was a somewhat bigger supermarket, which might come in useful for further provisions. Other than that, the road to the village was mainly lined with houses, semi built houses, and scrub land. Soon the fork leading into the village appeared. Ella noticed that the road continued on in the other direction, down towards the beach. She decided to explore that later on.

It wasn't long before Ella had reached the village square and saw the Alpha Bank ahead of her. She pushed open the doors and walked into the cool interior. Just inside the door was a reception desk with a dark curly haired Greek girl sitting behind it. Ella approached her; 'Kalimaira. Psackno yia keereah Michaelides, Nikki Michaelides, parakalo.'

(Good morning, I am looking for Nikki Michaelides please.)

The girl smiled and replied, 'Nay, Keereah Michaelides doolevvee etho, tha ferro tis.' (yes, Miss Michaelides works here, I will fetch her.)

She disappeared through a door to the interior of the bank and a moment later came back out closely followed by another woman, slightly older, who came over to Ella and introduced herself as Miss Michaelides, and asked how she could help Ella.

Ella shook her hand and said, 'etho kai pollee kairo, ee mitaira moo ixeerie ton pataira soo.' (a long time ago, my mother knew your father.)

'You are English?' asked Nikki.

'Yes,' replied Ella, a little relieved, she had been uncertain she could conduct the entire conversation in Greek. She continued, 'I wonder if I could talk to you about your father, and anything you might know of his life back then in 1961, when he was friends with my mother. Perhaps I could buy you lunch?'

Nikki smiled, 'that would be lovely. The bank closes from two in the afternoon until five, so if you come back at two this afternoon, we could go for lunch. I hope that will not be too late for you?'

'That would be great thanks,' said Ella, 'I had a large breakfast, so it will be fine. I will see you at two.'

Ella could see the bank was busy, so she said goodbye for now and left. She had the rest of the morning to herself. She could not see a tourist office in the square, so decided to ask at the hotel about the bus times. She walked back to the main road and followed it on through rough scrubland dotted with cactus plants, to the beach.

The beach itself had nothing of tourism about it at all. No kiosks, cafes or sun beds, just a long stretch of pebbly flat shore. It was very peaceful. In one direction it seemed to go on for miles before reaching a craggy cliff at the end of the bay. Towards the end of the beach that way, Ella could see the familiar blue rectangles of beach loungers for hire. Obviously that way lay tourism, cafes, water sports and ice cream. In the other direction, not far away, the continuing passage of beach was blocked from view by a pile of rocks. Ella decided to walk down to the rocks and see what was there and if the beach continued beyond. She had several hours before lunch with Nikki anyway. She walked down the beach to where the sea lapped the shore, the little stones making a little rattling noise as the sea drew in and out over them. Ella took off her sandals and paddled in the sea, walking along towards the pile of rocks. The water was still quite cold, but it was early in the season; later in the year it would be much warmer. It was not long before Ella approached the rocks she had seen before. There was, a little way up the beach, a little worn path through the rocks that presumably led out to the other side. She sat down on the beach just up from the sea, and waited a few minutes for her feet to dry, before brushing them off and putting her sandals back on. Then she walked up to the path. Wild herb bushes grew up the rocks on the shore side, and the smell they gave off as she brushed against them was heavenly.

Then she rounded a corner and almost gasped with surprise. There, unannounced by signage, on the beach was some sort of ancient Greek ruins. Columns rose into the sky, supporting nothing, others lay fallen on the ground. Rocks formed partial low walls, the remains of a building of some sort that once stood there. She scrambled down the last of the rocks to the site. Patches of marble were still visible on some of the columns and mosaic was intact in some floor areas, even some colour remained. It was hard to believe that so close to the sea, the weather and the water had not eroded almost everything. But here it was, remarkably well preserved.

In the water, another surprise greeted her eyes. A tiny island sat just a hundred metres or so out in the sea. On it was one building, a tiny little blue and white church. Tied to a rock on the island was a little row boat. Someone was obviously on the island, perhaps tending the church, or lighting a candle for the dead.

Just at the edge of the ruins on the beach was a tree, Ella did not know what type it was, but it's lush, spreading, dark green leaves offered shade, and on investigation, there was a bench beneath it. There was also a sign with some writing about the ruins. Ella walked over to investigate. The sign said the origin of the ruins was uncertain, and that possibly the Christian basilica of Saint Spiridon, for whom the village was named, had been erected on top of the original temple of Demeter. Aspects of both had been found in the same site. The temple ruins dated to 5BC whereas the basilica ruins dated to 5AD. The sign went on to point out which structures that could be seen now, dated to which era.

Ella walked around the ruins, soaking up the atmosphere, and trying to identify the different parts described on the sign. She sat on a wall in the hot sunshine and tried to soak up the feel of the place. Then she went and sat on the bench under the tree and tried to get a further impression. She had a bottle of water in her bag, that she had bought on her way from the village and she sat down now to soak up the atmosphere and rehydrate a bit. She drifted off into a reverie, this felt like a place of worship, and clearly the area was still being used today for religious purposes, as she watched an old man rowing the little boat back to shore from the church on the island.

But the day was getting along and it was time to be getting back and meeting Nikki for lunch.

Ella sat outside the bank on a bench in the shade of a large tree at five to two. She had time to cool down from the walk and have some sips of water. After five or six minutes, Nikki came out, and came over to Ella, smiling.

'Yassas,' she said, and Ella replied the same way.

'The restaurant on the other side of the square is very nice, shall we go there?' asked Nikki.

Ella agreed and they headed over and found a nice shaded outdoor table.

No sooner were they seated than a waiter came over to bring menus and ask if they would like a drink. Nikki and the waiter rattled away to each other in very rapid Greek, Ella caught the word Agglia (English) at one point, and portokalada (orange juice) at another. The waiter scribbled on his pad. Then he turned to Ella and asked her in English, what she would like to drink. As a point of principal Ella said, 'yia mena, ena leemonada, parakalo.' (a lemonade for me please.)

Then the waiter went away and they could talk.

Nikki began, 'we should decide what we want to eat, and then we can talk, or the waiter will come back and we won't be ready. He will be back soon with the drinks anyway.'

'What do you recommend?' Ella asked.

'Well I would recommend we get a fava (split pea dip) and taramasalata (cod roe dip) and share them as a starter with bread, then follow with souvlaki (pork kebabs) if you like those things?' said Nikki.

'I love all those things,' said Ella, 'yes, let's do that.'

'Okay then, I will order for us when he comes back,'
Nikki continued. 'So your mother was here in 1961,
did she stay long?'

'Well,' said Ella, 'I think she came over here at
Easter, and then stayed until autumn, it is possible
she worked in Manolis' bar during that summer.'

'What has she told you about it?' asked Nikki.

'Now that is the thing,' said Ella, 'My mother was
killed in a car accident in 1966, when I was almost
five, so she really didn't tell me anything.'

'What did your father tell you about her then?'

'I never knew my father. My mother did not put a
father's name on the birth certificate.'

'I am a bit confused,' said Nikki, 'how do you know
your mother was on Aegos in 1961 then?'

'I was brought up in a children's home, and I was
given a box from my mother's things, with memories
and suchlike in it. In the box were some photos with
the name of the island, Aegos, Agios Spiridos, and
1961 on the back. There was also a beer mat from
Manolis' bar, and some dried flowers. I wanted to
come here and see for myself where she had been,
maybe see if anyone remembered her. I have so little
of her life that I wanted to walk in her footsteps.'

Ella looked up and saw that Nikki had tears in her
eyes. Family was such an important thing to the
Greeks, Nikki probably would have thought it less
sad if Ella had had her arm cut off.

Just then the waiter came out with their drinks, and
they both thanked him. Nikki quickly gave him the
food order, and he was away again.

'That is so sad, that you had no one, no aunts or
uncles, no god parents?' said Nikki.

'No, my mother was an only child, and her parents
were already dead. She had never got round to
getting me christened, or saying which friends might

be good god parents. I was christened at the children's home because it was run by Nuns, and they thought I would go to hell if I died before I was christened.'

Nikki nodded, 'So how do you know your mother knew my father then?'

'Yesterday morning I went to buy some maps of the island, and I got talking to Bani and Haroula in their shop. They heard my story and looked at the photographs and said they recognised my mother. They said she had been friends with Heleni Argyros, Nikos Andreadis, Panicos Papadopolous, and your father Yiorgios Michaelides. They also said she had worked at Manolis' bar. They told me that your father Yiorgios sadly died ten years ago. I'm sorry.'

'Thank you,' said Nikki, 'he had a massive heart attack and went very quickly. The doctors say he would not really have known anything about it, and the pain would have been very brief. That much is a blessing.'

Just then the waiter came back out with the two dips, one pink, one yellow, and a basket of bread. He put down a small plate for each of them and hoped they enjoyed their meal. The pink taramasalata was decorated with black olives, and the fava was decorated with the customary raw onion. Nikki took a spoonful of fava and mixed some olive oil into it on her plate, then dipped some bread in it. Ella started on the taramasalata. When they had both served themselves and settled into the rhythm of their eating, the talk began again.

'I went to Manolis' bar yesterday and met his son. He is going to talk to his mother, and look for his father's photograph albums and meet me again this afternoon. I am going there after this, in fact. Also, I am staying at the Hotel Zeus, and I got talking to

Christos, and he has arranged for his father Yiorgos, to come and meet me at the hotel at five o'clock today. Apparently he knew everyone who came to the village, and remembers everything.'

'People will tell you all kinds of things,' said Nikki, a shadow seeming to pass over her face. We all have skeletons in our cupboards- that is the saying, yes?' Ella nodded. It was close enough.

'People will tell you lots of things; they like to gossip, and you have such a sad story, they will open up to you. They will probably say bad things about my father; he was the bank manager, and he was being investigated for fraud when he died. Actually we think that is what caused the heart attack. It was all very nasty. My mother and I do not believe my father had anything to do with it. My eldest brother was later arrested for the fraud, and is still in prison, he gets out soon, I think, but my mother has disowned him. She says he killed my father. I agree with her, but not everyone in this village feels the same way.'

'That is terrible,' said Ella. 'People can be very cruel; people's tongues are the cruellest weapon they have.' Nikki nodded and gave Ella a sad smile.

By now they had finished their starters and the waiter came and took the plates away. They spoke of how tasty it had been, and soon he returned with the plates of souvlaki. In the middle of each plate were four skewers of souvlaki, but like the fish the previous night, they were surrounded with rice and vegetables, chips, salad, tzatziki and lemon wedges, there were also strips of grilled pitta bread. Ella sighed; another huge but delicious meal. She valiantly began to eat. Nikki looked unfazed.

'Do you have the photographs on you?' asked Nikki.

'Always,' replied Ella, pausing to get them out of her purse.

Nikki looked at the pictures. 'Your mother was very beautiful. You have inherited her looks, but not her colour, you are much darker, more olive. You could be Greek. When were you born?' Nikki looked like she was thinking things through.

'I was born May 31st 1962,' replied Ella.

'When did your mother leave Aegos?'

'This photo of her and a man, says September 1961 on the back, and the one of just her, in what looks like a Greek restaurant, says November 1961, so I think she left shortly after that.'

'So you were conceived in Greece then?' smiled Nikki, 'No wonder you are so dark, you are one of us really, the island is in your blood.'

'I am hoping that I can find out who was my mother's lover back then. She cannot have told him about being pregnant, just ran away back to England. Perhaps there is still a hope I can find my father.'

'That is such a beautiful mystery, so very Greek,' said Nikki, 'everyone you tell will be so moved by it. I will tell my mother, and after you talk to Yiorgos tonight, between them and Bani and Haroula, soon everyone in the village will know your story, a lot of the rest of the island too maybe. Wherever you go people will want to drink raki (a spirit, another name for tsipouro) with you and talk about your mystery. Greek people will love it, and you too.'

Ella smiled and said, 'when I thought to come here, I was sure I did not have even a chance of finding anyone, but I have been here just two days and spoken to just a few people, and already you have given me hope.'

Nikki smiled and said, 'I am pleased you have hope, it is so important. Hope is one of the things that keeps us happy in life. But tell me, how come you speak Greek like you do? You have no Greeks around you at home.'

Ella replied, 'When I left the children's home, I was eighteen. I was not happy with the way the Nuns had taught me about religion, Catholicism just did not feel right to me. One day I went to the service at the Greek Orthodox church in my town. The people were very friendly, and took to me straight away, they thought I was Greek at first because of my colour. Even though the service was almost entirely in Greek, and I didn't really understand a word of it, it just felt right to me. The atmosphere, the incense, the icons; I felt so at home. I read some books. I work in a travel agents, so I started taking holidays on the Greek islands whenever they came up, and the church had a Greek language evening class, which of course I joined. After a while I was baptised Greek Orthodox, and I took communion with the others. I feel more comfortable amongst Greeks than with English people. I always thought it was a strange but beautiful thing.'

Nikki beamed at Ella, 'that is your Greek blood coming through. We think our blood is stronger and will always win out, so if you are half Greek, after a time you will become fully Greek. It is the natural way. Greeks always come home eventually too.' Nikki picked up the photo of Liz and the man and peered closely at it. 'I do not think this is Yiorgios, my father, though. It is a shame in a way, I would love to have you for a sister, you are lovely. I do not know who it is, it is very hard to tell.'

They had finished eating by now and Nikki ordered coffees for them both. The waiter brought the coffees with glasses of water, and a plate of fruit on the house, and a wallet with the bill discretely tucked inside. Ella swiftly picked up the wallet. The bill was twenty four Euros. She deftly pushed aside Nikki's attempts to pay half and insisted lunch was on her, as she had originally offered. She put thirty Euros in the wallet and nodded at the waiter, who came quickly over. She handed it to him, and he thanked her and went away.

'Thank you so much for lunch,' said Nikki, 'it was very kind of you. You must come to our house and meet my mother, she will remember things better than I can, and I know she would love to meet you. When are you free?'

Ella thought aloud, 'today is Wednesday, tomorrow I am going to Limonaki to meet Heleni. Friday I am going into Vathy to try and find Nikos. Saturday I am going to Agios Nikolaus to find Panicos. Sunday I would like to go to church, but I will be free after that.'

'That is settled then. You will sit with us in church and then come back to our house for lunch afterwards. This time lunch will be on me.'

'That would be absolutely lovely,' said Ella. 'I would really enjoy that. What time does the church service start?'

'It starts at seven thirty in the morning,' replied Nikki. 'Here is our address, just in case you miss church for some reason, you must still come to us anyway afterwards.' She handed Ella piece of paper on which she had written; Michaelides, Odos Argostoli 4, Agios Spiridos, Aegos.

Ella agreed to meet Nikki and her mother in church on Sunday morning, and with that lunch was concluded. Ella had a date at Manolis' bar. Nikki hugged her like a long lost relative, and kissed her on both cheeks as they parted.

Ella walked from the square to Manolis' bar, just down the road. The day was very hot, and being full of food, she was covered in a light sweat by the time she got there. When she got into the bar, Dimitris greeted her like a long lost friend, rather than someone he had just met yesterday. Ella thought how much she loved Greek hospitality. He offered her a drink on the house, but not wanting to take advantage, Ella said a coffee would be nice. Dimitris said that she looked very hot, and why not have an ice cream frappe and cool off. Ella said that that sounded lovely, and Dimitris turned to make the drinks. When he had finished he called out to Eleni, the waitress, to come and take over at the bar as he was having a break. He brought the drinks over to a quiet table at the back of the bar, and invited Ella to come and sit over there. Dimitris went back to the bar and returned with two tattered old photograph albums.

'Are you having a good day?' he asked.

'Very much so,' replied Ella, 'I just had a lovely lunch with Nikki from the bank, and in the morning I explored the ruins on the beach.'

'It is lovely down there on the beach opposite the little island,' he replied.

'That is a tiny little church on the island,' said Ella, 'do villagers use it? I saw a man rowing back from it, and wondered about it.'

'It is a little church for Saint Spiridon, and sometimes people go over to it and light a candle for the saint, or leave a little wax model of whichever part of them is hurting or sick, then the saint can heal it. Everyone in the village goes to the main church in the square for the services and the Thea Keynonya- holy communion, and that is where the Pappas- Priest goes too. But the little island church is for special requests, more old fashioned, superstitious kind of things.'

'I think I understand,' replied Ella. 'I would love to see the little church, do you think it would be alright for me to row over there?'

'There is no problem with you going over there, but you have to know where to put the little boat as some of the rocks are jagged. When we have talked and looked at these photos, I will take you, okay.'

'Oh that would be wonderful, thank you so much,' beamed Ella. 'It would not be putting you out too much, you are not too busy?'

'No,' said Dimitris, 'look around, it is not busy, it would be my pleasure to do it, and to be out in the sunshine for a little while. Anyway Greeks love any excuse to be in a boat on the water, even if only for a very short time.'

'You are very kind,' said Ella.

'I spoke to my mother last night, and she does remember your mother. She did work in the bar that summer in 1961. It was while my mother and father were courting, and Manolis often left Elizabett to run the bar for the afternoon, so they could go out on a picnic, or into town together. It was, as now, usually quiet in the afternoons. My mother liked Elizabett very much, she said they had many girls' talks together. There was a boy called Adonis that your mother was seeing romantically, but he was not from this island. He was a friend of Panicos and came over here sometimes. At least that is how mother remembers it, but she is ill now, and sometimes gets a bit muddled about things. Anyway, I found Elizabett in some more photos in these books,' Dimitris opened the books at marked pages to show Ella.

'This one is my mother and Elizabett. This one is Elizabett, Mother, Father and Panicos. Here is Elizabett with Heleni and Yiorgios. This is Elizabett with Nikos and Panicos.' Ella looked at all the photographs, but none of the men looked like the mystery man in sunglasses and a hat in her picture; he was taller and a different build. Ella was beginning to believe that this mystery man, Adonis, of whom there seemed to be no clear photographs, was the most likely candidate to be her father.

'There are no photos of this Adonis then?' asked Ella hopefully.

'Sadly no,' said Dimitris, 'he apparently only came to the bar a few times with Panicos. From what mother says, Elizabett saw him on her days off, mostly.'

'So what is the story, with your mother and this island,' asked Dimitris, settling back in his chair and beginning to roll a cigarette. 'Do you mind if I smoke?'

'Of course not,' answered Ella, and began once again to tell the tale of her mother, and her own connections to Greece, as she had told Nikki at lunchtime.

When she had finished speaking, they had finished their ice cream frappes, and Dimitris had smoked his cigarette. He looked moved and thoughtful. As Nikki too had said, he said, 'So you are half Greek, one of us really. And already Greek Orthodox too. We must go now to the little church, before the tide changes, the sea, she can be a bit awkward then.'

Outside the bar, Dimitris pulled out a little moped from a side alley. 'Hop on,'
he said, 'we will be at the beach in no time.'

Ella gave a little inward shudder; this would be her first time on the back of a Greek motorcycle. The tourists were reckless enough, but Greeks on motorbikes were just unbelievable. One time on the island of Kriti, she had seen a sight she would never forget. A man and his wife on a motorbike, two small children wedged in between them, and mother holding a baby whilst sitting side-saddle. Not a crash helmet in sight, a massive box of groceries bungee strapped onto the back, and the man was texting on his phone as he drove along. Reckless didn't even begin to describe it. Nevertheless, Ella took a deep breath and hopped onto the back of the bike.

There was no mention of crash helmets, and they raced away down the road to the beach. There was a side road Ella had not previously noticed, which led almost to the part of the beach where the ruins were. They walked down the beach together to the little rowing boat tied to a post on the shore.

'Jump in and I'll push her out,' said Dimitris, throwing his shoes into the boat and rolling his trousers up to his knees. Moments later, the little boat was bobbing on the waves as Dimitris jumped in and began to row out to the island.

As he rowed Dimitris said, 'It is a great shame to have a child without a father in Greece, I hope you soon find yours. My sister had a child and she would not say who the father was. My mother and father were furious, but she would not tell, so they sent her away to the next island, Kios, to live with an aunt. None of the family here have spoken to her since. I heard she had a little girl. She must be about nine years old now. I often think about her. It was probably for the best that your mother left when she did.'

'That is very sad,' said Ella, 'do you never think of going over to see her?'

'It would make my mother very angry if she found out, and she is already sick. Perhaps after she has gone, God bless her, I will see my sister and my niece once more.'

They arrived at the little island, and Dimitris zigg-zagged around some rocks before bringing the boat into a sort of natural harbour, where a branch had been wedged between some rocks to form a mooring post. He jumped out onto a flat piece of rock and tied the boat to the post, then held out his hand to help Ella out of the boat.

They climbed up the jagged volcanic rock to the little church. The door was not locked, why would it be in such a remote place anyway? Inside the church was dark and musty. Just inside the door was a brass stand, filled with sand and the stumps of candles. Alongside was a box of taper candles and a wooden box with a slot in the top for donations. Ella crossed herself the Greek way; three times, right to left, with three fingers pinched together as if taking a pinch of salt from a pot. The three fingers represent the Father, Son and Holy Spirit. Ella took a candle, crossed herself again and lit it for Elizabeth. Dimitris said, 'You should light a candle to the Saint to ask him for his help in finding your father. But come and see his icon first.' Dimitris walked to the front of the little church where an icon depicted Saint Spiridon. He had a long white beard, and was wearing what looked like an upside-down basket on his head, and holding a jewelled holy book. He looked like he might be frowning a little bit. Underneath the icon was a small bookshelf which was filled with a strange collection of bits and pieces; a wax leg, a doll's head, a toy car, hand drawn pictures, and all sorts of other offerings to tell the Saint what action was being hoped for.

'Saint Spiridon started life as a peasant shepherd,' began Dimitris, 'but later when his wife died, he entered a monastery and his daughter too, took religious orders. He is said to have converted a sceptical philosopher, by holding a brick and explaining how it was like the Holy Trinity, because it was fire, earth and water; three in one. At this point flames shot out of the top of the brick and water poured from underneath, and Spiridon was left with dust in his hand. He healed plague and other sickness, found lost jewels, turned a snake into gold coins for a poor man, could tell the future, cast out demons, raised the dead on occasion, and brought rain in times of drought. So you should ask Saint Spiridon to find your father and bring you to him, and perhaps he will hear you and help.'

Ella looked around the tiny little church. There were four wooden chairs for the tired faithful to sit on whilst they prayed to the Saint. There was an icon of Jesus, and one of the Holy Trinity, the Spirit represented as a dove. There was also one of Mary holding the baby Jesus. Mary was dressed in the blue robe and red cloak which is standard to Orthodox depictions, unlike the Catholic, pastel blue and white. There were some candles in stands, and a small empty table. It was very sparse by Greek Orthodox standards. Mary went to each of the four icons, Jesus first and Saint Spiridon last, and crossed herself in front of them and then kissed them. She lingered in front of the Saint's icon and in her mind told him what she most dearly wanted. Then she lit another candle to him and put a few Euros in the donation box.

Dimitris smiled at her when she had finished, and said, 'Now you will find your father. I am sure of it.'

They left the little church and Dimitris rowed them back to shore. When they got back to the bike, he asked her if he could drop her anywhere. Ella looked at her watch and seeing it was ten to five, said, 'If you could drop me at the Hotel Zeus, that would be great. I am meeting Yiorgos at five.'

Dimitris dropped Ella off at the hotel and she thanked him for a lovely afternoon.

Ella got into the hotel and went straight to the reception lounge area. An older man stood up and came over to her, extending his hand as if to shake hers, but instead just clasping it in both of his. 'I am Yiorgos, and you are Ella, yes?'

'Yes,' said Ella, 'hairo polee- very pleased to meet you.'

Yiorgos smiled. 'Christos told me you speak some Greek. Now let me get you a drink, and then we can talk- do you like Raki?'

'Oh yes, of course, it is a wonderful drink. It cures all that ails you and makes you feel good too,' replied Ella.

Yiorgos spoke quickly to Christos at the bar and then came and sat down with Ella on one of the comfortable sofas in a quiet corner of the reception lounge.

'So, have you had a nice day?' asked Yiorgos.

'Yes,' replied Ella, 'and it has certainly been busy.' Just then Christos arrived with a tray containing a small glass bottle of raki and two shot glasses, and three little bowls, containing olives, pistachio nuts and rusks. Yiorgos thanked him and poured out two shots of raki.

'Stin yammas,' (to our health) he said holding his glass up, and Ella said the same. They sipped the raki and gradually picked at the snacks as they talked.

'So,' said Yiorgos, 'tell me your story.'

Ella told the tale for the third time that day, and for the third time, got a similar response.

'So you are pretty much Greek then, practically a native of Aegos.' Yiorgos smiled. 'Who else have you spoken to already?'

'First I spoke to Bani and Haroula,' began Ella.

'They are a lovely couple,' said Yiorgos, 'but they put distance between themselves and the village when they moved away to New York. Not just geographical distance you understand. When they were leaving, they said they were never coming back, they would raise their children as American citizens. Local people felt a bit hurt and betrayed, but they threw them a leaving party anyway. Bani got very drunk and said some bad things about people in the village. Then after ten years things went wrong for them out there, they don't talk about it, but they came back. They couldn't have children. Now they are like outsiders, they will never quite fit in again.'

Ella was beginning to see that Yiorgos did indeed know everyone, but was also the village gossip. But she would let him talk, and speak ill of no one herself.

'Then I had lunch with Nikki Michaelides, and I am going to church with her and her mother on Sunday.'

'Nikki is a good girl,' began Yiorgos, 'but her family have had a lot of trouble. Her father was about to be arrested for stealing money from the bank while he was bank manager. The police were in his house when he had a massive heart attack. He never regained consciousness. They say he was dead before the doctor even got there. Then they arrested her older brother, as he had been stealing money and he is still in prison now. The family have disowned him.'

'She told me something about that over lunch,' said Ella. 'After lunch I saw Dimitris- Manolis' son, and he brought some photographs, and then took me over to the church on the island so I could pray to Saint Spiridon for help.'

'Well you will be lucky in your search then if you have done that,' said Yiorgos. 'Dimitris is a good boy, he looks after his sick mother. It is a shame about his sister Anna though. They sent her away to Kios when she got pregnant, and have never been in touch with them since. She refused to tell them who the father was, so they couldn't make him marry her, but I know she was seeing a married man at the time. His name was Panayiotis Kostas. A few years later, his wife died, something wrong with her chest, pneumonia maybe. He sold up and left the island. Maybe he went to Kios too, I never did hear any more about it. I like to think they are all together and happy now.'

'Everybody has their own troubles,' said Ella.

'Of course I knew Liz,' began Yiorgos, 'she was a lovely girl too. Always helpful, very friendly, talked to everyone, as much as she could, she never did pick up much Greek though. You are right in what you have heard and think; she was courting with a boy called Adonis. But he wasn't from this village. I'm not even sure he was from this island. He was best friends with Panicos, and quite good friends with Heleni. Maybe one of them has kept in touch with him and knows where he is now? Nikos was always the quiet one, it was hard to tell who he was friends with and who he knew. But Liz always had time for him. I think she cured him of his shyness that summer, he was easier around people after that.'

'I am going to see Heleni tomorrow,' said Ella. 'I bought some maps and I am looking forward to the walk. I will start out early before it gets too hot.'

'It is beautiful countryside between this village and Limonaki,' said Yiorgos. 'At one point, when you are at the highest place, you can look left and see Agios Spiridos and the coast on this side of the island, and look right and see Limonaki and the coast on the other side of the island. But it is a long walk. Make sure your shoes are comfortable, and you have a big bottle of water.'

It was getting late, and Ella wanted to freshen up and buy some supplies from the mini market before dinner. It seemed like she and Yiorgos had said everything they had to say for now, so she thanked him for his hospitality and explained she wanted to freshen up before dinner. Yiorgos hugged her like she was his own daughter.

Ella went up to her room and had a quick shower. It had been a long dusty day, and felt like three days rolled into one. She brushed her hair out and put on a cream jersey dress, she draped a pink shawl over her bag for later in case the wind got up. She put on her white sandals, which were very comfortable just because they were different from the ones she had had on all day. The maid had brought the dry washing in, and folded it onto a chair.

Ella left with a nod to Christos and headed for the little shop. She bought two bottles of water, two apples, and some biscuits. Then taking her supplies with her she headed down the road to Aphrodite's for dinner.

Carolina waved at her enthusiastically like a long lost friend, when she walked into the restaurant, and came over with a menu and settled her at a table.

'I have just got off the phone with my uncle Yiorgos, he has told me all about you. Can I bring you a glass of wine and talk with you while you decide what you want for dinner?'

'Of course,' smiled Ella, though truth be told, she was beginning to feel a little talked out.

Carolina quickly returned with two glasses of red wine, and sat down next to Ella so they could sit and drink together. 'I hope you don't mind, but Yiorgos will talk to everyone. It may help you in your search.'

'Oh that is quite alright,' said Ella. 'I honestly didn't expect everyone to be so helpful and friendly. It really is quite wonderful.'

'You know, it is very quiet this evening, and they can manage without me for an hour or so. I have not eaten yet, would you like to have dinner together?' asked Carolina.

'I'd love to,' said Ella. 'Only I feel like I have been talking nonstop all day, so I may not be the best company.'

'That is alright,' said Carolina, 'Yiorgos has already told me all of your story anyway. I could talk to you about the island, perhaps?'

'Yes,' said Ella, 'that would be really nice, thank you. What are you thinking of having for dinner? I will have that, as I like everything and am too tired to choose.'

'Well then,' began Carolina, 'we will have the grilled octopus in red wine starter, followed by Briam (a rich vegetable stew), that is not too heavy and will lift you and make you feel less exhausted.'

'That sounds lovely,' said Ella.

Carolina darted to the kitchen to put the order in, and returned with a jug of the red wine. They talked like old friends as they ate. The octopus was grilled to perfection, crispy at the edges, but moist with the wine in the middle. Carolina was right, it did lift rather than fill. The briam was delicious too. The sauce was thick and tomato flavoured, and all the vegetables were succulent and flavour filled. Even the grilled pitta bread that was served with it was fluffy and scrumptious. As they ate, they drank wine, and Carolina talked about the history of the island, Greek mythology, and how it had been to grow up in a small village. Ella found herself liking Carolina very much.

When they had finished, a waiter came and took the plates away, and Carolina ordered coffee and something about the house that Ella did not catch. She did not have to wonder for long though, because he soon reappeared with two coffees and two small terracotta bowls, which turned out to be full of yoghurt and pieces of walnut, drizzled over with golden honey.

'This yoghurt is made by a lady just outside the village who keeps goats, and makes her own yoghurt and cheese. The honey is from a village in the mountains, where the bees feed on heather and thyme. You'll see, you can taste the flavours in the honey,' said Carolina.

When Ella tasted the yoghurt dish, she proclaimed it the most sensational yoghurt she had ever eaten. She agreed that she could taste the heather and thyme in the honey. When they had finished, Ella got her purse out of her bag.

'No,' said Carolina, 'tonight dinner is on me, I insist. You know, if your mother had stayed here on the island we would have grown up together, as I was born in 62 as well. We would have been in the same class at school. I think we would have been best friends.'

Ella smiled at that and politely tried to protest weakly, but it was clear Carolina was having none of it. She thanked Carolina profusely, but tiredness was overcoming her, so she made her excuses. Carolina told her to come in later, the next night and she could meet Andreas, her brother. Ella agreed that she would.

She draped the shawl around her shoulders and strolled lazily back to the hotel. She said hello to Christos, but told him she was too tired even for a nightcap tonight, and headed up to her room. Within minutes of brushing her teeth and putting her slip on, she was asleep.

Chapter Three

Ella woke early, at 6.30 in the morning. She had been to bed early the previous night, and so was fully rested. She wanted to make an early start before the day got really hot. She packed a small backpack she had brought with her for excursions, with the maps, bottles of water, an apple, the remaining cheese pie, the olives and the biscuits. She also put in her purse, keys and sunglasses, and a large cotton scarf. This was multi functional and could be used to cover her head or shoulders if they got too hot, or to sit on to have lunch, or to wrap around herself if she went swimming, pretty much anything really. It weighed almost nothing and was very handy. Ella made herself a quick cup of coffee and got dressed. She put on a bikini, in case there was a chance to swim, khaki shorts, a loose white cotton peasant style blouse, white cotton ankle socks and a pair of deck shoes that were very comfortable to walk in. As an afterthought, she slipped a pair of light flip flops into the backpack. She combed her hair and put it into a ponytail, popping the comb into the backpack too. She was ready; she would breakfast a bit later on. Ella had already checked the maps and knew roughly where she was going, but she would check again over breakfast in the old town at the top of the hill. She started out along the track that she had taken on the first morning. When she reached the place where the track turned towards the village, and passed Bani and Haroula's shop, the track forked to the right and carried on as more of a walking path. This was the way Ella went. The path wound around slightly, sometimes passing people's gardens where chickens wandered about freely and the occasional goat was tethered on a long chain. In other gardens, vegetables grew. Most of the land was being used for something. Occasionally Ella would spot a 'day bed' under a tree in the shade. This tended to be an old mattress on crates, with a blanket or sheet thrown over it. Often the man of the house would doze out on this in the afternoon, it seemed like a comfortable cool place to have a 'chnoudee' –snoozy or siesta. The path began to wind upwards, and the shape of the old town could be clearly seen on top of the hill. It almost looked like a fort from this distance. Along the edges of the path there was now a rough stone wall, and on the right, just the other side of the wall, grew a huge cactus. Little red and black beetles were crawling on its big flat round pads. A little further on up the hill, one of the walled off areas was given over to boxes of bees. They were not bee hives such as Ella had normally seen, but just rough boxes on bricks dotted around amongst herb bushes. The few bees that were out, seemed hot and lazy, even this early in the day. On the left a garden was full of laundry, drying in the morning sun. A rope was strung between two trees, and on this were spread white sheets. All around the garden, clothes were spread over the top of herb bushes and other shrubs. Ella thought that this was a wonderful way to dry washing; the clothes spread out in the sun and scented with the aroma of herbs and flowers on which they lay, the plants getting some extra moisture and a little shade. She was momentarily in awe of the sheer functionality of it.

The hill got somewhat steeper and the path got more windy and crooked towards the summit. Then it suddenly became paved and open and she was in the old town. Ella walked through a couple of backstreets between densely packed, small, Greek town houses, and came across some shops. A little pavement café was just what she was looking for.

She sat down in one of the comfortable, padded, bamboo conservatory chairs. Soon a waiter came over.

They exchanged the usual 'kalimairas' and Ella ordered a sweet Greek coffee. She looked at the little menu card on the table and when the waiter came back, she also ordered a bougatsa, (a kind of custard pie). The Greek coffee was sweet and thick and delicious, and the water was iced and refreshing. Ella sat and enjoyed the breeze, and watched people of the old town slowly making their way about their morning business. The bougatsa was wonderful, Ella had worked up quite an appetite on the walk up the hill.

Ella got out the map and folded it until it showed only the relevant portions for her walk that day. It was about fifteen miles from Agios Spiridos to Limonaki, and she had already walked about two of them. The gradient showed that there was a little more uphill, but she had done most of it. She looked at the road that led through the old town, and related that road to her position at the café. If she followed the road round, it would eventually fork into two, and she needed to take the right hand fork. This meandered on for about two or three miles and then came to a left right junction. She would have to turn left there. After that, the road seemed to go uninterrupted to Limonaki. She was sure she would have to check the map again, but it seemed pretty straightforward.

She went into the café and asked for the toilets (poo eena ee tooaletta parakalo?) figuring she had better go now as there were not likely to be any en route. She purchased a can of drink; lemon tea, from the fridge and paid her bill.

Ella put on her backpack, after adding the can of lemon tea to it, and set off once again. Already two old men were sitting outside a kafenion drinking coffee and playing backgammon; the national pastime of the elderly. A taxi driver sat on a wall alongside his cab, working worry beads between his fingers. The road wound round the outside of the village, with an amazing view down to the sea and the village of Agios Spiridos. Just off the road was a sandstone formation in which the weather had eroded small caves. Two goats sat crammed into the shade of one such cave. They watched as Ella walked past in the sun, looking at her as if she were mad. In another cave, several chickens sheltered. Ella could see the end of the village now, and a final little mini market before the road stretched into the open distance. Ella couldn't resist popping in and buying herself a pistachio ice cream for the road. Walking along in the already hot sunshine, the ice cream tasted sublime. Now the walk had begun in earnest. The hot road offered no shade and climbed gradually uphill. After about half an hour, Ella had reached the highest point. As Yiorgos had said, she could indeed see the coast to both the right and left. She looked to the left and saw Agios Spiridos way down below, with the sea deep blue, and twinkling. Even the old town looked like it was some way below her now. She had not realised she had walked that far uphill. To the right she could see the Limonaki coast, but just rocks and sea. The half dozen houses that made up Limonaki village were not yet visible. Along the flat road, Ella could see several old fashioned windmills, and to the right there was a wind farm of about fifteen modern, white windmills. There was a good breeze up here, but still no shade. Ella was very glad she did not burn, but pulled out the scarf and slung it over her head and shoulders to prevent sun stroke. She also got the can of lemon tea while she was in the backpack. It was still cold, and very refreshing. She sipped at it as she walked along. The road continued, without any kind of shade. It was wild open heath up here, but so beautiful. The smells assaulted Ella; broom, thyme, jasmine, juniper, heather and a faint pine smell coming from a clump of pine trees she could see coming up soon on the side of the road. In fact the trees were the only kind of shelter for as far as Ella could see, and looked like the perfect place to stop for a pee. That accomplished, she walked on, the road once more hot and shade free. The smells of wild herbs and flowers got stronger as the sun got hotter. It was very heady and Ella felt like she could almost taste the wild herbs. The temperature had to be thirty eight degrees, or maybe even hotter, already.

She came to a wall forming the border of someone's land, and it was casting a small patch of shade. Ella decided this would be the perfect place to stop for a short rest, and a mid morning snack, and spread her large cotton scarf on the ground in the shade. From the backpack she took the cheese pie and a bottle of, now warmish, water. That all disappeared in no time at all, so she ate the olives too. Still slightly hungry, she ate the biscuits and apple for dessert. She washed it all down with a little warm water from the second bottle and put the rest back in the backpack to save for later. Some of the flaky pastry of the cheese pie had dropped as crumbs onto the ground, and now some large ants were carrying the pieces away. Ella watched them go about their business industriously. They were strange ants, the like of which she had not seen before. They sort of curled the back segment of their bodies upwards, so they looked somewhat like scorpions. Perhaps this intimidated the other insects, and gave them an edge in the bug world. More of the same type of ants were carrying a large dead beetle. It took quite a lot of them and they kept dropping it and having to start again. All around were bugs, butterflies and beetles. Their colours were amazing; brightly coloured butterflies, electric blue beetles, bright red bugs. Then Ella glimpsed the most beautiful little mantis. It had spotted the tiniest of little ants and was rushing over to catch it and eat it. Ella lay down to watch more closely. Then she saw a line of the tiny ants a little way away from the mantis. She put sticks and tiny stones in their path until the marching column of tiny ants was rerouted to directly in front of the mantis. The mantis could not believe his luck and started eating them one after the other. He would reach down, pick up an ant, hold it in his hands and munch it down and then do the same again. His strange little alien like, head bobbed furiously as he munched as many of the ants as he could. The small body of the mantis was almost transparent, and Ella could see a little black line in the middle of the mantis as his body filled up with the ants. Ella could have sat and watched the bugs all day, but she felt she should get on, collect her things and continue the walk to Limonaki.

The road began to take a downhill turn now, forming an S shape in the side of the hill. She could see the sea clearly below, breaking on the volcanic rocks. As she rounded the last bend on the lowest slope of the hill, Ella saw the small collection of buildings that made up the village of Limonaki. There really were only half a dozen houses, and something that might have been a taverna, and nothing else. Then there was a tiny harbour with a couple of small boats in it, and the sea, no more than that.

Ella walked down the last of the path and came to the first of the six houses. Outside, sat a little old lady dressed head to foot in black. She smiled a toothless grin at Ella.

'Kalimaira sas' said Ella, smiling back.

'na dicknete kauti, tha thelletay enna poto may krio nairo?' (you look hot, would you like a drink of cold water?) asked the old lady.

'Nay, efharristoe pollee,' (yes thank you) replied Ella, and the old woman disappeared surprisingly swiftly indoors to fetch the drink.

She returned equally quickly, Ella suspected the old woman had been watching her progress down the hill in the sun and had the drink ready. Typical of Greek hospitality that she would be so concerned and take such care. Ella drank the water.

'sey either may ta pothia, eckettay earthy toara?' (I saw you walking, have you come far?) asked the old woman.

'appo agios spiridos' (from Agios Spiridos) replied Ella.

The old woman tutted and made some little noises.

'afto eenai meea megalee volta.' (that is a long walk)

'nay' (yes) said Ella, 'alla ena omorpho.' (but a beautiful one)

The woman nodded, no doubt remembering the days when she could walk that far.

'serettay opoo spitty zee Heleni Argyrou?' (Do you know in which house lives Heleni Argyros?) asked Ella.

'ee teleftaya prin appo toe limanee,' (the last one before the harbour,) replied the old woman.

Ella thanked her, and thanked her again for the drink, and said goodbye. She began the walk along the road to the harbour. The houses were well spaced apart and it was a good ten minute walk to Heleni's house. As she arrived, Ella saw that the only building between there and the harbour, was a small café taverna.

Ella smoothed herself down and knocked on Heleni's door. She hoped someone was in after such a long walk, but she needn't have worried.

Heleni threw open the door and hugged Ella hello. 'Yiorgos rang me and said you were coming today Ella. I am so happy to meet you. Yiorgos told me all about you on the phone. I knew your mother very well. We were best friends that summer. Come inside.'

Ella felt somewhat overwhelmed yet relieved at the same time. She was not sure she could have told her tale in all its entirety once again, and the day was so hot and perfect. The walk had been other worldly, not seeing a soul for miles and miles, not even beasts or birds, except for bugs. It was like she had walked through another world, an in between world. A magical place of otherness.

Heleni said, 'there is the bathroom, why don't you freshen up after your long walk. I have put a towel and wash cloth in there for you. I have made some lunch, I was sure you would be hungry after all that exercise.'

Ella thanked her and took temporary refuge in the sanctuary of the bathroom. She needed the time out to collect her thoughts and to come back to this world, but a freshening wash would be nice too. Soon she had used the loo and given herself a quick wash down and freshen up, and combed her hair and plaited it, and she came back out to Heleni who was waiting in the huge kitchen.

'Sit down,' said Heleni smiling, 'you must need a good rest after that walk in the sun.' She began to serve up little plates of home-made meze.

She put out keftedes (little spicy meatballs), beetroot salad (a puree of beetroot and garlic), bread, olives, hummus (chick pea dip), gigantes (butter beans in a tomato and herb sauce), and kolokithi keftedes (little fried courgette balls) along with a jug of red wine, glasses and plates. Ella had not felt hungry, having had a good elevenses at the side of the road, but seeing all this delicious Greek food, that felt like hours, even days, ago and she was suddenly very hungry indeed.

They both sat at the table and began to drink the wine and eat the delicious home cooked food.

As they ate Heleni began to talk to Ella about her memories of Liz. 'We were such good friends. I had not met my husband Christos back then, and a small group of us were always hanging round together. We would meet up at the bar while Liz was working and then when she finished, we would all go somewhere together. Maybe we would go to the shop and buy a picnic, or bring things from home, then go to the countryside and laze around eating and drinking all afternoon, and into the long sunlit evenings. We especially liked the scented heath land you walked past on your way here today.'

'That was a beautiful place,' said Ella, 'I felt almost intoxicated by the smell. The aromas were practically palpable. I felt like if I breathed deep enough, I would fall into a magical drugged sleep, as if in a fairytale.'

'Yes, we felt that there too,' said Heleni. 'We felt like we were the artist crowd at the turn of the century. Sometimes I would scribble notes or poetry, Nikos would sketch with pastel crayons in a little notebook, Panicos would play his flute, and Yiorgios would sing traditional Greek songs, in his beautiful deep voice, or just sit and make little bracelets and necklaces out of flowers and grasses. We all wore them. We thought we were so Bohemian.'

'What did Liz do?' asked Ella, wondering if she was the only one with no artistic talent.

'Oh she danced,' said Heleni. 'She danced like an angel, moving and flowing with the grasses as if she was part of nature. Nikos drew pictures of her. I think she was our muse. I wrote poems inspired by the way she moved. Panicos played haunting melodies, he said were born out of her grace and movements. Yiorgios bedecked her with jewellery made out of nature's harvest. Liz was a Goddess that summer. She absorbed the spirit of the island into her soul and then danced it back out, and we all bonded through it.'

Ella suddenly could picture what Heleni described. It was like someone was running a movie in her head. She smiled. 'It sounds wonderful.'

'It was,' agreed Heleni, 'it was the perfect summer. Sometimes we went to the beach and swam in the sea, and lay on the beach to dry off and tan. Sometimes we would catch the bus into Vathy, and hang around the shops and cafes, smoking, and feeling like we were the coolest group the island had ever known. Or we would buy ice creams and wander out onto the harbour wall.'

'I'm going to Vathy tomorrow,' said Ella, 'it will be all the lovelier for knowing that I am walking in Liz's footsteps.'

Heleni smiled and gently touched Ella's arm, 'I am glad you are finding a little of your mother through our memories. Back then we talked and talked about life and what it all meant. About the afterlife and how we would be remembered. She would have loved that you have come on this quest, and are seeing the island as she saw it.'

'It does feel very special,' said Ella, 'it is not at all what I was expecting. It is so much better.'

'I was a little in love with Nikos back then,' began Heleni, 'but of course he never knew it. He was so shy and quiet. I thought he would just die of embarrassment if I ever said anything to him. I told Liz how I felt though. She said it was probably best if I didn't say anything, just spent time together. She said that if Nikos loved me, he would eventually realise it and tell me. But when Liz left so suddenly in the November, Nikos moved away too that winter, and he never came back. I think he missed Liz so much, the village just wasn't the same for him without her. Then I met Christos in January 62, and we were married soon after.'

'Why did she leave so suddenly?' asked Ella.

'I suppose we all thought it was because Adonis broke it off with her, and her heart was broken. But after Yiorgos told me your story last night, perhaps it was because, for some reason she couldn't tell Adonis, or any of us, she was pregnant with you.'

'Tell me about Adonis please,' asked Ella.

'Adonis was an old friend of Panicos. Their families knew each other somehow. They used to live on the other side of the island in Zanthos town, but then they all moved over to the island of Kios. The farming was better or something; they kept goats I think. Anyway, sometimes Adonis would hop on the ferry and come and stay with his old friend Panicos. That was how Liz met Adonis; Panicos brought him along one day when we were all going to the beach. I think she fell in love with him at first sight. I think Panicos was jealous at first as I think he had always been a little bit in love with Liz himself. She had never looked at him that way, and I think it hurt him a bit. I think he was a little angry at himself for introducing them too.

After that Adonis saw Liz as often as he could come over, but they always spent the time alone. Maybe Liz sensed that Panicos was a little bit jealous, or maybe she felt that the group of friends wasn't the right place for romance. We all still spent lots of time together on other days though. Adonis could not come over to Aegos so very often.'

'What was Adonis like?' asked Ella.

'He was tall, dark and very handsome,' replied Heleni. 'He was confident and funny. He was kind and considerate too. I know him more from how Liz talked to me about him, than in person, and she was very much wearing rose coloured glasses, but he did sound like a very nice young man. She told me about the first time they made love. It was in that very field we were talking of earlier, where the aromas of the flowers are overwhelming. You know, perhaps you were even conceived in that field.'

Ella felt that idea resonate with something deep and primitive inside her. Something she had felt whilst walking past the field. 'My mother kept some dried flowers, and thinking about it now, they looked like the flowers I saw growing in that field today.' Ella took out the photo of her mother and the unknown man and showed it to Heleni.

'Yes, that is Adonis, I think,' said Heleni. 'Adonis was the first for Liz. She said she had been a little frightened, but he was so tender and gentle with her, that she said it had been wonderful. She danced about for days after that first time. She danced as she worked in Manolis' bar even. The customers loved it, she was so beautiful.'

'Have you seen Adonis since then?' asked Ella.

'He came over to Aegos about two years later, but no one had an address for Liz, or even knew where she had gone. We never saw him again after that, he just went away again, and didn't come back. I don't know what happened between him and Panicos, but Panicos never spoke of him again. Soon after that Panicos moved away too. He doesn't come back to the village now either. When Yiorgios died, ten years ago, that was the complete end of our happy little group of the summer of 61.' Heleni sighed, thinking back to those halcyon days, her eyes misting over a little bit.

Heleni suggested they walk down to the little harbour. Heleni went to put some sandals on and came back with a bag, and Ella grabbed her backpack, and they set off. A couple of minutes down the road they passed the little taverna and Heleni shouted something to the owner who smiled and waved.

'I told Stavros to put the kettle on when he saw us coming back as we would stop in for a drink,' said Heleni.

They walked on for a few more minutes, then down a short slope and a couple of steps and they were at the little harbour. Limonaki really was a very small village. The harbour consisted of a stone walled jetty about thirty feet long, jutting out into the sea. A tiny boat with a motor and a sunshade was tied to a ring in the wall. Two other rings were empty. On the very small patch of beach in the lee of the harbour wall, a small rowing boat had been pulled up the beach until it was clear of the seaweed line.

Heleni and Ella strolled out along the short harbour wall. On the seaward side, waves slapped temperamentally at the wall, as if annoyed by its impediment of their progress to shore. In the quiet, clear, still waters of the leeward side, they could see little fish swimming about in the safe, calm shallows. Heleni pulled a piece of bread out of her bag and tore it in half, giving half to Ella. She broke little pieces off and dropped them in near the fish. The fish all came rocketing up to the surface, and grabbed the bread crumbs. More fish appeared. Ella moved along a few feet and did the same, and soon they were both attended by seemingly huge schools of little fish. It was quite something to see. Ella had seen similar scenes on nature programmes of piranhas, but this was little tiny young fish, and bread not meat; still it was fascinating to watch.

When they had fed the fish all the pieces of bread, they walked down onto the little harbour beach. There was not much there, just the rowing boat, its oars tucked neatly underneath it, and turned over to protect from the elements. At the end of the beach was a lime tree, the fruit still small and unformed. They looked amongst the stones, picking up the occasional pretty shell, or commenting on a shark's purse as beach combers often do.

'Is this a good place to swim?' asked Ella.

'Not really,' said Heleni, 'the water is quieter, but even here in such a quiet harbour, there will still be oil from the boats floating on the surface. Come round to the other side, where the sea comes straight to the beach. It is a bit livelier, but the water is cleaner and better.'

They walked back along the little beach until they came to the path before the harbour wall. There were five steps down from the path the other side, to a sand and stone beach. They walked along a little way until the stones thinned out and the beach became a bit sandier. Heleni stopped, 'This is a good place to swim.'

Ella got her big cotton scarf out of her backpack and laid it out on the sand. She placed her backpack on top of it, to secure it against any breeze, then took off her deck shoes and socks, followed by her shorts and shirt. In her bikini, she walked to the water's edge. Here it was rather stonier and had a slightly steep slope, but only for a couple of feet into the water, then it was clear and blue.

Ella picked her way into the water, which was cool, but not cold. In two steps she was in above knee deep water, but after that it flattened out and she had to stride out quite a way before it came up to her waist. Now it was deep enough to swim. She pushed off with a lazy breast stroke, half swimming, half floating, buoyed by the salty water. The incoming waves swelled as they passed her to break later at the shore. It was a strange sensation, but one she had always loved; that feeling of being lifted up as a wave passed underneath her. Now she was used to the water temperature, she felt warm. She turned and floated on her back, the sun beating against her face and chest. If she had normal English skin, she would have been burning by now, between the sun and the salt in the water, but instead she knew she was just turning a deeper olive colour. At the shoreline, Heleni was paddling in the shadows, with her skirt hitched up around her thighs. Ella decided to swim back to shore. Actually, very little swimming was required. She swam a stroke or two and then let the next wave carry her along a bit. In no time at all her feet were touching the sandy seabed. She stood up, took a step or two towards the pebbly slope, then a wave knocked her over. Laughing, she went to stand up again as another wave came and knocked her back down. This went on for quite a while, the sea buffeting her playfully, and Ella laughing so much she was getting mouthfuls of water. She wondered nonchalantly, if it was possible to drown laughing in very shallow water. It probably was, but she was enjoying herself too much to worry about that. She looked up and could see Heleni was laughing too. Eventually she half dragged herself, and half crawled up the stones. She sat on them, more exhausted by the effort of getting out of the water than by the swim itself. She faced the sea and let the waves wash over her up to her waist. Underneath the stones were sucked and moved about by the tide and it felt like a deep tissue massage; it was really a very pleasant sensation. After a little of this she got her breath back, and accompanied by Heleni, both still laughing, they walked up the beach and flopped down on the cotton scarf.

The two of them sat peacefully, enjoying the sunshine, Ella drying off rapidly.

'That was fun,' said Ella, 'I never thought I could drown while being unable to stop laughing.'

Heleni laughed, 'it was pretty funny to watch too.'

When Ella's bikini was dry, which did not take long in the hot sun, she pulled her shirt and shorts back on, and took the flip flops out of the backpack. She pushed her decks, socks and the cotton scarf into the backpack, and they headed back to the path, Heleni sitting on the edge of it, to dust the sand from her feet before putting her sandals back on.

They walked back along the path until they arrived at the little café. Stavros the owner, rushed out and kissed Heleni hello, then introduced himself to Ella. He made a point of seating them at the 'best' table, with a view out over the harbour. 'Vleppo peegez koleebee,' (I saw you swimming) said Stavros, 'eetan toe kreeo nairo?' (was the water cold?)

'leego, stin protee,' (a little, at first) replied Ella. 'na paree exo eetan asteeo.' (getting out was funny.)

'eestay aggleetha?' (are you English?) asked Stavros.

'Nay,' (yes) replied Ella. 'tha meeno ston agio spridos.' (I'm staying in Agios Spridos.)

Heleni spoke in very rapid Greek to Stavros for a short time, and then turned to Ella and asked her what she would like to drink. Ella replied that she would like a frappe please. She heard Heleni order two sweet frappes and two Baklavas (very sweet Greek pastry.)

Shortly, Stavros brought the frappes, along with a jug of iced water. He went away and then returned almost immediately with two plates of baklava and two forks, baklava being too sticky with honey, to pick up in your fingers.

Heleni and Ella ate the sticky dessert, both thoroughly enjoying it. The cold, sweet frappes were delicious too. Ella got out her purse and tried to take out money to pay the bill, but Heleni wouldn't hear of it and pushed her purse back into her backpack.

Heleni got her purse out, but Stavros came over and said that there would be no bill, it was on the house. It was quite comical really, a rush of people all trying not to let anyone pay.

Ella said, 'But you have no customers, how can you give us all this on the house?'

Stavros grinned and said, 'In a few weeks, I will be packed all day long with tourists. I will have to hire someone to help, it will be so busy. They will hike here, then rest for hours, buying food and drink before they hike back again. They will drive here for lunch, afternoon tea and even dinner. It is my pleasure to have you as my guests now, while it is quiet. I was very entertained watching you get out of the sea; I laughed along with you both. Heleni has told me your story, and I very much hope you find your father while you are here. If you do find him, bring him here for a coffee one day, yes.'

'Oh yes,' said Ella, 'If I find him, I will bring him to meet everyone who has helped me in my search.'
After a little longer chatting and passing the time of day, Ella and Heleni said goodbye to Stavros, and walked back up to Heleni's house.
'I should probably be starting back soon,' said Ella. 'I don't want to be walking on those unpaved, unlit roads in the dark.'
'Oh don't worry about that,' said Heleni, 'Christos will drive you back when he gets in from work.'
'I don't want to put you to any trouble,' said Ella.
'Nonsense, it's no trouble at all. You must be quite tired from all that walking already today, and swimming too.'
When they had settled on the sofa, Heleni brought pictures of her grown up daughters to show Ella.
'This is my eldest Maria. She teaches archaeology at the university in Athens. This is my other daughter, Zacharoula. She is a gynaecologist at the hospital in Thessaloniki. Maria is getting married this September.'
'What clever daughters you have,' said Ella.
'Yes, I am very proud of them,' said Heleni.
The day seemed to have flown by and it was no time at all before they heard Christos' car pulling up outside. He came in and was introduced to Ella. She heard Heleni summarising her story to him in Greek. She was beginning to recognise parts of it in Greek now, she had heard people saying it so many times. It was easy to pick out names like Elizabett, Mitaira (mother), Pataira (father) and Adonis. Other bits were not so familiar. Christos drank a cherry juice that Heleni had poured for him, as he listened. At the end he spoke to Ella and said, 'I hope your story has a successful outcome, I wish you all the best.'

Ella thanked him, and Heleni told Christos she had said he would drive Ella back to Agios Spiridos. Christos said that of course he would, no problem. Heleni said she had to get on with dinner, and hugged Ella and wished her well in her search. Ella said goodbye, and got into the car with Christos. As they passed the old woman in the first house of the village, Ella waved at her sitting out on her porch, and the old woman waved back, smiling a toothless grin.

Christos asked where Ella wanted to be dropped, and she said the big supermarket on the main road if that was okay. Ella thanked him and got out of the car. Christos waved as he drove off. Ella headed next door, to Zefiros restaurant, where she had decided to have her dinner.

As it was still relatively early; most tourists and Greeks alike, seemed to prefer to dine late, with all the restaurants getting busy at 9pm, Zefiros was pretty quiet. Just a couple who looked German, eating a huge meat platter at an outside table, and an old man at the bar drinking coffee and raki. Ella took a seat at an interior table. After a very short time the waiter came over and bid her 'Kalispaira' (good evening), and Ella replied with a 'Kalispaira sass.' The waiter handed her the menu he had brought over.

'tha thellartey katty na peeittay?' (would you like anything to drink?) he asked.

'enna heemo roddokeeno parakalo,' (a peach juice please) replied Ella.

The waiter thanked her and went away to get the drink while she browsed the menu.

Ella decided on Cretan rusk soaked in tomatoes and herbs, and topped with chunks of feta cheese as a starter, followed by liver cooked in lemon and herbs.

When the waiter came back with the peach juice, in a tall glass clinking with ice, Ella placed her order for dinner.

It was not long before the waiter returned with the Cretan rusk salad, and put it down in front of her saying 'Kalee orexee,' (enjoy your meal.)

The rusk was very tasty. The hard chunks of bread had soaked up the juices from the ripe, succulent tomatoes. The rusk was softened but not soggy. Ella thought it could stand a little olive oil and wine vinegar, and dressed it accordingly. Now it tasted even better, the sweet tangy vinegar punctuating the other flavours, and the peppery crisp olive oil coming through in highlights. There was an obligatory dollop of tzatziki on the side of the plate, always a bonus. Ella finished the salad and sat sipping her peach juice for a few minutes, until the waiter deemed the length of time since she stopped eating, appropriate to collect her plate, and ask if everything was ok, in halting English.

'ottee etan meea pollee oraya salata,' (that was a very nice salad) replied Ella, indicating Greek was okay for the duration of the meal. The waiter smiled and went away again.

After another few minutes he brought out the liver. It had been fried in lemon juice and herbs, until the outside was crispy, while leaving the inside soft and pink. It was a dauntingly huge piece of liver, that filled most of the platter in its own right. Squeezed around the edge of it were, chips, rice, salad, tzatziki, lemon wedges and tomato wedges. Ella declined the offer of bread and went to work on the large plateful of food. Surprisingly she managed it all. The liver melted in her mouth, and having a piece of each accompaniment with each mouthful, it all disappeared in no time at all. Ella was hungrier than she had thought. She thought it must have been all that walking and swimming that had worked up such an appetite.

After she had finished, the waiter left it a few minutes before coming and taking her plate away and asking if there would be anything else.

'borrow na echo to logareeazmo, parakalo,' (can I have the bill please) replied Ella.

The bill arrived in a wallet. The waiter also brought a shot glass of raki, on the house. When he walked away, Ella looked at the bill. It was thirteen Euros, so she tucked fifteen into the wallet and took her raki up to the bar where she sat down next to the old guy.

'Kalispaira,' she said to him, and he replied in kind.

'Melenee Ella Hudson,' began Ella, but she didn't have to go any further.

'Ah,' said the old man, his face lighting up with interest, 'Yiorgos told me about you. I am very pleased to meet you. I am Yiannis Zefiros, and this is my restaurant. Did you enjoy your meal?'

'Very much so,' replied Ella. 'The rusk salad was very tasty and the liver melted in my mouth.'

Yiannis smiled. 'So tell me, how is your quest progressing? What have you discovered today?'

Ella told him about her trip to Limonaki and how Heleni had told her about Adonis being her mother's lover.

'After Yiorgos spoke to me today, over coffee in the kafenion,' said Yiannis, 'I thought about your story that he had told me, and remembered that I did meet Elizabett. I hoped you would come into my restaurant so I could talk to you, but if you had not I would have left a message with Yiorgos the next time I saw him.'

Yiannis ordered two more rakis for himself and Ella. Ella was glad she had only had peach juice with dinner, she did not like to get drunk.

'I remember,' began Yiannis, 'one night that summer, Elizabett and Adonis came here for dinner. It was very romantic. Someone was playing bouzouki. Anyway, when they had finished their meal and were drinking wine and eating baklava, Adonis got down on one knee and proposed to Elizabett. Of course she said yes, and cried a little bit. Everyone in the restaurant cheered. It was very moving. I often wondered what happened next, because I never saw them again after that.'

Ella was shocked, her foundations felt a little bit rocked. Why had Adonis and her mother got engaged, but never married? Why had her mother returned alone to England? Fleetingly she worried that Adonis might also be dead. Perhaps he had been dead a long time. Suddenly Ella felt sadder than she had since her arrival.

'I wonder what happened next as well,' she said. 'Do you remember which month that was?'

'I think it was August,' replied Yiannis.

Ella thought that at least Adonis had not died very suddenly, because they were still together for a few months after that. She still had further enquiries to make, she would not let her hopes be dashed, or get too high just yet. Ella thanked Yiannis for the drink, and for putting another piece in her jigsaw puzzle, and left.

Outside the night was now much cooler, too cool for the shorts she wore. She took the cotton scarf out of her backpack and tied it around her waist to form a long skirt, which was much more comfortable.

Ella walked back along the main road towards the hotel. It did not take long before she reached Aphrodite's restaurant. It was quite late now and the place was fairly busy, but Carolina noticed her, and waved her over to the bar as soon as she came in.

'Kalispaira Adelphi mou,' (good evening my sister) she said, hugging Ella and kissing her on both cheeks. 'How are you today? Have you had a good day?'

Ella replied that she had had a very nice day, and took a seat on one of the bar stools. Carolina called to a man at the end of the bar to come over, and introduced him to Ella as her brother Andreas.

'So you are the fisherman,' said Ella, and Andreas beamed at the recognition. To a Greek, to be a seafarer, and to catch fish, are amongst the best things there are to be. After all, it was good enough for Jesus.

'I have had some of the fish you caught; the octopus and the barbouni, both were delicious.'

'I cannot take credit for the flavour of them,' said Andreas, 'I just catch them. God grows them, and Carolina cooks them. They make a good team.' Ella and Andreas both laughed.

Carolina came over to them from the other side of the bar, having concluded the business that had been occupying her at the till. 'Now, what are we having to drink?' she asked.

Andreas asked for another bottle of Mythos beer, and Ella said that that sounded nice, and that she would have the same. Carolina got the drinks and brought her own cup of coffee over to where they were sitting.

'So,' asked Carolina, 'tell us how your day has been?'

Ella told them all about her walk over to Limonaki, and they agreed it was a very beautiful walk. They were familiar with the scented fields, and the views to both sides of the island. She told them about meeting Heleni, and how Heleni had confirmed that Adonis was indeed Liz's lover. She told them about her swim in the sea and how funny that had been, and they laughed along with her at the retelling of it. She told them how Heleni's husband had saved her the walk, and driven her back. Then she told them about meeting Yiannis Zefiros. She told them how Adonis had proposed to her mother in his restaurant.

Carolina clapped her hands and made an expression of joy, then said, 'But why do you look so sad, Adelphi mou?'

'Well,' began Ella, 'they never got married. I am worried about why that was. My greatest fear is that Adonis died suddenly, and that was why Liz returned to England, single and pregnant.'

'But that may not have been the reason at all,' said Carolina. 'Perhaps she was worried that his family would not, or even did not accept her, because she wasn't a Greek girl, or even Greek Orthodox, so they couldn't get married in a church unless she was baptised.'

'I'm not sure she was even Christened in any church actually, and I'm told she spoke very little Greek,' said Ella.

'So that may well have been the problem,' said Carolina.

'Or he may have said he was not ready to start a family,' said Andreas, 'and she got scared when she found out she was pregnant. She would not have qualified for any medical help or hospital bills as a tourist, so maybe she went back to England for medical care. Maybe she meant to come back but never did.'

'There are so many possible reasons,' said Carolina, 'you could drive yourself crazy thinking and worrying about it. The best thing to do, is to carry on making enquiries, as you have, and see what happens. Do not worry, let the drama play itself out in front of you, and it will all come out how it is supposed to in the end.'

'Yes, of course you are right,' said Ella. She felt less despondent now she had talked with Carolina and Andreas. She was glad she had come in for this drink and chat.

'Where are you going tomorrow then?' asked Carolina.

'I am going into Vathy to see if I can find Nikos Andreadis,' said Ella. 'He too is a fisherman, and works out of the harbour there apparently.'

'I will be having a drink in the Hotel Zeus bar tomorrow night with Christos,' said Andreas. 'I only see him now and then in tourist season, but we always have a drink together in the hotel bar on Friday nights. Come and say hello when you get back, and you can tell me how it went, and I can tell Carolina.'

'I will do that,' said Ella. 'I haven't yet got around to finding a bus timetable. Can you tell me what time the bus gets to the stop outside, to go to Vathy please?'

'They are frequent,' said Carolina. 'From seven in the morning until nine at night, they run every half hour. They stop outside here on the hour and the half hour. It is only a Euro to go to Vathy. The last bus leaves Vathy at nine thirty to come back, but if you happened to miss it, a taxi would only cost about seven Euros. Make sure you agree the price with the driver in advance though.'

'Thank you, that is very helpful,' said Ella. 'How about the other villages, how are the busses to them?'

'That is trickier,' said Andreas. 'You have to go into Vathy bus station, then get a bus out to the village you want from there. Sometimes with the closer villages, it is easier to pay a few Euros and get a cab, instead of spending hours on a bus. Certainly if you

are coming back in the evening, a cab works out better.'
Ella thanked them both, wished them a good night and headed back to the hotel for a much needed shower and sleep.

Chapter Four

Ella woke bright and early, feeling refreshed from her sleep. She pulled her swimsuit on and went down to the pool for an early swim. The old guy who cleaned the pool, smiled and waved and called kalimaira to her. She responded, thinking that was another one Yiorgos had been chatting to, but she didn't mind, not at all. The more people who knew her business, the more chance she had of success.

After her swim she went back up to her room to shower and change, and there was a little white cat sitting outside her door in the small porch area. It was a mainly white cat with tabby splodges on its sides and on one ear and the tip of its tail. It was very clearly a boy cat, one glimpse at it and Ella decided it must walk like John Wayne. She gave it a quick stroke, and it showed no sign of leaving. When she went inside, it just sat down at her door. Ella got a small bowl and filled it with milk, and put that outside for the cat. He was all over it, drinking it quickly as if it might be taken away again. Ella decided he must be feral and hungry. He did have a bit of a round saggy tummy though, so perhaps he was just opportunistic.

Ella showered and dressed, washing out her swimsuit and some other bits while she showered. She put on a long skirt and an embroidered blouse and her brown sandals. She tied her hair up into a high ponytail. Ella hung the washing out on the line and then grabbed her purse and keys and headed out to the local mini market. As she left, the cat, who appeared to have taken up residence outside, and was obviously waiting for her reappearance, took to once more rubbing around her legs. 'Alright, I'll get you something,' she told it, 'I'll be right back.' The cat sat down to resume his wait, clearly understanding fully, the universal language of food.

Ella walked round to the shop, saying good morning to the owners as she entered. She put a couple of spanakopittas (spinach and cheese pies) into her basket, added some fresh milk and a packet of ham. She picked out two packets of biscuits she liked and then added a bag of cat biscuits. That would be enough for now, she thought.

When she got back to her room, the little cat was still sitting outside, the milk bowl, now fully emptied and licked clean. Ella greeted him with a stroke and told him to wait there a minute as she had something for him. He obediently sat back down and assumed the waiting cat position.

Ella got a small plate and poured some of the cat biscuits onto it. Then she decorated the top of the biscuits with a torn up strip of ham for good measure. Taking that and the milk carton out to the porch, she put down the biscuits as the cat once more rubbed against her legs, half trilling, half purring. She tipped some more milk into the bowl and went back inside leaving him to it.

Now at last, it was time for her own breakfast. So much activity and all before eight in the morning. Ella made herself a cup of coffee, and cut some of the bread she had bought previously. She drizzled olive oil over each slice and added some ham. She added a spanakopitta for good measure and took the whole lot out onto the balcony. When she had eaten all the food and drunk the coffee, she came back in and made herself a cup of tea, and had a couple of the biscuits on the side. It was still too early for there to be more than a solo swimmer in the pool, but plenty of towels were thrown proprietarily over the sun beds. Ella grinned at the idea some people had of a holiday. She would be bored out of her mind sitting around a pool all day and occasionally going in, then eating chips and drinking in the bar all night. Each to their own she thought. She would be out of a job if those people didn't come into her shop at home and buy their annual package holidays.

Ella peeked out onto the front porch. The cat was gone and both the plate and bowl were empty and clean. Ella picked them up and washed them up along with her own plates and cups. Everything put away, she gathered what she would need for the day; a bottle of water, an island map, the one with the capital, Vathy, on the reverse side of it, purse, keys, sunglasses, a big, light shawl scarf- handy if she was going into a church, that was pretty much all she needed.

Ella left the room and walked down the main road to the bus stop. It was eight twenty five and there should be a bus to Vathy along soon. At eight thirty five, she started to wonder if it had come early and she had missed it. Then, just when she was convinced that was the case, and she would have to wait until nine, she saw the bus coming along the road towards her. Of course, she thought to herself, it was running on Greek time.

The bus pulled up and the door opened. Ella climbed in.

'eena eeseteerio stin Vathy parakalo,' (a ticket to Vathy please) she asked the driver.

'ena evro,' (one euro) he replied, pulling a ticket out of a machine beside him and handing it to her. She handed him a one euro coin and walked down the bus until she found an empty seat. She sat beside the window and watched the surrounding countryside. The countryside was volcanic and beautiful, much like all the other islands she had visited. The hills rose to either side, covered in lush green shrubs and herb bushes. Occasionally she could see several goats grazing on the slopes. Houses came and went in clusters as the bus drove through little villages, stopping from time to time when there was another passenger or two to pick up. All the houses looked unfinished, roofs left flat with iron rods poking out skywards. She had discovered on a previous visit, that this was, in fact, a tax dodge. If the houses were left unfinished, as if another storey was going to be built on top, then the tax was lower than it was on a finished building. In the village main streets, there was always the same clusters of shops, cafes and a bank. Whenever the bus stopped to pick someone up, or more rarely drop someone off, all the cars and bikes behind tooted with annoyance. In the countryside they passed olive groves with chickens running free range beneath the trees. Side roads led off into the hills, to inaccessible little villages that Ella yearned to see and explore. From time to time they passed an Exo petrol station. The bus would seem to be engulfed by countryside one moment, with tall cypress trees and geometric shaped pines that looked like they went on for miles and miles, then suddenly they would round a bend in the road and be in another village. At other times they travelled parallel to the coast; the sea, beaches and rocks passing by the window. Then after about half an hour, the countryside wasn't there anymore. What had at first, seemed like another village, had become denser and denser with houses. Ella realised they must be in the suburbs of a big town, probably the capital Vathy, where the bus was headed. The bus climbed up a hill and at the top Ella could see Vathy below them. The harbour formed a deep horseshoe shape, the name Vathy meaning horseshoe. The dark blue harbour was dotted with boats of all sizes; fishing boats, pleasure boats, and on a concrete jetty at the far end, a ferry, loading up to take passengers to one of the nearby islands. A road ran all around the harbour, and on the other side of that a town sprawled inland. As the bus came down the hill, all the cafes, shops, restaurants and other establishments came into view as the bus drove past them. At the middle of the bay, the bus pulled off the road into a large parking area. The bus driver called out 'Vathy' and came to a stop, turning the noisy engine off. Everyone rushed to get off, and Ella let them. She was not in a big hurry to get anywhere. As the bus emptied, Ella picked up her bag and got off herself. She left the bus park and crossed the busy road to the waterside opposite. There was a bench looking out onto the harbour, and she sat on that to get her bearings and have a look at her map, as well as enjoying the view and taking in her surroundings. On the town map, the fishing harbour was marked as the opposite side of the ferry jetty. She looked over that way. It was quite a walk, and she reckoned it would take her at least an hour to walk round there. Still it would be a pleasant walk along the edge of the harbour, a nicely paved promenade talking her all the way round to it. Ella drank about half of the bottle of water she had brought; she could easily buy more in any café or shop. The view out from the harbour to sea was lovely. The harbour itself was in a natural valley, with dark green forested hills rising up either side of it, and the town rising up the hill behind Ella.

She put the map and water bottle back in her bag and stretched, before setting off on a gentle walk around the harbour. As she walked along, she noticed there were little mini jetties jutting out all around the bay. To these were tethered the pleasure boats and other private craft. At each jetty, stone steps came up from the water's edge to join the promenade on which she walked. Dotted along the promenade were little mini parks, small planted areas with benches, or play areas for children. Every five hundred yards or so there was a periptero (a kiosk selling tobacco, newspapers, chocolates and drinks.) Ella stopped at a planted garden area and finished her bottle of water. The day was getting hot now, and there was little or no shade on the promenade. After she had rested for a few moments, she started off again, stopping at the next periptero and buying a bottle of fizzy orange and a bottle of water. She was nearing the ferry jetty now. The ferry was just leaving and she could hear the engines churning up the water of the harbour as it got ready to leave. She could smell the faint whiff of diesel in the air from it. She stopped to watch it pull away and out to sea; boats had always held a fascination for her. On deck, passengers watched the harbour as they moved away from it. Soon the boat was well on its way to leaving the bay entirely. Ella wondered which island it was going to; Kios maybe?

Ella continued her walk. As she approached the ferry jetty, there was a widening of the roads leading out to the jetty. She had to cross to the town side of the road, and then walk along for a couple of hundred yards, skirting cafes that sprawled tables out onto the pavement. Finally she was past the ferry entrance and could cross back over to the seaward side of the road. A little further and there was a path down to the fishing boat harbour. The path wound downwards until it was a concrete jetty pushing out to sea, parallel to the ferry jetty. All but the highest slopes of the town were out of view from down there. Fishing boats were moored along both sides of the jetty. Ella read the Greek names painted onto the sides of them. They were called ordinary Greek names like Yiorgos, Yiannis, Eleni, or Anna in the main. Sometimes they were called after the saints; Agios Spiridon, Agios Dionysus, Agia Irenaeus, Agios Gerasimus, or more originally Delphini –Dolphin. The first few boats were empty, but at the fifth a man sat on board sorting out and mending his nets.

'Kalimaira sass' Ella called to him. He called Kalimaira back.

'serettay Nikos Andreadis?' (Do you know Nikos Andreadis?) she called to him. 'aftos einay enna psarass etho' (he is a fisherman here.)

The fisherman shrugged, it seemed he did not know him.

Ella continued along the jetty calling out the same greeting and question to every manned boat she passed. She was getting nowhere. No one knew Nikos it seemed. She was beginning to wonder if he didn't fish out of Vathy after all. She got all the way to the end of the jetty, where the view was terrific, but it was marred for her by the fact that she had come to a complete dead end in this part of her quest. She turned to walk back along the jetty, feeling a bit dejected. Still, it wasn't a wasted trip, she could spend the day exploring the shops of Vathy and having lunch somewhere nice. She was jolted from her reverie by one of the fisherman calling to her from a boat she was passing.

'Ela, Kireeay,' (come here Miss) he called.

'Nay,' (yes) she replied walking over to the side of the boat he was working on.

'Are you English?' he asked her.

'Yes,' she replied, 'I am staying in Agios Spiridos for a few weeks.'

'This Nikos, you are looking for, do you know him?' he asked.

'I have never met him, but he was a good friend of my mother, many years ago,' replied Ella.

'Do you know where he is from, how old he is?' asked the fisherman.

'He is from Agios Spiridos, but he moved out here to Vathy in about 1962, I think. I guess he would be about sixty or so now.'

'Ayah,' exclaimed the fisherman, 'that would be Andreas. When he first came out here, there were too many Nikos already on the fishing boats, so we called him Andreas, as his name was Andreadis. I had forgotten he was called Nikos, until you said where he was from and how old he was.'

'Do you know where I can find him?' asked Ella.

'He has his own boat now. It is called Heleni. He will be out on it until tonight. He usually comes back about five o'clock, then sorts out his catch and his nets for an hour or so. He moors over there by that green post,' he said pointing back along the jetty a way. 'If you come back around five o'clock, you should find him then.'

'Thank you so much,' said Ella, 'I had pretty much given up on finding him when you called me over.'

'You did look sad. I suppose it is important that you find him.'

'Well really, I'm looking for someone else, that I hope he knows, but I want to meet all my mother's friends from the old days, and that way get to know her a

little better myself. She died when I was just a baby really,' said Ella. 'I hope he remembers those days.'
'I'm sure he will,' said the fisherman, 'Greeks are like elephants, they remember everything.'

Ella thanked him and walked away back down the jetty towards the town. She was going to have time for some shopping and lunch after all. She thought it strange that Nikos had named his boat Heleni. Perhaps he too had had feelings for Heleni, and her love from back then was not unreciprocated, just unspoken between them. How interesting that he had left without ever saying anything to her. Ella thought that was kind of sad.

She crossed the road and walked along a bit further round the bay to see what else was there. She rounded a turn in the road, a sort of kink in the curve of the bay, and saw an old castle fort jutting out from the hillside out into the harbour. Ella stopped at the next café along the road for a Greek coffee and water, and a piece of kadaifi (a kind of shredded wheat pastry with lots of honey and spices), and whilst having her mid morning snack, noticed just how many cats there were in this part of the town. They were everywhere. Sitting around the café tables poncing for food scraps, sitting on the harbour wall on the lookout for early returning boats filled with fish, loitering by single fishermen who were fishing off the harbour wall, sunning themselves in optimum spots, they really were everywhere. As she sat there in the café, a man went by on a bike with a cat sitting on the handlebars, with the confidence of a cat who regularly travelled in that fashion.

When Ella had finished in the café, she walked towards the castle. When she came to a mini market, she popped in and bought a bag of cat biscuits. She did not like to be empty handed of treats and have nothing to give, when there were this many cats around.

She walked along until she came to the castle. As she got closer, she could see it was divided into two areas either side of the road. There was an arch across the road, which made the road effectively too low and narrow for any cars, busses or trucks to pass through. From this point on, one was on foot or on motorbike or bicycle. Ella could also see donkeys laden with baskets on the narrow pathways the other side of the arch. She walked through. It was like walking backwards in time, into history. On her left, towards the harbour, was a gated area, where one had to buy a ticket to visit the old historical harbour castle ruins. A sign beside the gate said 3 Euros. But on the right hand side going up the hill, the town had moved into the castle. Shops and cafes filled the medieval streets, and disappeared off into a maze. Ella decided to explore that later and find somewhere nice to lunch. But first she thought she would explore the castle ruins. She bought her ticket at the little ticket booth. It was very pretty; marked Castle of Saint George, 3 Euros, Number 16, on a background picture of a piece of jewellery found on some archaeological dig. Ella had quite a collection of this style of ticket back home, from previous travels. She tucked it safely into her purse and walked into the castle grounds.

She came out into a walled garden. All around her the high stone ramparts of the old castle rose skywards. The central garden area was tall with grasses and wildflowers. At various points, stone steps led up to the ramparts. Ella walked through the grass towards some steps, pausing when she saw movement in the grass. She watched, and a large tortoise came scuttling through to an open patch. A tourist had also seen the tortoise, and was frantically fishing his camera out of its case, to take a photograph. But the tortoise either was not feeling photogenic, or was in a rush to get somewhere, and had disappeared into more long grass before the man could get his camera out and focus. Beaten by a tortoise, Ella smiled. The tortoise was going pretty fast though, its reptilian body supercharged by the hot sun. Ella climbed the steps, noticing all the heraldic emblems engraved into the stone walls of the old castle. When she reached the top, the view from the battlements out over the harbour and out to sea, almost took her breath away. She stopped to have a drink of fizzy orange and fully take in the views. She could see the whole of Vathy bay laid out beneath her to one side, the coast stretching back along the island in front, and to the other side the vast blue expanse of sea, and the distant outline of the island of Kios on the horizon. She imagined how it must have been to stand here watching out for the ships of invaders, on watch all day with the sun beating down on her, or on watch all night by the light of the moon, getting bitten all over, and chilled by the wind off the sea. Ella walked along the ramparts to the far end, where steps descended down the outside of the wall to a garden area surrounded by sheer cliffs on one side and the harbour waters on the other. Here there were more cats than ever. In the centre of the garden area was a huge tree, some of its branches propped up by poles to stop it falling over under its own weight. There was a sign by the tree, saying it dated back to the time of Socrates and that the philosopher himself used to sit underneath the tree and teach his students. Ella doubted this was true on several levels, but liked the idea nevertheless. She sat down on a nearby bench and got out the cat biscuits, sprinkling them about her for the cats. She was soon surrounded by a veritable carpet of cats, in all states of repair. Cats missing an ear or an eye, or a tail or a leg. Big cats, scrawny cats, pregnant cats, kittens, wary cats, friendly cats. The cats of the world had united in this harbour side garden, it seemed. Ella fed them, as fairly as she could, until the whole bag of biscuits was gone. Gradually most of the cats drifted back to whatever they had been doing before. A few hung around nearby hopefully, but with the kind of attitude that said; 'we've got nothing better to do anyway.' Ella enjoyed the feel of the sun on her shoulders and the potent smell of the jasmine growing up the cliff walls. After a while, Ella felt it was time to go and explore the town within the castle.

She walked back to the ticket office and out through the gates into the maze of tiny walled streets. It felt somehow surreal, like she was on a giant film set. Tourist gift shops set in a medieval fortress seemed so odd. Other places seemed like they had been there forever. A restaurant with rickety wooden chairs and bare tables sprawling out into the narrow street, almost blocking it, a line of octopuses, (chtapothia) hanging on a string across the street drying- being watched wistfully by a local cat or two.

Every available nook and cranny of the castle had been utilised in some way for modern shopping. In one place clothes hung from crumbling ruins. A small boy played accordion in a corner for tips. A mother cat fed her kittens in the shade of an alley too small even for shops. Elsewhere doors were walled up. Little gardens and archaeological digs could be looked down on from above but were closed to entry by tourists. There were shops selling olive oil products, and Ella walked into one of these. They had soaps and creams made from olive oil and scented with local herbs. There were dried herbs packaged prettily to take home as souvenirs. Salad tossers, bowls and masks made from olive wood. Everything you could imagine to buy as a souvenir, plus the usual selection of tacky stuff that some tourists seemed to prefer. Ella looked at the white statues of Greek Gods and Goddesses, and browsed the Greek cookery books, chuckling at some of their strange translations. In the end she bought several boxes of mountain tea, a strange kind of herb tea that tasted of mountain herbs, and if brewed strongly enough, faintly of incense. She also bought a tub of Stefi Olive oil moisturiser. She had long since used the last of a pot she bought on a previous trip, and had never found anything to equal it back home. Ella continued walking through the narrow walled streets which every now and then opened out to reveal a little walled garden or a small church hidden in the midst of the streets. Finally she came to a really quiet point at the far end of the castle town. There, almost jammed up against the cliff was a deserted little restaurant. It looked perfect for lunch and Ella picked a nice table and sat down. The cliff was on her left with scented jasmine clinging to it. In front of her she could see some of the streets she had walked along on her way there. Soon a waiter arrived, immediately speaking to her in English. Obviously she was in a very touristic zone, but never mind, it was very nice just here, and the smells drifting out from the kitchen were very tempting. The waiter greeted her and gave her a menu, asking her if she would like a drink while she was waiting. Ella ordered a half litre jug of local village red wine, which amounted to about three glasses. Over the course of a lazy lunch, three glasses would be fine.

She browsed the menu and decided after a lot of going backwards and forwards, on tyrokaftairee (a spicy cheese salad, where the cheese is blended with green chillies and herbs) as a starter, and moussaka (meat and aubergines layered in a cheese sauce) as a main. Moussaka was generally considered a very touristy dish, but as it seemed to be tourist central here in the castle, Ella decided to go with the flow. Often what was cooked most regularly, was freshest and tastiest. When the waiter came back out with her wine she gave him her order. While Ella waited for her food to arrive, she sipped at a glass of wine and enjoyed the peaceful ambience of this quiet little corner of the busy town. Soon the waiter brought out the tyrokaftairee with a bread basket and a side plate with cutlery wrapped in a serviette. Ella dipped the bread into the cheese salad dip and found it to be as good and tasty as she remembered from previous holidays.

Later on, the Moussaka proved to be very good too. Ella now felt completely full and thought a gentle stroll was required for the next hour or two before she would begin to feel comfortable again. When she asked for the bill, the waiter brought a plate of juicy red watermelon, on the house. Ella was very relieved it was not Ravani or some other filling dessert; watermelon she could manage, it was practically a drink anyway. Ella finished her wine and the watermelon, and paid the bill, which was a very reasonable twelve Euros, so she left fifteen, and got up to go. The waiter called after her goodbye, and wished her a nice day, so she turned and smiled, and waved back at him, calling 'Yassas.'

Ella made her way back through the medieval castle maze of streets, until she came to the main arch which led back into the more modern part of Vathy town. She immediately sensed she was in the local's area now. People around her now were speaking Greek, not English and German like they had been. She turned off the main road, and began walking uphill through the streets which were lined with normal shops; greengrocers, butchers, bakers, hardware, hairdressers, clothes shops. She passed a school whose gates were already locked for the day-the children started very early and went home for the day at lunchtime. They did get a lot of homework though. Ella carried on through the streets, passing what looked like a town hall, then coming abruptly upon a little fenced off town park. She went in through a gate and was once more in a peaceful garden of scented plants and cool shaded benches. She decided to sit for a while and drink some water; she needed it anyway after the wine at lunch time. It was so tranquil here in the heart of the sprawling town, bustling with daily business, the little park forming an oasis of calm and shade. There didn't seem to be any other people in the park, but there were plenty of birds, cats and insects. Plenty to sit and watch as she drank her water. Ella walked on through the park, which had areas of plants and trees, areas of rocks formed into little gardens, a children's play area and some stone benches around a fountain. At the far side there was another gate by which to exit. Ella came out that way onto a street that looked deserted. There were four shops; a travel shop, a finance broker, a barbers shop, and a cake shop (zacharoplasteeo), of which only the cake shop looked open. More out of interest than anything else, Ella wandered inside. It was nothing like the cake shops back home. There were pastries mainly, and some cakes, but they did not look sweet and gooey like the cakes Ella was used to, but almost savoury or dry sponge. There was nothing of the cream filled bun, or iced cupcake in this shop. The smell of fresh coffee filled the air, overwhelming the smell of cakes and pastries. Everything for sale looked homemade, not mass produced. Ella asked for two bougatsa (custard filled pastries) in a box to take home, and a coffee. She paid, then the man who ran the shop gestured to her to take a seat outside and he would bring her coffee out to her. A moment later he came out with two coffees and two iced waters, and sat down at the table with her. Shortly after that a woman brought out a plate with two pieces of some sort of pudding on it, and two forks. The man said that she must try his pudding on the house. He said it was a new recipe and he wasn't sure if he was going to sell it yet, so he would be very pleased if she would taste it. Ella did not really have room yet, but did not wish to be rude. She took a fork and tried the dessert. It tasted like a heavily spiced bread pudding, but lighter than the traditional English dessert. It was very nice, not the usual honey laden Greek dessert, but more like a sponge cake flavoured heavily with cinnamon and cloves. 'It would be nice with Tsai (Greek tea) I think,' said Ella.

'Yes,' agreed the man, who had already introduced himself as Agamemnon, 'I think so too. The spices are the same as the ones used in the tea. My wife thinks it is nicer drizzled with honey, and served with very sweet Greek coffee though.'

'She has a sweeter tooth than you, I think,' said Ella smiling.

'That is true,' Agamemnon replied. 'We lived in England, in London, for a few years, when we were younger. When we were first married we couldn't afford a house, and my uncle let us live above his Greek restaurant in London rent free, as long as we helped in the restaurant. He paid us a little too, and we saved up until we could afford to come back home and set ourselves up here.'

'Did you like London?' asked Ella.

'It was rather too cold and wet for me,' said Agamemnon, 'but my wife loved the English cream cakes and sweet iced cakes. She put on a lot of weight while we were there. I think she would go back in a moment if she got the chance. She did not mind the weather so much. But I was sad, I missed the eelioss' (sun).

Ella chatted with Agamemnon a bit longer, about London and Greece, then excused herself, saying it had been wonderful to meet him, but that she had an appointment with a boat that was coming in, and had to make her way back down to the fishing harbour. Agamemnon wished her well, and she wished him well back.

Ella made her way through the streets heading downhill, knowing that would bring her out somewhere on the main harbour road. It wasn't really possible to be lost when the sea was downhill. Sure enough, after a while, she came out on the main road, along a bit from the fishing harbour. She looked at her watch; she had half an hour before Nikos' boat was due in. The fishing harbour was about twenty minutes walk away, even a gentle stroll should get her there a little early, so she could be in position when the boats came in.

Ella positioned herself by the green post she had been directed to earlier, and watched the first of the evening's returning fishing boats chugging slowly into the harbour. The first boat arrived and tied up. A man hopped onto the pier to tie the boat in position. The rest of the crew passed buckets and boxes out to him. He sat on a box and started to gut the fish they had caught, with a knife. Soon he was surrounded by cats, which seemed to have instantly appeared out of nowhere. He threw the guts behind him on the ground and the cats descended on them for their dinner. Soon another guy joined him gutting the catch, while a third hauled up a bucket of sea water to wash the fish with. It was a hive of industry, the cats playing their part, and cleaning up the guts almost as soon as they went down. As soon as the job was finished the cats moved along the jetty to the next boat that was just pulling in. When the fish were all cleaned, the first man took them away in a box down to the parking area at the road end of the jetty. Presumably they were going to be refrigerated for sale the next morning, or possibly being taken to restaurants for that very evening. The second man washed, stacked and cleared away the remaining boxes and buckets and then also left the boat, presumably making his way home. The third man sluiced down the boats deck with water, and sat down to sort out the net and get it ready for the next fishing trip. That was pretty much the pattern in one form or another as each boat came in. The cats were getting quite full now, and strolled lazily to each new boat, no longer bothering to fight for the scraps.

Time was getting on and Ella realised it was almost six. She wondered if Nikos was staying out all night. Just then she saw a boat coming towards the part of the jetty where she sat. Sure enough it was the Heleni.

Ella waited until the boat had tied up and a man had climbed off and settled to the task of gutting fish. She wandered over to him and said, 'Kalispaira,' (good evening.)

He looked up at her briefly and grunted roughly, 'kalispaira sass.'

'eesettay Andreas, Nikos Andreadis?' (are you Andreas, Nikos Andreadis?) Ella asked.

'Nay,' (yes) he replied, not adding anything else, but looking at her a little more closely this time.

'Eemay Ella Hudson. Ee mitaira moo eetan Elizabett Hudson.' (I am Ella Hudson. My mother was Elizabeth Hudson.)

Nikos stopped what he was doing and looked more closely at Ella. 'Yes, you do look like her,' he said in English, 'but more Greek. Is she here with you?'

'Sadly not,' replied Ella, 'she died when I was only four. I have come to this island looking for people she knew back in '61, to try and get to know her better. I'm told you and she were good friends that summer.'

'Yes we were,' said Nikos. One of the cats came over and nudged against him as if to tell him to get on with gutting the fish. Nikos picked up his knife and another fish and dutifully resumed his task.

'I can see you're busy now, but can I buy you dinner when you have finished, and we can talk a little?' asked Ella.

Nikos thought for a moment then said, 'I'm hardly dressed for a city restaurant. I usually cook myself dinner on the boat here from my catch. I tell you what, you go down to the shop and buy some tsipouro or whatever you like to drink, and some bread, and come back here and I'll cook us both dinner.'

'That sounds lovely,' said Ella. 'Can I leave my bags on the boat while I go to the shop?'

'Endaksee (ok) of course,' said Nikos.

Ella took her purse out of her bag, and lowered the other bags onto the boat. She waved at Nikos and headed off down the jetty to the mini market.

In the mini market, Ella bought a bottle of tsipouro, a loaf of bread, then for good measure, some onions, tomatoes, peppers and olives, and a block of feta cheese. Whatever Nikos planned to cook, there should be enough to go with it now, thought Ella. Ella walked back to the boat. Nikos was back on board. The cats had done their cleaning job, there was not a scrap of fish guts in sight. The cleaned fish had been stashed away in cold boxes, the deck scrubbed, and Nikos was currently folding up his nets. As Ella approached he finished with the nets and pushed the now tidy pile of netting to the back of the boat. He helped Ella down into the boat and indicated a clean place for her to sit. She handed the bag of groceries to him, and he grinned. 'You have a good meal in here. Along with some of my fish, we shall eat well tonight.

Ella offered to help with anything but Nikos refused, telling her to relax while he made dinner. He got out a little camping stove and put a frying pan on it. He poured a little olive oil into it from a tin he obviously kept on the boat for such purposes. Then he added two large sardines to the pan. He cooked them slowly, turning them carefully twice. When they were cooked, he put them on plates, and put a little more oil in the pan. He added some squid he had prepared earlier and cooked it for just a few moments so it wouldn't be rubbery. He added some to each plate, tore a lump of bread for each plate, turned the gas off and handed a plate to Ella. He rummaged around for a couple of forks and knives and tin cups. He handed Ella a shot of tsipouro in a tin cup, and said, 'Stin yammas.' (to our health.)

Ella replied the same and they began to eat and drink. Nikos produced a pot containing sea salt to sprinkle on the fish. Ella sensed that Nikos wanted to eat for a bit before he got talking, so she ate quietly enjoying the wonderful flavours of just caught fish.

The squid was melt in the mouth perfect, and the sardines were very tasty, though the little bones were a bit fiddly.

When they finished, Nikos threw the fish heads, tails and bones up onto the jetty for the cats, who made short work of them. Nikos produced a large cooking pot and scraped the oil from the frying pan into it, adding a little more as well. He roughly chopped the onions and peppers into the pot and began to cook it over the gas stove. Ella watched, a little surprised; she had not been expecting two courses. Nikos produced three slabs of swordfish steak from a cold box, which he had also prepared earlier, and cut them into chunks, throwing the central bone onto the jetty for the cats and the chunks into the pot. He added the roughly chopped tomatoes and some water and left it to cook. While it cooked he cut the feta into chunks and put some on each of their plates along with the olives. He poured a little more tsipouro into their mugs. Ella remembered the bougatsa in her bag and realised they were heading into the realms of four courses, and smiled. The sun was beginning to set, but the water in the harbour was very calm and the boat bobbed gently, soothingly.

'What can I tell you about Elizabett?' began Nikos, thinking back through the mists of time. 'She was very beautiful. I drew lots of pictures of her that summer. She danced like an angel. You know, before Elizabett, I could hardly talk to anyone. I used to go to Manolis' bar and sit at one end with my drink, and then leave again, saying no more than a few words all night. Elizabett came over and talked to me. She didn't mind when I didn't, couldn't answer, just chatted away to me like I was her oldest, best friend. After a while I forgot about being shy. I felt like we had been friends for ever and it was so easy to talk to her. I think I was a little bit in love with her for that. My life opened up because of Elizabett. Then she introduced me to the others, slowly one at a time, when it was quiet, so I would not feel overwhelmed. First Yiorgios, then Panicos, and finally Heleni. Before I knew it, I was part of a group of friends. My world was suddenly a different, more colourful place, and all thanks to the kindness and care of Elizabett. Of course there was never anything more than friendship between us. I think she was closer to Panicos for a while, but that all changed when Adonis came along.'

Nikos paused to look in the cooking pot. Obviously he decided it was ready and found two bowls to serve it in. He handed Ella a bowl of the chunky fish stew, and tore off another chunk of bread to go with it. He smiled and said, 'Kalee orexee.'

The stew was delicious. Ella had never eaten swordfish so fresh, and the vegetables complimented it perfectly. They did not talk again while they ate. Ella got the feeling Nikos liked to appreciate his food while he ate it, and fully immerse himself in the tastes and sensations. That was fine by her, the food was good. It was nice to give it the attention it deserved. When they had finished, Nikos poured them a little more tsipouro each. Ella remembered the bougatsa, and got the box out of her bag. She offered one to Nikos, who beamed at her. 'I love bougatsa,' he said. 'What a treat. I hope you haven't got any more surprises though, I'm full.'

Ella smiled and said that that was all, and added that she was full too. 'I notice your boat is called Heleni,' she said, 'is that after Heleni from Agios Spiridos?'

'Yes,' said Nikos wistfully, 'I was very much in love with Heleni back then. But when Elizabett left so suddenly, all my confidence seemed to leave with her, and I thought I could never tell Heleni how I felt. I heard she married someone else the next year anyway.'

Ella thought it was probably best not to tell Nikos how Heleni had felt about him. It was too late for it to do any good now, and might just cause him pain. 'Did you meet Adonis?' she asked.

'Only once,' said Nikos, 'when we all went to the beach together. I could see that Elizabett was immediately very taken with him, but I don't know what happened afterwards.'

'Well,' said Ella, 'it has been lovely to meet you and I must thank you for the wonderful dinner, but I should be getting back, as it is getting late. Where can I get a taxi from?'

'I will show you, if you wait just a moment longer,' replied Nikos.

Nikos busied himself putting away the plates and cups and the little stove. He collected up the boxes containing the fish and put them up on the jetty. Then he climbed up himself and took Ella's bags from her and helped her up too. They walked down the jetty together. At the end of the jetty Nikos asked her to wait a moment while he put the boxes in the back of a flat bed truck. Then he walked on with her to the main road. Three taxis were parked near the entrance to the ferry jetty. Nikos went over to one and spoke to him rapidly in Greek for a few moments. He came back to Ella and said, 'He will take you to Agios Spiridos for six Euros.' Nikos hugged Ella and she got into the taxi, waving goodbye to him as it pulled away.

The roads looked different at night, the hills making dark brooding shadows to the sides. Even when there was a view of the sea, it sat there like a black carpet, merging with the black sky. Every now and then they would pass a roadside shrine with a little oil candle flickering away inside it. These shrines marked places where people had died in road accidents. The Greeks were very matter of fact about death; build a shrine, light a candle at the important times of remembrance, go to the remembrance services in church, take the mixture of wheat, raisin, almond and pomegranate to commemorate the dead, and then move on, get on with life.

Ella half dozed in the taxi. She was full of food and tsipouro, there was nothing much to see, and the taxi was comfortable. Shortly she came out of her reverie by the taxi driver asking her, 'poo tha pas sto agios spiridos?' (where abouts in Agios Spiridos?) 'Zenothotheo Zeus parakalo,' (Hotel Zeus please) she replied, pulling out her purse.

When they pulled up outside the Zeus, shortly afterwards, the taxi driver said six Euros, and Ella gave him seven fifty and got out.

She went into the hotel reception and called hello to Christos and Andreas who were sitting at the bar, saying she would be back down to have a drink with them in a couple of minutes.

Ella went up to her room and put down her shopping. She had a quick wash and brush up and changed into a dress and flip flops. She picked up her purse and keys and headed down to the bar. She greeted the men with a 'kalispaira' and sat down beside them, as they greeted her in the same way.

'So tell us about your day,' said Andreas.

Ella told them about her day exploring Vathy, and the old town and castle. They both agreed it was a very beautiful part of the city. Then Ella told them about meeting Nikos, and having a wonderful dinner on his boat. She told them that she did not feel she had found out anything new, except where to find Nikos, but that she had coloured in her picture of her mother's life a little more.

'This morning there was a white cat with tabby spots outside my room,' said Ella. 'Is it the hotel cat? I hope it was okay to feed him?'

'Oh that is Bob,' replied Christos. 'He is no one's cat, but he hangs around the hotel and befriends the tourists who sometimes feed him. I think he fattens up all summer and almost starves all winter.'

Ella smiled at the idea of him being called Bob. In Greek that would be spelt 'mpwmp.' 'How did he come to be called Bob,' she asked.

'Years ago, a little girl who was staying here started feeding him, and she called him that. It just kind of stuck to him I suppose. He has been Bob ever since,' replied Christos.

Ella finished the Metaxa she had ordered, and said she really should be getting to bed as it had been another long day. Andreas and Christos wished her good night and hoped she had a good day tomorrow.

Chapter Five

Ella awoke at seven o'clock to the sound of tapping,
which stopped, then shortly afterwards, started again.
She soon realised it was coming from the door to her
room, and hopped out of bed to see who was there.
She opened the door, but no-one was there. Then
she looked down, and Bob was standing there
looking up at her expectantly. He had been knocking
on her door with his paw, telling her it was breakfast
time. Ella laughed.

'Ok Bob,' she said, 'I'll get your breakfast, hang on a
minute.' Bob went and sat down on the porch in the
shade.

Ella poured a bowl of milk, and a plate of cat biscuits,
and tore another slice of ham over the top. Bob was
dining well again it seemed. She took the dishes out
to the porch and put them down beside Bob, who ate
furiously, as if he hadn't eaten in at least a month.

Ella decided not to go for a swim this morning,
perhaps she would swim in the sea later on. She
showered and plaited her hair, then dressed in her
bikini, over which she put a floaty skirt and t-shirt,
with a flimsy cotton jacket, a mere wisp of material
that flowed behind her in the breeze. She slipped on
her white sandals. Now it was time to think about her
own breakfast.

She cut a slice of bread and poured some olive oil
onto it. It was going hard. She put the remains of the
loaf into its bag to take with her on her outing today.
She was sure there would be some time later to feed
the fishes. She added the remaining spanakopitta to
her breakfast plate, and the remains of the halva.
She shook some of the rusk pieces into a bowl and
poured olive oil over them, putting them back into the
fridge to soak. They would be very tasty when they
had softened and soaked up the oil. Ella made

herself a strong cup of coffee to go with her breakfast, and then took the whole lot out onto the balcony. She waved down to the pool guy, who smiled and waved back.

Ella sat and ate her breakfast and looked at the rock formation. She could see several faces in it now too, as well as the original lizard shape, looking as if it was ready to break away from the other rocks and rush off on a Godzilla style rampage at any moment. One of the faces looked directly at the lizard, as if to say, 'I'm watching you lizard, you don't rampage on my watch.' Another face seemed to stare directly at Ella, whilst another looked off into the distance as if keeping lookout.

Ella finished her breakfast and collected Bob's dishes from outside. Bob was nowhere in sight, off about his business of the day no doubt, or perhaps getting his second breakfast from another willing tourist. She washed everything up and put it away. She put together her bag for the day; purse, keys, sunglasses, big cotton scarf, an apple, a bottle of water, the bag of old bread. She put away the things that had been left about from the previous day; dry washing, purchases, clothes and shoes, and made a neat pile of items she needed to hand wash, but had forgotten about when she showered this morning.

Ella headed down to the bus stop, but the one on the other side of the road this time. Agios Nikolaus, where she was going today, was the next town along the coast in that direction, and she took an educated guess that busses passing through Agios Spiridos would carry on to Agios Nikolaus.

After about ten minutes a bus came along. It had Agios Nikolaus written on the destination display on the front, so that guess had worked out about right. It pulled up alongside her and she climbed on. It was one of the old fashioned style of busses, less modern and coach like, more old school bus style. There was a conductor, who waved her on to a seat, nodding as if to say, you can pay me when you have settled down. Ella took a seat next to a huge open window, that was blowing warm air into the bus. The old style busses had big windows, whereas the more modern coaches had little individual air conditioning vents that blew cold air onto your face, and could be twisted to a different direction or turned off entirely. Luckily her hair was plaited, or else it would have been blowing all around her face. The conductor came over to her. 'Agios Nikolaus, parakalo,' she said. 'efdominda lepta,' (70 cents) he replied, pulling a ticket from a little booklet. Ella gave him a one euro coin, and he fished out thirty cents change from his belt bag.

The countryside around her was very similar to the views on the journey into Vathy, but Ella didn't really have time to enjoy the views as Agios Nikolaus was only ten minutes drive down the road. In no time at all, they had reached the outer sprawl of the town and were pulling into a large bus garage parking area. The conductor called out 'Agios Nikolaus.' Everyone rushed to get off. Greeks were always in such a hurry, even the language came out in a rush. Ella thought that the heat should surely slow them down a bit, but perhaps like the lizards and the tortoise, they were supercharged by the sun.

Ella was last off the bus. She headed over to the main building, where the ticket office, a small café, and toilets were located. She went up to the ticket office, they didn't have any other customers. 'pssackno yia Panicos Papadopoulous. Eenay enna odigoss leofoureeou etho,' (I'm looking for Panicos Papadopoulous. He is a bus driver here) said Ella.

'Nay, ton sairo,' (yes I know him) said the ticket office attendant, 'perimenettay ena lepto,' (wait a minute.) The woman pulled out a stack of forms from under her desk and ran her finger down them. 'eenay odigeesee ena leofourio yia Zanthos simaira. Aftoss tha eenay peeso sto pemdee kay missee.' (He is driving a bus to Zanthos today, he will be back at 5.30,) she said.

Ella thanked her and left the bus station. She had the day ahead of her to explore Agios Nikolaus. Where to begin. Just outside the bus station was a town map, her position at the bus station clearly marked on it. As she was looking at the map, a road train pulled up in the road beside her. Ella had encountered the road trains before on other islands, and fondly referred to them as Happy trains. This was because she was sitting in a bar where the bar owner was a friend of hers, when she saw her first road train go past. Evgennia, the bar owner, had laughed and said, 'there goes the happy train,' waving it at as it passed. The children on it waved tentatively back at her, but the adults looked sullen and bored. Ella had asked her why she called it the happy train. Evgennia had replied that she called it that because everyone on it always looked so miserable. Ella had been calling the road trains, happy trains ever since. A road train was actually a modified car or van chassis that had been rebuilt to look like a little train. It pulled along a half dozen little trailers with seats and roofs, and took tourists on a slow ride around the town. Generally a happy train ride cost about three or four Euros for the full loop around the town, or you could pay less and use it as a form of transport from A to B. Ella loved the funny little things, and it was a good way to see what the town had to offer. The full circuit lasted anything from twenty to forty minutes, depending on the town. The passengers were disembarking, apart from the odd one or two who wanted to get off elsewhere. The back seat in the last carriage was empty. Ella liked this seat, it had the best views she felt, as she hopped on. Soon the driver walked down the train collecting fares from new passengers. Finally he got to Ella. 'ee pleeriss diadromee pross ta peeso etho,' (the full ride to back here,) she said to him. 'Trio evro' (3 Euros) he replied giving her a ticket. He walked slowly back down the length of the train allowing anyone else who wanted it, to get on, and climbed into the driver's seat. He rang a little bell and the happy train got underway. Greek music piped out of little speakers attached in the roof of each carriage. Ella smiled, she loved the twee little trains.

The train drove slowly through the town centre, passing shops and tavernas. It passed shops displaying handcrafted jewellery and pottery, and a bar that advertised a resident rock band every Thursday night. Tourist shops with inflatable crocodiles and ducks, for the sea or pool, flashed by in a blaze of colour. Every kind of Greek shop was mingled with shops with gaudy tourist displays, street cafés, craft shops and the occasional glimpse of a town square or small park area. It was really quite beautiful. Greeks and tourists alike sat outside at cafés and kafenions. Ella smiled to herself as she read the board of one café, proudly announcing its sale of 'stuff on toast.'

The train was passing through the town centre now and coming towards the coast, through fields growing courgettes, squashes and tomatoes. Dogs wandered about, taking themselves for their daily walk. One ran alongside the train happily for a little way.

Then the train turned left onto the main coastal promenade. People shouted and waved at it as it passed, and Ella smiled and waved back. A brown sign reading Aphrodite's rock pointed seawards at a large rock rising out of the sea just off the coast. Ella could see that the promenade path was deeply cracked in places; clearly there had been some earthquake activity here in recent years. The train turned left again, and Ella noticed that on the right, a coastal path led off to what was clearly an archaeological site. A nearby brown sign said that it was the Archaeological site for the Palace of the Kings. Ella decided to buy another ticket back to this point and explore the site, after the happy train had finished its circuit. She strained to see the site, but could really only see columns rising and little else. The train passed through fields and alongside the army barracks, then turned back towards the town. It passed through an area of houses that had big gardens, filled with trees laden with fruit and olives. The train went off down a side road, that was really no more than a dirt track, and laboured its way uphill for a little while, taking in a bit of the countryside surrounding Agios Nikolaus. Eventually it rejoined the main road for a very short time; luckily as it held up the traffic with its slow progress, and was soon pulling up once again in front of the bus station. Ella remained in her seat and bought herself a one and a half euro ticket to the coast path for the Palace of the Kings. It wasn't long before the happy train was letting her off at the start of the coastal footpath. It was a lovely path to stroll along. Cracked paving had been laid and there were benches every hundred yards or so. Birds, insects and lizards were everywhere, and it made for a very interesting walk. A skylark sat on the nearby fence of the archaeological park and sang as she walked by. Later a kite posed within about a foot of her so she could have a good look at it.

After a time Ella arrived at the entrance to the park. She bought her ticket for three Euros forty, another of the pretty picture series, this one depicting a pair of large pithoi (big ceramic pots about seven foot tall, used to store oil and wine) on a mosaic background. Then she was inside the park.

First there was a path of ancient stone leading up to a roped off, excavated area. Ella walked up to it and saw the most beautiful set of floor mosaics, all in separate room areas. The path wound off to the right through some olive trees then became more built up, with actual walls standing alongside the columns. This, the little signs said, was the storage area. There were pithoi of all sizes here from small three foot high ones, to huge eight foot high ones. There was a large flat stone and a sort of lipped stone bowl; the sign said it was for grinding olives to make oil. Further into the main building area, and the signs started to talk about the various rooms of the palace, how this room was a receiving hall, and this a bedroom or bathroom. Another was a spa, with a massive mosaic floor that the sign said was a bathing pool. Ella wandered about the main palace for a while, reading the little signs and taking in the atmosphere. It was amazing how much was preserved here. She climbed up some steps and was in an open outdoor area which the sign said was some kind of forum, where the king held audiences, and passed judgement in cases. From here some steps led down into an area surrounded by trees. It was like a long street on the perimeter of the palace, and the sign said it was probably some sort of common market area, outside of the palace itself. Ella sat down on a rock wall and placed her hands flat alongside her. She closed her eyes, and was instantly transported to another time. She felt the hustle and bustle of the market, heard the people shouting, could almost smell the fish and spices and bread, could almost feel people jostling against her. She let the atmosphere soak into her and explored the rest of the site with different eyes. In most of the world, history seemed as far away as the hundreds or thousands of years that separated it from now; here it felt like it was just a breath away. Ella continued to walk through the site. She came to an area marked as the temple, where there was a huge female statue. It was robed, but the head and arms had been broken off. There was an altar area, and huge columns rising skyward. She passed an area that looked like an amphitheatre, and she was in a market square, or so the sign said. This was more than a palace, it was a whole town. There were very few visitors walking round the site, and for a moment or two, Ella felt like the past was more alive than the present. She came to a burial area, but it was no ordinary burial ground. Stone steps led down into tombs underground, through a labyrinth of tunnels and caves, to the shelf that marked the final resting place of a king, or someone of high importance. If she had felt in awe before, this place just about finished her off.

Ella carried on walking through the site, past arches, mounds and caves that alone would have impressed her, before she saw everything else. There was so much here, and she was just expecting a dry archaeological site, as per the brief mention given in her tour guide. She found herself walking through gardens now. Palm trees and wild herb bushes alongside fragrant flowers, cypress trees, olive trees and things she had no idea what they were, but which smelt divine. There was a big stone arch through which she could see the sea. As she walked through it she saw a one way metal turnstile and it led out into the harbour. It was a really pretty little harbour, dotted with luxury boats, and she saw a taverna on the harbour front that looked just perfect for lunch. Ella was about as full as she could get of history, and now she needed to be full of lunch too. She left the park and made her way down to the taverna.

It was a lovely little harbour side taverna, with comfy conservatory, armchair style, seats. Ella sat right by the water's edge where she could see all the boats, or peer down into the water and see the fish swimming about. The waiter came over and after a quick greeting in Greek, he asked what Ella would like to drink, she asked for a 'hema karasseeoo' (cherry juice) and the waiter nodded and handed Ella a menu.

She studied the menu for a little while, but before the juice arrived she had decided on horta, (variously translated to English on menus as grass, weeds or wild greens. Generally it is mainly wild spinach and similar wild edible greens, steamed and served with lemon and olive oil. Horta are sold for about 15p for a big bunch in supermarkets.) Ella thought she would try the stuffed squid (calamaries) for the main. The waiter came back with the iced juice, and took her order.

Ella sipped at the cherry juice which was bitter sweet and delicious, and reminded her of some sweets she used to love to buy when she was a child. They were a rare treat as she had to save up pennies to buy them.

A large pleasure cruiser was just leaving the harbour, packed with tourists, no doubt off for a beach barbeque on some deserted stretch of coastline, followed by swimming off the boat in the afternoon. Ella hoped she would be going on a boat soon, other than the ferry to Kios, which she would no doubt do in the next couple of days, as she missed the feel of water underneath her. Swimming was fine, but boats were better. Perhaps that was her Greek half coming through.

The waiter came back with a bowl of horta and a basket of bread, and wished her the standard 'kalee orexee.'

The horta tasted fresh and earthy, seasoned with the crispness of the lemon and the peppery flavour of the olive oil. Ella added a little salt to perfect it. Even with a couple of slices of bread, it disappeared very quickly. Ella realised she had been quite hungry. The waiter took the bowl away shortly after she finished, and she told him the horta was 'oopairochoss' superb, and he smiled and did a funny little bow.

In the harbour someone was pottering about on the deck of his boat, and someone else was just coming off of their boat with a shopping bag, obviously out to get some supplies. A small fishing boat chugged back into harbour, pumping out little flumes of black diesel smoke behind it. They had likely caught enough fish early on, and decided to call it a day. The waiter arrived with the stuffed calamaries on a platter. Four squid, filled so they were fat and round, coated with breadcrumbs, sat in the middle of the plate. Around them were a small salad, some tzatziki, some chips, some warmed pitta bread slices, and lemon wedges. It looked and smelt wonderful. Ella could barely wait for the waiter to go away so she could dive in. She cut open one of the squid, to reveal a very dark looking filling. It was impossible to tell what it was by looking. Ella tasted it. And then to confirm, tasted a second mouthful. It was absolutely heavenly. The filling, she surmised, was the tentacles chopped and mixed with the ink for colour, onions, herbs, salt, breadcrumbs and a little wine. The ingredients were clearly quite plain, but the end result was off the scale of good tastes. The main course disappeared almost as quickly as the starter. All that was left on Ella's plate were lemon skins. She had finished everything, including her juice. It was with some reluctance that she ordered a coffee and asked for the bill. It was with some joy, that she saw the coffee and bill arrive along with a slice of ravani topped with ice cream, on the house.

The bill only came to thirteen Euros, but Ella left fifteen and got up to walk away, sighing with satisfaction. She strolled around the harbour, looking down at the boats and reading the Greek words that spelt the boat names, to herself. She walked until she was out on the far arm of the harbour wall, then sat down on the edge of the wall, legs dangling over the water, and took the stale bread out of her bag. She broke off little pieces and began to feed the fishes. Soon she had gathered quite a crowd of little fish who had come to feed. Occasionally a bigger fish came along and ate one of the smaller fish, but generally the little fish were having a good time feeding. Eventually all of the bread was gone. Ella got her apple out of her bag and ate it. She felt like she was having a bottomless pit day today, regarding food; nothing seemed to fill her up. She finished the apple, and threw the core into the water for the fish. They had a good go at it, in their frenzy, before realising it wasn't bread. It was pretty much gone by then though.

Ella wandered lazily back down the harbour wall, stopping at the first café she came to for a cup of tea. After that she walked along the promenade until she came to the beach. She walked down a few steps onto the beach, and wandered down to the sea edge. Ella took off her sandals and paddled along in the sea as it lapped over her feet. She looked for shells and pretty stones glimmering in the water, occasionally stopping to pick one up and examine it for a moment before dropping it again. The day was getting increasingly hot and seemed to be getting a heaviness to it. Ella decided to go for a quick swim to cool off. She spread her large scarf on the pebbles of the beach, putting her bag and sandals on it. She stripped down to her bikini and added her clothes to the pile. She was not worried about crime, as it was practically nonexistent here. Ella waded out into the sea, which was a nice gentle sandy slope this time. Nearer the harbour wall there were more rock pools, but here, further along, it was sandy. When she got to thigh deep in the water she began to swim, the cool water very refreshing against the oppressive heat that was still building. There was still not even one cloud in the sky, but the pressure said a little rain was coming. Off the coast a tourist pleasure boat cruised by. Ella could hear the guide shouting through a megaphone to the passengers; 'Agios Nikolaus, Gerald Durrell, Lawrence Durrell, The Garden of the Gods, filmed here,' –tourist data, shouted in passing, places visited for a brief moment. Ella grinned.

Ella swam back to shore, and sat on her scarf for a while. She was not drying as quickly as usual, the humidity in the air had increased. Ella decided she was about as dry as she was going to get and pulled her clothes on over her still slightly damp body, she could dry as she walked. As Ella stood up, she realised the air pressure had increased significantly. She felt like a giant hand was pushing her back down again. She collected up her bag and things, and started to walk up the beach towards the promenade. There was so much pressure now, it was actually quite hard to walk, such an unusual sensation. A large dark cloud loomed on the horizon. It had appeared out of nowhere, so was probably coming in quite fast. Ella looked along the promenade for a bar or café. The nearest was about a hundred yards away and was an ouzerie; perfect she thought, and began the laboured walk towards it through the heavy air.

But before she had quite got there, the rain suddenly began. Huge heavy drops came down hard and fast like a power shower. Ella ran the last bit to the ouzerie, but was still soaked; at least it would be impossible to tell swimming wet, from rain wet, she thought to herself. She went through the door, automatically shaking herself like a wet dog. It was hot and humid indoors, and she took a seat by the window. The rain was coming down in heavy sheets. A waiter came over and greeted her, making a comment about the rain. Ella ordered a small carafe of ouzo, and settled down to watch the downpour. The waiter brought the little jug of ouzo along with a small glass and a large jug of iced water and a little bill rolled into a shot glass. Ella thanked him and mixed herself an ouzo and water. The day outside was not quite as cloudy as the drink in her glass, she thought, smiling. Then suddenly the rain just stopped. The sun came out again straight away, and for a moment or two the promenade steamed with evaporating moisture. Then, as if nothing had happened, normal Greek weather was resumed. It was hot and sunny, the ground was dry, and people emerged and went about their business dressed for summer as usual. That was how it rained in Greece in the summer. It practically never happened, but if you were indoors in a shop, you could easily miss it and never know it had happened at all. Except until two or three days later, when a new crop of mosquitoes hatched out and bit you raw. Ella made a mental note to herself to apply some of her mosquito repellent for the next few days. She did not like the DDT based products and so made her own. It was a few tablespoons of cloves soaked in alcohol in a jar for a week or so, then a little olive oil, a few drops of lavender and a drop of tea tree were added to it and it was shaken well and sprayed on. More effective than the shop bought preparations. If she did get bitten, and she did have a few bites on her legs already, there was a Greek after bite lotion that didn't contain much except ammonia. Ella jokingly referred to it as her tube of wee cream. It was very good though, and instantly soothed bites.

Ella poured herself another ouzo and water. The waiter brought over a tea plate of things to nibble, alongside the drink. This was the way in ouzeries. Greeks do not like to drink without food, so little bits and pieces are served gratis, along with the ouzo, to avoid drunkenness. The small plate contained a tablespoonful of some sort of lamb stew, a few pieces of rusk, a fried cheese ball, and some olives. Ella picked at the food, which was all very nice, and made an interesting accompaniment to the aniseed flavour of her drink.

When she had finished her ouzo and the nibbles, Ella put money in the shot glass to cover the bill plus fifteen per cent tip, waved to the waiter in acknowledgement, and left.

There was plenty of time yet, as it was still early afternoon, so Ella decided to walk back to the town centre. She started out along the promenade back towards the harbour, but shortly saw a sign pointing upwards through shop lined streets to the centre of town. The shops nearest the promenade were all tourist shops and cafés, but as she got more into the heart of the town, the shops became chic little Greek clothes shops and shoe shops. Ella window shopped as she walked along, but then spotted a dress she simply couldn't resist. It was a classic line in white with gold ribbon trim, in the sort of style the Greek Goddesses wore in paintings. It was absolutely perfect for a party or formal dinner, and at forty Euros, not hugely more expensive than clothes at home. She went into the shop.

The shop assistant greeted Ella and asked if she could help her.

Ella replied, 'otee to lefko foremma sto paratheero, borrow na to thokimazow parakalo,' (that white dress in the window, can I try it on please?)

'vevayuss,' (of course) said the shop assistant, 'ti megeethoss eenay aisee?' (what size are you?)

'Agglia dekatessera, Ellada, xero, sarranda deo.' (UK 14, Greece, I think 42) replied Ella.

'Yes that's right,' said the shop assistant, changing to English, 'one moment, I will get it for you.'

The shop assistant returned with the dress in Ella's size, and directed her to a dressing room. While she had been waiting, Ella had spotted a dress of the same style in bright blue with gold trim, but shorter, for day wear. She asked if she could try that one too. The assistant told her she would get it for her while she changed.

Ella went into the changing room and tried on the dress, it looked fantastic on. The assistant called from outside to say she had the other dress and Ella went outside to get it.

'Oh, you look like a Greek Goddess in that dress,' said the assistant, 'with your dark hair and olive skin, it suits you perfectly.'

'Yes,' smiled Ella, 'I will take it.' She took the blue dress and returned to the changing room. The blue dress looked almost as stunning as the white one. Ella decided to treat herself and buy that too. She took both dresses out to the till and waited while the assistant wrapped them in fine tissue paper and packed them into a stiff paper bag with the shops logo on it. She paid the seventy Euros and left, smiles all around. Ella was glad she had brought extra money with her on this trip. It had not been as expensive as she thought it might be, and there was room for some little luxuries and treats.

Ella continued her walk through the shopping centre. Suddenly a pair of sandals in a shoe shop caught her eye. They were gold and flat, and had gold ribbons that tied criss cross up the calves. They would be absolutely perfect with the white dress she had just bought. They were only twelve Euros; a must have. She went into the shop to see if they had her size, 38, which of course they did, and soon she had made another purchase.

Ella continued to walk through the winding streets, following the signs for the city centre. It was not too much longer before she recognised one of the main streets she had passed through earlier in the day on the happy train, and now she had her bearings, and knew her way back to the bus station. She wandered through the streets, window shopping, and was drawn into a shop selling handmade lace and embroidery. She looked around for a while, but in the end, couldn't resist a beautiful little white lace shawl to go with her new dress, for only seven Euros. For the amount of work that must have gone into making it, it was priced ridiculously cheaply.

Ella walked on through the shopping centre, stopping twice more, once to buy some lavender and thyme, olive oil soap, and once to pop into a greengrocers shop, and buy a bag of cherries. Finally Ella arrived back at the bus station with a bit of time to spare. She used the public bathroom and freshened up a little bit, but quickly, because Greek plumbing has a rather pungent aroma, which one wants to get away from quite quickly.

Ella bought herself a cup of lemon tea from the café, and after she had drunk that it was twenty past five. She went to sit on a bench outside and watch for the return of Panicos' (number forty two) bus from Zanthos.

After about fifteen minutes, Ella watched the number forty two bus pull into the parking area. A middle aged looking guy with a bald head was driving. He looked portly but friendly. He wore sunglasses pushed up onto the top of his head. The bus disgorged passengers from both front and middle exit points. Panicos got out and opened the luggage compartment and reached deep inside for bags, boxes and packages, passing them to a pressing crowd of passengers. Soon all the passengers and their belongings had dispersed, and Panicos straightened up, stretching his back and pushing the luggage compartment closed. Ella walked over to him and said, 'Yassas, psackno yia Panicos Papadopoulous.' (hello, I'm looking for Panicos Papadopoulous.)

'eemay Panicos,' (I'm Panicos) replied the man, 'borrow na sass voytheesou?' (can I help you?)

'Melenee Ella Hudson, ee mitaira moo etan Elizabett Hudson.' (I'm Ella Hudson, my mother was Elizabeth Hudson) said Ella.

'Was?' said Panicos in English.

'Yes,' replied Ella, 'sadly, she died in 1966.'

'But you must have been just a baby then?' said Panicos.

'I was four and a half years old,' answered Ella.

'That is very sad,' said Panicos. 'I suppose you know I knew your mother?'

'Yes,' replied Ella, 'I have met some of her other friends from that time. I wonder if I could perhaps buy you dinner, and you could, in return, tell me what you remember about my mother?'

'That would be lovely,' said Panicos, 'let me just hand in my tickets and things, and get changed, and I will meet you out here in about fifteen minutes.'

Ella sat back down on the bench and watched the busses coming in and going through the routine of sending people off with their packages to the rest of their evening. The bus station worked like a finely tuned machine, with bursts of chaotic activity followed by quiet lulls. Before long, Panicos returned, dressed now in slacks and a white cotton shirt, and carrying a jacket. Ella gathered up her shopping bags and walked over to meet him.

'I know a nice little restaurant down by the sea, does the most delicious kleftiko, (a tender lamb dish) if you don't mind the walk,' he said.

'a nice vradini volta (evening stroll) would be lovely,' agreed Ella.

Panicos insisted on carrying her shopping for her, and they set off, Panicos pointing out various buildings, statues and parks to her, along the way.

It was an interesting walk and Panicos took her on a slight detour to point out a particularly special park with a statue of Odysseus in the centre of it. They sat on a bench for a while to rest and admire the marble, and how beautifully it had been worked. After a minute or two a little three legged ginger cat hobbled over, and began to rub around Panicos' legs.

Panicos got a napkin out of his pocket, and unwrapped it, to reveal a lump of cooked chicken. He tore it into little pieces and fed it to the little cat piece by piece, the cat taking each piece delicately from his fingers. When it had finished, the cat settled down for a wash.

'I always stop here on my way home from work,' said Panicos, 'and I have been feeding this little guy every day for a couple of years. I even come by on my days off. We have become quite good friends I think.'

Ella smiled.

The cat finished washing, rubbed against Panicos once more, then hobbled off about its business.

Panicos and Ella continued their stroll down to the seafront. The taverna that Panicos liked, obviously was a regular stopping point for him too, as the waiters greeted him with friendly comments, and quickly seated him at an obviously favourite table, outside, but against the wall of the taverna, with a lovely view of the sea, and all the people taking their own 'voltas' along beside it.

The waiter asked if Panicos wanted his usual drink, and he in turn asked Ella if she liked Mythos beer. She said that she did, and Panicos ordered two of them.

The waiter handed them menus, and went to get the beers. Panicos put his menu down on the table, and asked Ella if she liked saganaki (a fried cheese dish) as it was also particularly good here. She replied that she did, and Panicos offered to order for them both, which Ella was more than happy for him to do. When the waiter returned, Panicos spoke very quickly to him in Greek, as Greeks are inclined to do. Because the words sort of roll together, it is a language that is automatically spoken quite fast. Ella caught the words saganaki, Greek salad, kleftiko, mythos and lots of twos. Moments later the waiter was gone again, and they sipped the cold beers.

'So you want me to tell you what I remember about your mother,' began Panicos. 'It was a wonderful summer, we all went out together all the time, hanging out in town cafés or at the harbour, going swimming, picnics in the country, long hikes into the mountains, and through the woods. I remember how your mother danced when I played the flute, and Yiorgios sang. I had a big crush on your mother, and I was trying to build the courage to ask her out on a proper date, just the two of us, but I was afraid she would not want to do it in case it spoilt our friendship. Then foolishly, I introduced her to my friend Adonis. Adonis Zacharoulis. He had come to stay with me like he sometimes did, from the island of Kios. She fell for him straight away, and I realised I had never had a chance with her. She had never once looked at me the way she looked at Adonis.'

Just then the waiter arrived with the salad and saganaki, along with a basket of bread and plates. Panicos told Ella to help herself, and waited until she had taken what she wanted before filling his own plate. The salad was crisp and tasty with chunks of cheese crumbled into it. The purple olives in the salad were rich and delicious. The bread was very good too, not the usual kind, but a slightly sweeter version, topped with sesame seeds. The saganaki was melt in the mouth scrumptious, not at all greasy like one might expect fried cheese to be, but crispy on the outside, and soft and melty on the inside. They both ate their food with murmurs of appreciation.

'What happened with Adonis?' asked Ella. 'I wonder why my mother came home that November?'

'I don't know what happened between them. But I do know your mother was very upset. I saw her on her own one night just before she left, and the mere mention of Adonis' name sent her into floods of tears, so I didn't press her, I thought she would tell us, her friends, in her own good time, and it was best to leave it then. I wished I had pressed her though, because she left shortly after that, and none of us ever found out why. Adonis came over to the island again, shortly after she left, and when he found out she had left, he got very angry and refused to talk about it too. But his face went black like a thunderstorm. When I tried to talk to him, he told me it was none of my business, and he never again came to visit me after that. I often wondered what happened to both of them.'

Ella told him her story, and all the things she had found out on the island, and how she was trying to find Adonis because she thought it likely he was her father. Panicos listened attentively, looking at times, more like a concerned uncle than anything else.

'No wonder she was upset,' said Panicos, 'if they had fallen out and she was pregnant, and he didn't know, that would explain why she cried the way she did, and why she left too.'

'I wonder why she didn't tell him?' said Ella.

'Are you going to Kios to try and find him?' asked Panicos.

'Yes, I think I must try, but I don't really know where to begin,' sighed Ella.

'Well back then, his family lived in the town of Kefalos,' said Panicos. 'You might try there to start with. Ask at the town hall.'

'Thank you,' said Ella, 'that gives me somewhere to begin at least.'

The waiter arrived to take away their dishes and empty beer bottles, and shortly returned with two more beers, and then two portions of kleftiko. The kleftiko was cooked in foil and slow roasted. The foil was pinched closed, so the lamb steamed as well as roasting slowly, and fell off of the bones. It was served in a rich gravy, with a basket of Greek bread. Ella tried the lamb, it was tender, moist and delicious. The gravy tasted of meat juices and herbs. Ella opened out her paper serviette, and every time she found a piece of fat, she put it in the serviette, along with pieces of thick bone, and occasional small pieces of meat. Panicos looked at her questioningly.

'I too, have a feline friend,' Ella said, smiling at him. 'His name is Bob, and he relies on the tourists to feed him up in the summer, and keep him going through the winter. This morning he knocked on my door, to wake me up to feed him.'

Panicos laughed. 'The cats of Greece have big personalities. They are very hard to ignore. They keep the rats down too.'

Panicos added some of his own thick kleftiko bones and fat to Ella's parcel. 'He will make short work of this you know.'

'I'm sure he will,' agreed Ella.

When they had finished the meal, Ella triple wrapped her parcel for Bob, and slipped it into her bag. Panicos asked if she would like a coffee, but she declined, saying it was too late in the day for her to drink coffee as she would never sleep. Panicos asked if she had tried Kumquat liqueur, which was

made on another Greek island. Ella replied that she
had not, and Panicos ordered two of them.

The drink was very sweet and had a strange, slightly
bitter, orange taste. It was a bit of an assault on the
palate, but very nice nevertheless. Ella heard
Panicos asking the waiter for the bill. 'This was
supposed to be my treat,' she said, reaching for her
purse.

Panicos waved her away, saying, 'if I let a pretty lady
buy me dinner in my local restaurant, I would never
hear the last of it. They would mock me for years,
honestly, it would be terrible. Anyway it has been my
pleasure, let me get it, please.'

Ella knew when to retreat graciously, and thanked
him for his generosity.

When they had finished, they left and walked to the
water's edge, watching the sea slapping against the
wall, it was a soothing sound that really came into its
own under cover of the night. 'I was told you had
gone to live in Athens,' Ella began, 'I'm glad you
came back here, I might never have found you in
Athens.'

Panicos looked sad for a moment.

'I'm sorry,' said Ella, 'did I say something I should not
have?'

Panicos smiled at her, and laid a reassuring hand on
her arm. 'It makes me sad thinking of Athens, but that
is my fault, not yours,' he said. 'I was a very foolish
man in Athens. I had a music shop, a house in town,
a wife and a child, a daughter, not much younger
than you. But I also had another passion. I liked to
play cards. It started off as a once a month thing, just
playing for lepto (change) with friends, but soon I
started playing with real card players for money. I just
couldn't stop myself. I thought about my beautiful
wife and daughter, my house and my little musical

instrument shop, but I just couldn't stop. Then I hit a losing streak, and first I lost my car, then most of the stock from my shop. In the end I lost the shop and the house too. When they came to take the house away, that was the first time my wife knew anything about any of it. I should have talked to her sooner, but I was a proud man. I kept thinking that my luck would change soon, it had to. I would win it all back, my wife need never know anything about it. I would buy her a boat, and take them on a lovely holiday around the islands. But I was deluding myself with dreams. When they took the house away, she left me and went back to her parents with my daughter. She said she never wanted to see me again. Her brother and father came and gave me a beating, and told me to never look for her, or go near my daughter again. I came back to Aegos because I didn't know what else to do.'

Ella sighed and said, 'that is such a sad story, I'm so sorry. Perhaps one day your daughter will come and find you, like I am looking for my father. Maybe she will not hold a grudge against you, but just want to know you as you are now.'

'That is my dearest wish,' said Panicos, 'but it is getting a little late now. But perhaps, perhaps.'

'Well she is missing out on a wonderful father,' said Ella, 'Perhaps you will be a token uncle to me. I have no real family left now, unless I do find Adonis.'

Panicos gave Ella a little sideways hug, 'I would love to be your uncle, anipseea mou,' (my niece) he said.

They looked at the sea a little longer, watching the lights of what looked like a cruise ship, out near the horizon.

'Where are you staying?' Panicos asked.

'At the Hotel Zeus, in Agios Spiridos,' replied Ella, 'But there is no rush, we can walk a little more if you like? I can get a taxi back if I miss the last bus.'

'A niece of mine will do no such thing,' said Panicos. 'I will drive you back, it is just up the road in any case. But yes, let's stroll along the seafront a little longer. It is right that you should be my niece anyway. For the longest time, Adonis and I were close, like brothers.'

Ella slipped her arm through his, as they walked companionably along. After a while they came to an area where a block of apartments fronted the sea. 'This is where I live,' said Panicos, pausing to write his address and telephone number on a piece of paper which he gave to Ella. 'Call me anytime you want, even if you just want a chat. This is my car here.'

Panicos put Ella's bags on the back seat of the car and opened the front passenger door for her. She got in. He drove the short journey back to Agios Spiridos and parked outside the front of the Zeus hotel, getting her bags out for her. She hugged him goodbye, promising to see him soon.

Ella went through reception and straight up to her room. Christos was not about, perhaps he was out back putting out beer bottles, or washing glasses. The bar was deserted.

But Bob was waiting on her doorstep. 'You are a clever cat, aren't you Bob,' she cooed at him. 'How did you know I had a treat in my bag for you? Did you smell me coming out of the car?'

Bob looked at her with his head on one side, as if to say, 'I knew you had a treat for me when you were setting it aside in the restaurant, in the next town, my dear.'

Ella unwrapped the meat, fat and bones, and tipped them directly onto the stone tiled floor. Bob wasted no time getting stuck in, and was still purring and eating simultaneously, when Ella shut the door and went to bed.

Chapter Six

Ella woke up very early, before even Bob was ready to come knocking at the door. She showered and dressed in a long skirt and long sleeved peasant blouse, and a pair of beige pumps. She plaited her hair. By the time she had done all of that, she could hear plaintive little miaows coming from Bob outside. She could even see the tip of his paw trying to push through the tiny gap under the door. He was very good at cute, she had to hand it to him. She prepared a bowl of biscuits and ham, and a bowl of milky water and took it out for him. He let her give him a little stroke before he got down to proper eating. Ella hand washed her clothes that needed it and hung them out on the line, then got her purse, keys, shawl and sunglasses. Bob had eaten everything and gone, and the bowls were empty, so Ella washed them up before she left. It was seven o'clock now, and church was due to start in half an hour so Ella started walking down to the village square. She arrived with ten minutes to spare, but the chanters had already started up inside the church.

Ella walked into the cool dark church, stopping just inside the door to face the iconostasis (a large wooden carved wall decorated with icons, behind which the Priest performs his Holy functions) and crossed herself. She lit three candles; one for her mother, one for a beloved cat who had died not long ago, and one for the hope she would find her father. She walked round the perimeter of the church, crossing herself and kissing the icons in the prescribed order. Finally she did a sort of semi curtsey and crossed herself in front of the iconostasis, then looked around. Nikki and her mother had not arrived yet, so Ella took a seat about midway down the church, next to the aisle. At half past seven, a little bell rang inside the iconostasis, and the Priest and the Deacon (his assistant) began to chant verses of preparation. The chanters sang answering verses. Ella knew from experience that this could go on for about an hour before the mass started. The church only had a handful of people in it apart from the chanters and the Priest, and they were universally old women. Ella knew it would fill up as the long service continued. Two and a half to three hours was about average for a Greek Orthodox service. At about quarter to eight, Nikki and her mother came in. Nikki saw Ella and waved, then they both embarked on their own personal round of candle lighting and icon kissing. Nikki finished quicker than her mother, only kissing a few icons, she considered especially important; whereas her mother was doing the full circuit. Nikki came over to sit beside Ella, and hugged her hello, kissing her on both cheeks. She asked how Ella had been, and how she was getting along with her enquiries. Ella replied that there had been some developments, and that she would tell them about it over lunch. At that point Nikki's mother came over, and introductions were made, and hugs and kisses exchanged. This was not looked on as unusual in any way, Greeks often chatter during the service, and children tend to run about and do pretty much what they want. Then the Priest came out to cense the church and its occupants with incense and everyone stood up. They all turned to face the Priest as he sensed each corner of the church, crossing themselves as he walked past them. Then the Priest waved the censer at the congregation, censing each person in turn, the people bowing and crossing themselves as he got to them. Then the Priest went back into the iconostasis and everyone sat back down. At half past eight, the bell rang, more furiously this time, and everyone stood up, The Great Doxology had begun. The chanters answered the Priests chants with Kyriay elayson (Lord have mercy) and See Kyriay (to you Lord) or Amen. The job of the congregation was to stand up and sit down whenever the Priest came out, and cross themselves in the right places; doxa patree kay yio kay agio nevmatee (Glory to the Father, Son and Holy Spirit,) and paneyegeass (the virgin, all holy, our lady) and a couple of other places. Also they had to turn and face the Priest whichever part of the church he was in and cross themselves as he passed by them. The Priest brought out a golden book (The Bible) and everyone queued up in the aisle to kiss first it, and then his hand. When everyone had returned to their seats, the Priest came out and censed them again. The service continued along these lines, interspersed with the reading of the gospel. The men of the church holding banners and holy symbols in front of the iconostasis as the Priest inside performed the sacred ritual over the bread and wine.

Nikki asked if Ella had eaten or drunk anything that day and Ella replied that she had not, so Ella said she should come up for communion with her and her mother. The children were taken up for communion first, and those of the congregation who had observed the proper fasting and other rules, went up after them. The communion was a mixture of Greek bread soaked in Commanderia wine (a kind of rich sweet sherry) and water. After this there were some more chants and responses, and then the Priest came out to give a chunk of bread to anyone who wanted it. This was considered the gift of the Church and everyone participated. Collecting the bread, and kissing the Priests hand as he said chronia polla (many years) in blessing, was easier said than done.

No orderly queue here, like in her church at home, but a mob descending on the Priest from three sides. He had to swing from side to side like an automaton, handing out bread to the congregation, which immediately afterwards dispersed. There was no collection plate like at home, and Ella put some money in a collection box by the candles instead. The three of them emerged into the bright, hot, sunlight of the village square. Nikki led the way to a car parked on the edge of the square, and helped her mother into the front seat, holding the back door open for Ella. They drove a very short way down some side streets, and then parked up again. Nikki helped her mother out of the car, and she scuttled off into the house, to the kitchen no doubt; where a traditional Greek woman, spends an inordinate amount of time.

Inside Nikki gave Ella a glass of commanderia, and a glass of water. Both were very welcome, as Ella had had nothing since she woke up, apart from communion. She ate her church bread with the drinks. She had been too dry for it to be possible to eat it before then.

There was a lot of clattering about from the kitchen and adjacent dining room, but Nikki assured Ella they could do nothing to help her mother, she would not hear of it. Finally she called them into an early lunch. It was only about eleven o'clock, but no one had eaten because of communion, so they were all ready for the food.

On the table, Nikki's mother had laid out bread, keftedes (meatballs), loukaniko (Cypriot village sausage), salad, spanakopitta, hummus, tzatziki, taramasalata, olives, chicken pieces cooked in tomatoes and herbs, and dolmades. There was also a big carafe of red wine, and another of iced lemon water.

Nikki's mother invited Ella and Nikki to help themselves, and so Ella put a little of everything on her plate, and wine in her glass. The food was home cooked and wonderful, some served hot, some served cold, not especially based on whether or not it was a salad. Ella could not believe how good it all tasted, and gave her profound compliments to Nikki's mother.

'So,' began Nikki, 'What have you found out since we last spoke?'

'I think I have discovered that my father was a man called Adonis Zacharoulis, who lived with his family on Kios,' said Ella.

'Oh,' said Nikki's mother, 'I think I met Adonis once in the bar, when I was there with Yiorgios, he seemed nice enough.'

'I am booking a ticket to Kios for two days, to try and find him,' said Ella. 'I'm told his family lived in Kefalos town.'

'If you go to Kefalos, go to Demeter's bar and ask for Allessandro and Ireni. They will give you a room for the night for a very good rate. Tell them Athena Michaelides from Agios Spiridos on Aegos sent you.'

'Thank you,' said Ella, 'that will be very helpful. I spoke to Yiannis Zefiros, and he remembered Adonis proposing marriage to my mother in his restaurant. But no one I have spoken to knows why they did not get married, and why my mother was upset, and went back to England.'

'That is indeed very mysterious,' said Nikki.

'I hope I can find out what happened, and I hope I can find Adonis,' said Ella. 'Also, I hope he will be happy to meet me.'

Nikki and Athena nodded sagely.

'We hope so too, for you,' said Athena.

Nikki agreed.

While they had been talking, they had been helping themselves to several platefuls of the delicious food, and had now eaten their fill, which was most of what Athena had put out on the table.

'That really was 'fantastiko' -ena nosteemo yevma,' (a wonderful meal) said Ella, patting her tummy, and drinking some water, before Nikki refilled her wine for her.

Athena would not hear of any help in clearing the plates. 'I'm only putting them in the kitchen for later,' she insisted.

Then after a short while, Athena re-emerged with coffee and Baklava. As they ate the Baklava, Athena said, 'traditionally Baklava is made with thirty three layers of filo pastry, eva yia kathay chrono tis zoiss too Christoo, (one for each year of Christ's life,) so it is perfect for dessert after church.'

Ella expressed her surprise, she had not known that. When they had finished, they took their wine out into the garden, and sat in the sunshine dappled shade of the grapevine trellis.

Athena said, 'I liked your mother Elizabett very much. I was courting Yiorgios, and sometimes I would sit in the bar while she was working, and tell her about my feelings. I wondered if he felt the same about me, and she said she could see in his eyes that he did. That gave me confidence, and made me feel happy, and she was right. He asked me to marry him that Christmas. He hid a ring in with other gifts. He had already asked my father of course.'

'I have met most of her friends from that summer I think,' said Ella, 'and they have told me some lovely things about her. I feel I know her so much better now and I am so grateful for that.'

Nikki and Athena smiled at Ella.

Ella thanked them both again for a wonderful lunch, and excused herself, saying that she had to get back into the village, and book a return ferry ticket to Kios. They hugged her, and hoped she would visit them again soon, and urged her to let them know what happened on Kios. Ella left, filled with a warm glow of friendship, wine and food.

Coming out of the house, Ella was momentarily disorientated, but she soon found her direction towards the village square through a maze of little back streets lined with low walls, plants, olive and lemon trees and, just about everywhere she looked, cats; and on to the little travel agents shop, which she had noted previously was open on a Sunday, between two and four in the afternoon. It was just coming up to two now, so that was perfect.

The woman in the travel office smiled and greeted her in English. She actually had no accent, and Ella assumed she was an ex pat, living and working in Greece.

'I want to take a ferry to Kios tomorrow morning, as early as possible, and come back on Tuesday evening,' Ella said. 'Is that possible? I know some ferries only run some days, at certain times.'

'It should be okay,' replied the assistant, 'let me check.' She reached for a pile of timetables, and ran her finger down a page, looking at the times. 'Yes, there is one that leaves from Vathy tomorrow, at nine in the morning, getting to Samios in Kios at about ten o'clock. Coming back, it leaves Samios at five o'clock on Tuesday evening, getting back to Vathy at about six o'clock.'

'That sounds perfect,' said Ella, 'how much will it cost?'

'Are you going as a foot passenger or taking a car?' asked the assistant.

'A foot passenger,' replied Ella.

'That would be eight Euros each way,' said the assistant.

'That's great,' said Ella, 'I'll buy those tickets now then,' and she pulled a twenty euro note out of her purse. The assistant wrote out the tickets and gave her change. 'Do you have a little map of Kios by any chance?' asked Ella, 'just one showing the main towns and villages.'

The assistant produced a little folded paper map, with a rough map of Kios on one side, and a lot of adverts for restaurants and shops on Kios, on the other side, and handed it to Ella along with the tickets in a wallet. Ella thanked her, and was about to leave, when as an afterthought she asked, 'where are you from, if you don't mind me asking?'

'Originally, I'm from London, but I lived in Brighton for many years. Then I came to Greece working as a tour rep, and when I decided I wanted to live here permanently, this job came up. I've been here eleven years now. I married a Greek man after the first two years. It's a good life. I wouldn't go back now, even if you paid me.'

'Not even with all the troubles in Athens?' asked Ella.

'That business doesn't reach out to the islands,' said the assistant, 'and times are hard all over aren't they?'

'Yes,' agreed Ella, 'that's very true.'

Ella thanked the woman, put her tickets away in her bag, and left.

She walked on down the road until she came to Manolis' bar, and went inside. Dimitris saw her and shouted a greeting, like a long lost friend. 'Sit down,' he shouted, waving her to a table, 'I will bring you over a frappe.'

Ella sat herself down where he had pointed and watched him busily making the drink. He called to the girl who worked there, and told her to take over as he was going on a break, then came over to Ella's table carrying two ice cream frappes.

'You don't mind if I join you and talk?' he asked.

'Of course not,' said Ella, 'I came here to see you.'

'Are you hungry? Have you eaten?' asked Dimitris.

'I am so full,' replied Ella, 'I just had lunch at the home of some other friends I have made.'

'That is very good. Greek home cooking is a treat, unsurpassed elsewhere. Now tell me, how is your search going?'

'I have met most of Liz's friends from back then I think. They are all very lovely people, and they have told me lots of things about her. I feel I know her so very much better now. It is looking very likely that Adonis Zacharoulis was my father, but I have not been able to find out where he lives yet, or even if he is still alive. He lived with his family on Kios, back then, and I have a ferry ticket to go there tomorrow. I also found out that he proposed marriage to Liz, but I don't know what happened after that, or why she came home.'

'So it is still the big mystery,' said Dimitris, sipping at his frappe and rolling a cigarette.

'I do not wish to offend you,' began Ella, 'but I remember you told me your sister was sent to Kios to live with your Aunt. I wonder if you would like me to take a message to her for you?'

Dimitris lit his cigarette and puffed thoughtfully. Ella sat quietly, drinking her frappe, and let him think it over.

After a while he said, 'I think that would be a lovely idea, and my mother would never have to know. Should I send a gift as well as a letter, do you think?'
'I think that would be a very nice gesture. Perhaps include something for your niece?' said Ella.
'Are you busy this afternoon?' asked Dimitris.
'Not at all,' replied Ella, 'why, what can I do for you?'
'Will you come into Agios Nikolaus with me, and help me buy presents that they would like?' asked Dimitris.
'I would love to try and help you find the perfect gifts,' said Ella. 'I was there just yesterday myself, and bought some lovely things in the shops. Also I have made an uncle there,' and Ella went onto explain about meeting Panicos. 'He knows the area very well, and probably has the day off today; if I phone him, he might be able to meet us for coffee, and tell us the best places to shop.'
Dimitris grinned, and showed Ella to his office phone, where the necessary call was made. Dimitris wrote the name and address of his aunt down on a piece of paper for Ella. In no time at all, Ella and Dimitris were on his bike, heading down the road to Agios Nikolaus to meet Panicos for coffee.
Panicos greeted Dimitris, looking at him like a father might look at his daughter's suitor. But he was friendly enough, and very pleased to see Ella again so soon.
'I am glad you called me, I hoped to hear from you again, but never thought it would be so soon. It is good that you are including me in your life like this,' said Panicos.
Ella gave him a hug, and they sat down and ordered Greek coffees all around. Ella introduced Dimitris, telling Panicos that Dimitris was Manolis' son.

'I can see the resemblance, now you say that,' said Panicos. 'I was sad to hear about your father's death.'

Dimitris thanked him and explained about his sister, and her estrangement from his family.

'It is very sad when family lose touch for whatever reason,' said Panicos. 'I, myself have a daughter I never see. Ella has done the right thing suggesting you make contact via her, in the form of a letter and gifts. She is a wise young lady.'

Dimitris agreed.

'I bought a lovely handmade lace shawl, in a little shop yesterday,' said Ella. 'Perhaps something like that would be nice for your sister?'

'That does sound nice,' said Dimitris, 'a pretty gift made with care and intricate attention. But what to buy for a nine year old girl?'

'There is a bookshop in Makedonias Street, that has a big collection of children's books, and there is a small toy shop in Perseus Road. Perhaps you could find something there, a doll maybe?' said Panicos.

'I think you should include a gift for the man in your sister's life,' said Ella, 'I'm sure there will be one.'

Dimitris looked surprised, and Panicos looked at Ella quizzically, but did not say anything.

'That is quite probably true,' Dimitris said, 'a bottle of Metaxa maybe?'

They all agreed that they had the basic shopping list drawn out, and set off to find the various shops. Shopping was so much easier with a plan of action, and within the hour they were back at the original café. Dimitris had bought a beautiful shawl for his sister, a story book and a very pretty doll for his niece, and a bottle of seven star Metaxa. Ella pulled out a packet she had bought while the men were busy buying the Metaxa. It was a nice little writing pad, decorated with vine leaves. She gave it to Dimitris saying, 'why don't we leave you here to have a drink and write a letter, and we will go and find a nice box for you to pack your gifts in?'

Dimitris looked lost. 'But I have no idea what to write,' he said.

'Just write what is in your heart,' said Ella. 'Start with Dear Anna, and the rest will come to you. You'll see.'

Ella and Panicos left him to it. Ella looked back, and could see Dimitris was already scribbling away.

'Where can we buy a nice gift box?' she asked Panicos.

'I know the place,' he replied leading her through the streets. 'Why did you say that about a man in her life?' he asked.

'I spoke to someone in Agios Spiridos, and he knew who the father of her child was. He is one of those people who knows everything about everyone actually. Anyway, after she was sent away to her aunt's on Kios, things changed for the father. You see he had been a married man, which was why she wouldn't tell anyone who he was. He could not be forced to marry her, it was just not possible as he was married already, and all telling her parents would accomplish, was to bring shame and unhappiness on everyone involved. So she kept quiet and let them send her away instead. But not long after that, a couple of years maybe, the man's wife died, of pneumonia I think. He left Aegos soon after the funeral. They had no children, and he just sold up and left. It is possible he went to Kios to be with Anna and his daughter. Perhaps they even married.'

'You are quite the detective aren't you?' said Panicos, admiration in his voice. 'And you have told Dimitris none of this?'

'No,' replied Ella. 'It is not my place to tell him. It is for his sister, if she wants him to know.'

'You really are very wise,' said Panicos, 'I am very proud to have you for my niece. What else have you found out during your enquiries and kept to yourself?'

They had reached the little shop selling stationery now, and were picking out a nice box for the gifts.

'Well,' said Ella, 'I found out that Nikos loved Heleni, and named his boat after her, and Heleni had told me that she had loved Nikos, but did not have the courage to tell him. But since she is now married to someone else, I didn't tell Nikos that she had loved him too. I wanted to, but I thought it might just hurt him, and open old wounds.'

'I think you did the right thing,' said Panicos. They were walking back towards the café, when Panicos gave Ella the box and said, 'hang on a moment,' and dived into a mini market. He came out with something wrapped in paper. 'We must just stop by and feed Ginger,' he said.

They went into the little park, and sat on the bench facing the Odysseus statue. Soon the little three legged ginger cat came hobbling over. Panicos stroked it in greeting, and unwrapped the paper, tipping its contents onto the ground in front of the little cat. It was a portion of raw minced meat, and the little cat went at it like it was Christmas.

After they had finished in the park, they headed back to the café, to find Dimitris finishing a glass of Mythos beer, and reading through his letter.

'I have finished,' he said, 'would you like to read it?' Ella replied that she thought it was too personal, but Dimitris begged her to make sure it was alright, so she read it through, and declared it perfect. Between them they packed the box with the gifts and the letter.

Panicos said, 'I will take Ella and the box, back to her hotel in my car, and you go back on your bike.'
Dimitris agreed, and told Ella to come and see him as soon as she got back from Kios, and she assured him that of course she would.
Panicos and Ella arrived back at the Zeus hotel at about half past five. Christos was already manning the empty bar, and waved hello to Ella. She told Panicos, she would just take the box and her things, up to her room, and then join him at the bar for a drink.
Ella put down her things, and Dimitris' box, and had a quick freshen up, then went back down to the bar.
Bob had not made an extra appearance –obviously realising there was to be no extra food.
Panicos was sitting at the bar chatting to Christos in Greek, and drinking an Alpha beer.
'I see you two have already met,' grinned Ella.
Panicos and Christos grinned conspiratorially back at her.
Ella ordered a beer for herself, and while Christos was getting it, said to Panicos, 'I wondered if you were in a hurry to get back? If not, Christos' cousin Carolina, owns a nice little restaurant just round the corner from here, and perhaps you would stay and have dinner with me. You bought me dinner yesterday, so perhaps you'll let me return the favour tonight?'
'I would be delighted,' Panicos beamed a radiant smile at Ella. 'But that is two or three hours away yet. Why don't you let me drive you out to see a sight or two, then we can come back, and have dinner in the evening?'
'That sounds lovely, let's finish these beers and go.'

Ella and Panicos chatted with Christos for a little while, as they drank their cold Alpha beers, then went out to the car.

Panicos took the road towards Vathy, but soon turned off down one of the little side roads that Ella had thought looked interesting, and had wished she could explore, while she had been sitting on the bus. The road was very narrow, and wound tightly round the hillside. As they climbed, trees on the hillside were on one side of them, and a sheer drop down the cliff, on the other side. There wasn't even any sort of guard rail, to stop cars going over the edge. Ella shuddered at how it would be if they had to pass someone on this road. But the views down to the sea and the little villages were amazing. From up here, the island seemed so much smaller, and so much more could be seen, all at once, in one breath taking view. They rounded another bend, and Panicos pulled into the parking area in front of what looked like a small shepherds hut. When they got out, the smell of wild flowers, heather and jasmine nearly knocked Ella off her feet. The hut turned out to be a tiny shop, with a little old man sitting inside. It sold honey, and beeswax candles, honey soap, and honey biscuits. The old man and Panicos spoke rapidly, then the old man brought a bowl of almost black syrup and a small spoon for Ella to taste it.

'It's honey from his bees. Try it, it's delicious,' urged Panicos.

Ella dutifully took a taste. 'It *is* delicious. Rich and dark, like syrup, like toffee. I have never tasted honey like this in my life.'

The old man looked pleased.

'I never buy my honey anywhere else.' Panicos picked four tins off of the shelf as he spoke, and paid the old man for them. Ella bought a packet of honey biscuits, as she was a little bit peckish now. It had been an early lunch, and looked like it was going to be a latish dinner.

They went outside to look at the bees behind the hut, as a coach roared past on the road, taking the bends at breakneck speeds. It was empty apart from the driver, who was obviously on the way home after driving a tour about all day, and in something of a rush to get there as well.

'Are there many accidents on these roads, with people driving like that?' asked Ella.

'Every few years or so, someone goes over the edge,' shrugged Panicos. 'Sometimes they are killed, sometimes not. You will see the little shrines all along the roadside to people who died here.'

They went and looked at the bees. There were a half dozen or so little hives, but one was bigger than the others, and of particular interest, because it had a glass panel in place of one of the sides, and Ella could look inside, and watch the bees going about their business. 'How fascinating,' she proclaimed. Neither of them gave a thought to the fact that they were not wearing protective clothing, and bees were flying about all around them. It seemed perfectly natural to be standing there amongst all the activity. The bees were not interested in them, just the flowers, and the work they had to do.

Ella and Panicos admired the panoramic views silently for a while, then went back to the car.

A little further along the road, and they drove into a fairly small mountain village. There were a few tourist shops, but they were all closed up now, it being Sunday evening. Nevertheless, the village was still very pretty.

'There are several really pretty mountain villages on the island,' said Panicos. 'Some have walks that lead up to them, through mountain paths and areas of woodland. It is a wonderful hike, perhaps you would like to come on one with me, one day?'

'I would most definitely love to do that,' enthused Ella, 'let's arrange it when I get back from Kios.' Purposefully she didn't talk about what she might or might not find on Kios, and what the outcome might lead to. Panicos did not mention it either. He could see she was nervous about finding Adonis, or not finding him. For Ella's part she was happy to have found an uncle, who already felt more like a family member, than anyone had to her, in a long, long time.

'The mountain villages make wonderful things, in part because they always have, and in part, to sell to the tourists. I come to this village to buy sweets; little baked honey and nut clusters that are wonderful. Also I buy Commanderia wine up here. They also make the nicest Greek bread I have tasted anywhere. They have hand crafted lace and woodwork too'

'I will make sure to come back and buy some of those things,' said Ella, 'it sounds very much like the sort of things I would want to buy.'

They continued along the mountain road, which still wound tightly round the hillside. At one point, they met a jeep coming the other way, but neither vehicle made anything of it. The jeep speedily reversed back into a wider spot, where a bit of hillside had been hacked away, leaving tree roots exposed, and Panicos swiftly passed him. They came to a parking area, or a passing area for bigger vehicles, on the side of the road. Panicos pulled over and stopped. Over the edge of the mountain, was the most amazing view. For as far as Ella could see, there were fields, all divided up, and growing different crops. Here and there, were poly-tunnels and windmills. Clearly the plain was devoted to growing food, but it looked like a very wholesome way of doing it.

'That is Mareesee plains, where all the food for the island is grown,' said Panicos. 'It is organic farming, none of the crops are sprayed, no chemicals at all. The government has banned the use of pesticides and GM crops. The water runs down from the mountains all around the plains, and is held underground by natural rock. The white mountain in the distance, melts a lot of snow throughout the year, which helps keep the water table filled. Beside each windmill is a well, and the windmills bring up water to irrigate the crops. There is a network of irrigation pipes running all over the plains. The more sensitive crops are grown in the poly-tunnels, we even grow bananas in them. The windmills also power cooling systems for the tunnels when required.'

Ella said she thought it was all wonderful, and that she had noticed the fruit and vegetables tasted so much better on the island, than at home. She passed Panicos a honey biscuit, and they sat and nibbled, quietly taking in the scenery.

After a while they set off again. The shadows were starting to get longer, and Panicos said he had one more thing he wanted to show her before it got dark. They drove along the mountain roads, Panicos slowing, when he saw goats in the trees at the roadside, or chickens in the grass near the road edge. Ella wasn't sure if he was slowing to show her the wildlife, or in case the animals darted out in front of the car, causing an accident to all concerned. She suspected it was probably the latter option, but all the same, it was nice to go slow and see the animals.

At last the road stopped winding around the mountains, and was back at approximately sea level once more. They drove along country lanes, past houses growing crops in their gardens, or having one tethered goat, or a few chickens. They drove through mile upon mile of olive groves, and lemon and lime trees.

Then the road opened out to a vista of scrubland that was like it had been transported straight out of a desert somewhere. Tall cactus plants with giant pads dominated the landscape. Dry grasses grew where they could, and little flowers that liked it dry, somehow managed to thrive. In the distance Ella could see the sea. Panicos parked at the edge of some sand dunes. The area was fenced off, and there was a small garden shed sized hut a little way away. They walked over to it. Inside were posters and information describing how this beach was a sanctuary for the loggerhead turtles. No one was allowed on the beach except the people who worked to help protect the turtles. Little wire cages had been put over the spots on the sand where turtles were known to have laid their eggs, to protect them from other foraging wildlife. It was deserted and very beautiful for that.

'When they are laying their eggs at night, at the right time of year, you can come and watch quietly from here, it is quite something to see. Also the night they hatch is quite the sight too,' said Panicos proudly.

'I would love to see that,' said Ella wistfully.

'Perhaps you will,' said Panicos. 'Who knows, maybe you will still be here when they hatch? Maybe you will never leave?'

'I think I would dearly love that,' said Ella. 'This island has worked its way into my soul. I can see why my mother loved it here.'

The sun was dropping into the ocean, and night was beginning to fall, so they decided to drive back to Agios Spiridos, and go for dinner. Panicos drove back a different way, along the coast road. It was quicker and easier, only taking about half an hour, but still very pretty views of the coast, and the little coastal villages, which Panicos reeled off the names of, as they drove through. He seemed to be rather enjoying the role of tour guide. It was not long before they were bypassing Agios Nikolaus, and then turning into the little village of Agios Spiridos.

'Where is Carolina's restaurant?' asked Panicos, 'I will drive directly there.'

Ella told him the way, and they parked outside. Carolina came rushing over as soon as they walked through the door, to greet them, and to be introduced.

'This is Panicos, one of my mother's friends from that summer,' began Ella. 'He was best friends with Adonis for many years, and so I have adopted him as my uncle.'

'aftee eenay meah pollee kallee anipsia,' (she is a very good niece) smiled Panicos.

'I am going to Kios tomorrow to try and find Adonis, but for now, I am very hungry,' said Ella, turning to Panicos, 'how do you feel about the fish meze?'

'Sounds great.'

They sat down and Ella turned to Carolina and said, 'We will have the fish meze please,' (which is a huge two person dish, comprising seventeen different plates of which many are fish) then asking Panicos whether he would prefer wine or beer. Panicos said it was for her to choose and so she ordered a half litre of red wine.

Carolina smiled and said, 'You are hungry. Have you had a busy day?'

'Yes, it has been very busy, and very long. I was up very early for church, and then had an early lunch with Nikki and Athena Michaelides. Then I went shopping in Agios Nikolaus with Dimitris, then Uncle Panicos took me on a little tour of parts of the island. It has all been lovely, but lunch seems like it was two days ago.' Everyone laughed.

'I'll bring you out the first cold courses and some wine, right away then,' said Carolina.

In no time, good to her word, Carolina returned with plates, cutlery and glasses, a basket of bread, and the wine. She went straight back to the kitchen and returned with a lovely Greek salad topped with feta cheese, a plate of taramasalata, a plate of olives, and a plate of fava. 'That should start you off nicely,' she said, 'kallee orexee.'

Panicos and Ella helped themselves to salad, and dipped their bread in the dips. Although they were not rushing and were drinking wine as well, they had demolished the starters, and were nibbling their way through the olives in no time.

But Carolina was obviously watching, as the next, cooked, course came out immediately, and she swiftly swapped the empty dishes for full ones. There were calamaries (battered squid rings) decorated with lemon wedges, saganaki (battered cheese) and grilled crispy octopus.

Ella and Panicos made fairly short work of this course too.

'What time is your ferry tomorrow morning?' asked Panicos.

'It leaves Vathy at 9am,' said Ella between mouthfuls. 'But I am going to go early, so I can say hello to Nikos before he goes out fishing on his boat.'

'I don't have to go to work until midday tomorrow,' said Panicos, 'I could drive you to Vathy if you like? I would dearly love to say hello to Nikos again, after all these years.'

'That would be wonderful,' replied Ella, 'I was thinking of leaving the hotel at seven.'

'That's fine, I'll be outside at seven then,' grinned Panicos. Suddenly his world was filling up with friends, and friends that felt like relatives again, and it was all thanks to Ella. He felt quite content, somewhere deep inside, and it was nothing to do with the food, wonderful though it was.

Carolina cleared the plates once again, and brought out the next course, which comprised courgette and scrambled egg with herbs, hummus with warmed pitta bread, prawn saganaki (nothing like cheese saganaki but prawns in a spicy tomato sauce), and cheese balls, (deep fried balls of cheese and potato.) Ella and Panicos had by now, slowed down a little bit, but were still not in the least daunted by the quantity of food. Ella was beginning to suspect Panicos might have missed lunch because of her visit, and was glad she had ordered the large meze.

'So what is your plan when you arrive at Samios in Kios?' asked Panicos.

'Well,' began Ella, 'I have an address for Dimitris' Aunt in Samios. I will go there first, and find out where Anna lives now, then deliver her parcel. Then I thought I might go to the town hall, and find the address for Adonis' family in Kefalos. Then I'll go to Kefalos and book into Demeter's for the night as recommended to me by Athena Michaelides. Then I will see what else I can find out.'

'That sounds like a sensible plan of action,' said Panicos, 'When do you come back?'

'My ferry gets back to Vathy at 6 o'clock on Tuesday evening.'

Panicos nodded to himself.

Carolina came out to clear the empty plates again, and this time to ask if everything was alright, and if they were ready for the next course. Ella and Panicos both assured her that the food was wonderful, and that they were indeed, ready.

The next course comprised fried whitebait (marides), courgette fritters, battered barbouni strips, and a shellfish salad. This course took a little longer. In fact they were still nibbling at it, when Carolina brought out the final course, and squeezed it onto the table. A huge sea bream covered an entire platter, and little bits of lemon, pickled samphire, capers, tomato and pickled garlic, decorated the edge of the platter. Carolina squeezed a final plate of spicy fried potatoes, alongside everything else. 'That is everything,' she said.

'That is plenty,' said Ella, 'it is all delicious, thank you.'

Panicos and Ella slowly ate and drank their way through the rest of the food and wine, before finally slouching back, stuffed, into their seats.

Carolina came to clear the wreckage of plates that covered their table and they both told her how wonderful everything had been. She asked if they would like a coffee, and Panicos accepted, while Ella declined, choosing instead a mint tea. Ella excused herself for a moment to go to the bathroom. On the way back she paused to chat to Carolina at the bar, and paid her forty Euros for the meal, which included a good tip. She said that if she did things that way, Panicos would not be able to insist on paying when the time came, as it was already taken care of. Carolina smiled in acknowledgement.

Ella returned to the table just as the hot drinks arrived. Carolina also brought two pieces of ravani topped with ice cream. Ella wondered where she would put her piece. Panicos, who clearly had a sweet tooth, did not appear to have the same problem. Ella ate half of her cake, but then stopped, declaring herself full to the brim, and defeated. Panicos finished hers too, quite happily.

Carolina came over and sat with them to chat for a little while, and ended by saying 'kallo taxithee,' (have a good trip,) and instructing Ella to report back to her when she got back.

'I have been told to do that by a lot of people,' said Ella, laughing, 'perhaps I should throw a town meeting, or have a party.'

'That is not such a bad idea,' said Carolina, a seed of something, clearly planted in her mind.

'Well, I should be getting back,' said Ella, 'early start tomorrow.'

'tow logareeazmo parakalo,' Panicos said to Carolina.

'Ochee. Ella echee eethee katavleethee,' (No, Ella has already paid,) replied Carolina, winking at Ella.

'sass poneeree mikrow aleppoo,' (you sly little fox,) said Panicos, laughing.

They said their farewells and went out to the car. Panicos drove round the corner to the hotel. He thanked Ella for a lovely dinner, and promised to meet her at seven in the morning.

Ella waved him off and went into reception. She walked into the bar and said hello once again, to Christos.

'Did you have a nice dinner?' he asked.

'It was wonderful,' replied Ella. 'We had the fish meze.'

Christos made appreciative groans, obviously clearly remembering the last time he had had the meze.

'Where did Panicos take you on his little tour?'

'We went to a mountain village, and to a place where they sell the most amazing honey I have ever tasted, and you can see into the bee hives.'

'I know the place,' said Christos, 'his honey is indeed very good, the best.'

'We went and looked at the Mareesee plains, and then at the bay where the turtles lay their eggs.'

'Ah that is called Fissaria Bay,' said Christos. 'It is protected now, but the new government is not sure it will stay that way. That want to allow moderate building, but the environmentalists are fighting them, saying that any building will destroy the turtles.'

'That is terrible,' said Ella.

'Sometimes tourism is not such a good thing, when they want to build more and more hotels everywhere,' said Christos.

Ella sighed.

'But Mareesee plains are a triumph though,' he said, wanting to end the conversation on a high note.

Ella changed the subject, 'tomorrow I am going to Kios, and staying over for one night. Do I need my passport back? And should I leave the room key here?'

'Neither should be necessary,' replied Christos, 'but I will fetch your passport for you anyway, and you can take it just in case anyone asks. You might as well leave the key at the desk in the morning. It is one less thing to carry, and it saves any trouble if it were to get lost, or dropped overboard or something.'

Ella agreed, and Christos got her passport for her. She had eaten and drunk far too much to have room for a nightcap, so she said goodnight to Christos, and went up to her room.

There was no sign of Bob, which Ella was not especially surprised about as she had no treats for him. That cat was psychic, she was sure of it. She tipped the last of the biscuits into a bowl for him, and shredded the last of the ham on top. She put the bowl in the fridge overnight. She poured the last of the milk into a bowl and put that back in the fridge too. Bob's breakfast was ready, so he wouldn't get forgotten if she was in a rush in the morning.

Ella packed her rucksack with a change of clothes and shoes, a wash bag, a bikini, her big scarf, money, tickets, passport, sunglasses, the map of Kios, and the biscuits and bag of cherries, and a bottle of water. She placed the rucksack alongside Dimitris' box, then showered, and sat outside on the balcony while her hair dried, sipping at a cup of herb flavoured mountain tea. She had coated herself in her anti mosquito preparation, to avoid being the main course for the insects, as she sat outside in the very pleasant night breeze. The palm tree in the garden below made slapping noises with its fronds. It was a relaxing sound, that when Ella closed her eyes, sounded exactly like the pitter patter of rain on the windows, back home. How wonderful to have to sound of rain, while sitting in the dry heat, caressed by a gentle breeze. It was very soporific, and Ella soon felt the need to clean her teeth and go to bed. She did not forget to dry her toothbrush, and add it to the wash bag. She did not forget to set her alarm for six thirty either.

She lay a while, listening to the night, and thinking back through the day. She had taken a risk leaving the patio doors open, and the air conditioning off; she might well wake up bitten all over. But the night was so comfortable, and the sounds from the nature happening outside, so relaxing, that she just had to take the risk. She soon fell asleep, covered by just a cotton sheet.

Chapter Seven

Ella woke to the sound of her alarm, which always made her think of the kid's show Captain Pugwash. As it went diddlydee diddlydee, she always awoke, half finishing the musical phrase in her mind. Not the worst way in the world to wake up, even if it was early and she was a little bit groggy. She padded out to the loo, still half asleep really, but awake enough to remember to put the loo roll in the bin, not down the toilet. Greek plumbing cannot deal with toilet paper, and tourist misdemeanours were largely responsible for the blockages, and subsequent terrible smells, that arose in the height of the summer months, when the weather could really cook, and accentuate the aroma. By the time Ella had washed and emerged from the bathroom, Bob had his paw under the door and was meowing quietly. Ella opened the door and he looked up at her. She risked reaching down and picking him up for a cuddle. Bob purred, perfectly amenable to the idea.

'I won't be here tomorrow morning Bob,' Ella told him, 'I have to go away overnight. When I come back I'll buy you a special treat, okay.' Bob looked up into her eyes, and purred happily. Ella got his breakfast out of the fridge, and put the two bowls down on the porch for him. He went straight at it, not in the least bothered by the temperature. Perhaps it was the cooling cat version of an ice cream frappe, thought Ella. She got the bowl of olive oil soaked rusks out of the fridge, and ate them quickly on the balcony, with a cup of black coffee, before dressing in culottes, sandals, a t-shirt, and light cotton cardigan, and dragging her hair roughly into a ponytail. That had used her half hour window, so she threw the washing up in the sink, and grabbed her bag and the box, and headed down to the hotel reception. She handed her room key to the girl on the desk, and went outside to where Panicos was already dutifully waiting in his car.

'Kaleemaira anipseea mou,' (good morning my niece,) he said, as chirpy as someone who had already been up for half the day.

'Kaleemaira oh theeoss mou,' (good morning my uncle,) replied Ella, putting her things in the car and smiling back at him.

Ella got into the car and they headed off towards Vathy. It was already a lovely clear day, despite being very early and the sun not being at its full heat yet. The roads were quiet, with only a few people heading into town early. As most shops opened at about seven anyway, the commute for those workers had already happened. Opening early meant they could shut for a long lunch, and afternoon nap, and cooling off time, followed by another opening for business in the late afternoon through the evening. So after only about a twenty minute drive, they were already pulling into the fisherman's parking area at Vathy harbour. Ella left her things in the car and walked down the jetty with Panicos until they came to the green marker post. The Heleni was still moored to the post, Ella was pleased to see. She would have hated to have found it gone to sea already, and Panicos to have had a wasted trip. Just when she had decided that Nikos must not have arrived yet, he stood up on the deck of the boat, caught sight of Ella and waved enthusiastically, peering to see who it was with her.

As they drew nearer Panicos called out, 'Yassoo palio feelo mou, Niko,' (Hello my old friend Nikos.) Nikos peered at Panicos curiously, then suddenly recognised him, 'Panicos,' he shouted, jumping up onto the jetty, and giving him a big hug.

Ella stayed a while, filling Nikos in on what she had been doing since she saw him last. The ferry was already in port, and as it was now gone eight, Ella decided to go and embark. Panicos walked back to the car with her to help her with her things, telling Nikos he would return to catch up properly very shortly.

Panicos carried the box, and Ella carried her rucksack, having got the outward ferry tickets out, to carry in her hand. When they got to the boat, a man tore her ticket in half and gestured her aboard. Panicos handed her the box and wished her a safe journey, and good luck, (kalo taxithee kay kalee ticky.)

Ella walked onto the boat, along the side of the same ramp which the cars used to embark. She came to some stairs and climbed them, going through a door into the main interior deck. The toilets were to her left and right, and then the area opened up into a large area, divided into seats, some with small low tables in the middle of them, others just banks of seats. At the far end was a small bar and restaurant, currently giving off an alluring smell of coffee. Also at the far end of the room were two more doors. Ella took one and went up some more steps to the open deck. More seating was available up here, and Ella took a bench seat facing out to the sea, placing the box and bag alongside her. She could see the fishing boats occasionally coming in or out of the harbour from here, but not the fishing jetty where Panicos and Nikos were doubtless catching up the years.

People gradually drifted upstairs, filling the seats around her, or just having a look around before going back to the interior deck. Ella had biscuits, cherries and water, so did not feel the need of the interior deck and its café. She preferred to make this outward journey, watching all that went on around her from the open deck. Perhaps she would use the café on the return evening trip.

At nine o'clock sharp, the engines, which had been ticking over for some time already, notched up a gear and Ella felt the ferry begin to move. It pulled slowly away from the dock, and Ella realised she was now at sea, between islands, no longer on Aegos. It was a strange feeling, especially as land was still right there, close enough to reach by a short swim. Ella loved the feeling of being at sea. As the ferry pulled out of the harbour she looked down and there was Nikos, standing beside Panicos on the Heleni, both looking up at her and waving. Nikos had brought his boat out into the harbour a little way, so she could easily see them both. She waved back, laughing. What lovely, friendly people they were; it brought a slight lump of emotion to her throat, as they waved her away. Soon they were out of sight, and Aegos was fast becoming a long stretch of coastline, and not much more. In the distance, Kios was similar but smaller.

The sea breeze was very refreshing, and gave Ella an appetite, so she ate her biscuits and cherries, and drank her water, watching the coast of Kios getting clearer by the minute.

By quarter to ten, Samios harbour was fully visible as they pulled into it. Rows of prettily painted, pastel coloured houses seemed to be stacked up the hillside of the bay. Ella thought it a stunningly pretty sight, as the ferry manoeuvred into its position in the port. So did all the tourists and day trippers on board apparently, as they crowded the deck to take photographs.

Finally they were docked, and the engines turned off. The ramp was lowered, and an announcement made, first in Greek, then in English, and finally in German, for passengers to go to their cars to be ready to disembark, and for foot passengers to disembark right away. Ella collected her things, and made her way to the lower deck. At the harbour side, Ella soon came to a queue of taxis available to hire. She leaned in to the one at the front of the line and asked him in Greek, how much to the address she had for Lula, Dimitris' and Anna's aunt. The taxi driver told her four Euros, and she agreed that price and got in. The taxi driver did not drive off right away, but waited for the rest of the foot passengers to disembark first. Ella was not surprised, taxis often waited to get a second passenger who could also be charged a full fare to go in the same direction. They considered themselves as small busses, one supposed. This was especially common behaviour at ports and bus stations. Apart from a large family who all piled into the taxi behind, there were no other customers for the taxis. As soon as this fact became clear, the taxi driver put down his paper and started the engine and drove off.

They drove up steep streets, with barely any room either side of the car, turned, drove along a way, then back down a way. This maze like journey went on for about five minutes before the driver pulled up in front of a house, which Ella could have easily walked to. She paid him and got out, and he raced off.

Ella pushed the doorbell of the address she had been given by Dimitris, and after a minute or two, a frail looking, elderly woman came to the door.

She opened it saying, 'Nay, borro na sass voitheesou?' (Yes, can I help you?)

'Psackno yia tin Anna Kostas,' (I'm looking for Anna Kostas,) asked Ella, somewhat nervously, as she was playing a hunch on the name here.

'Zee katta meekos tou dromou stow numero exi,'
(she lives along the road at number six,) said the
woman.

Ella thanked her and turned away.

'eesay fillee tiss?' (are you a friend of hers?) asked
the woman.

'ockee, alla echo enna doro yia ekeenie appo enan
feelo,' (no, but I have a gift for her from a friend,) said
Ella.

The old woman nodded, clearly satisfied with that
answer, and went back inside, closing the door
behind her.

Ella walked along a few doors and rang the bell at
number six. A woman slightly younger than her,
opened the door saying, 'parakalo?'

'Anna, Anna Kostas?' asked Ella.

'Nay,' (yes) said the woman quizzically.

'Melenee Ella Hudson,' began Ella.

'You are English?' interrupted Anna.

'Yes,' said Ella, thinking that speaking in English
would make this a lot easier. 'I have a gift for you
from a friend.' Ella held out the box to her.

Anna took the box from her, saying, 'how curious. A
friend sending a gift to me via an English person. Do
come in, and have a cup of coffee.'

Ella followed her inside, to a large comfortable
kitchen, where Ella was invited to sit at the table.

Anna placed a cup of coffee and a glass of water in
front of them both, before sitting down. She had not
yet opened the box.

'So who is this friend that sent you?' she asked.

Ella took a deep breath, 'your brother Dimitris, from
Aegos.'

Anna gasped, then quickly collected herself. 'How do
you know Dimitris?'

Ella told her own story once again, as quickly as possible, and Anna visibly softened. 'There is a letter in the box too,' she added.

Anna opened the box and took out the letter. 'Do you mind if I read it now?'

'Of course not,' replied Ella, taking out her map of Kios to look at. She sipped at her coffee as Anna read, stopping now and again to discretely wipe away a tear before it dropped onto the letter. She finished and looked at the gifts. 'This is a lovely surprise,' she said, 'I suppose I have you to thank for him finally doing this.'

'Well only, you know, men sometimes need a little nudge to their thinking. He felt he could not upset your mother by coming to you directly.'

Anna nodded. 'Could you stay a little longer, while I write a note for you to take back to him please.'

'Of course, it is no problem,' said Ella, relieved it was all going so well.

'Would you like a piece of bougatsa?' asked Anna. Ella replied that she would love a piece, and Anna gave it to her and invited her to take a look around the garden while she waited, and see the rabbits and chickens. Ella went out into the little garden that was half stacked up the hillside behind the house. It was tiny really, just room for a small table and chairs, some pots of herbs, a hutch with several rabbits in, and a caged area with four chickens pecking about. It was tiny, but in practical terms, it provided meat, herbs and eggs, and a place to sit in the sun, which Ella did, as she ate her bougatsa.

It was not very long before Anna came out to join her. She passed a letter to Ella.

'How did you know my name was Kostas now?' she asked.

'Yiorgos who owns the Zeus hotel, told me what he thought he knew about the past, and after he said Panayiotis Kostas left the island immediately after his wife died, I sort of assumed and guessed the rest.'

'You didn't tell any of that to Dimitris then?'

'No, it was not my place to gossip.'

'I have told him all about it in my letter. I hope he understands how it was.'

'I'm sure he will. He misses you very much, I think.'

'I miss him too,' said Anna. 'It is a shame my daughter is growing up without her uncle. She will love the gifts though.' Anna jumped up as if she had just thought of something important. Either that, or left a pie in the oven which was now burning. She ran into the kitchen and returned with a photo that had obviously been taken quite recently, of herself, Panayiotis and her daughter. 'Give him this too, please.'

'Of course I will,' said Ella smiling. 'Now I should be going, I have quite a lot to do. Could you possibly tell me the way to the town hall please?'

'I can do better than that,' said Anna, 'I will take you there on my scooter.'

'That is very kind of you, thank you,' said Ella.

'After all you have done for my family, it is absolutely nothing,' said Anna.

They headed out on Anna's scooter, down the steep, narrow streets, along the main harbour road, narrowly missing wandering tourists. Sometimes Ella just shut her eyes and prayed. They turned down a slightly wider road, that was obviously the main street, and parked outside a large building.

'This is the town hall,' said Anna, 'would you let me come in and help you? Perhaps it will be easier.'

Ella agreed that it probably would be easier, as her Greek was not wonderful, and readily accepted the offer of help.

They went inside, and Anna rattled off a lot of Greek at the woman at reception, and was told a lot of things in return. She turned to Ella, 'The records of who lives on the island, and where, are upstairs. Shall we go and look?'

They walked upstairs, and into a room that Anna led them to, which held the records. They wandered along looking at the letters on folders, past Alpha, Beta, Gamma, Delta and Epsilon, until they reached Zeta.

The folder marked 'Za' was near the beginning of the section. Anna pulled out a pile of papers, and looked through until she found the name Zacharoulis, then those that said A.Zacharoulis or Adonis Zacharoulis. There were three. Two were Adonis Zacharoulis, and the other was just A. Anna wrote down all three names and addresses, and handed the piece of paper to Ella. Two of the names were in Kefalos.

'So what are you going to do next?' asked Anna.

'I am going to Kefalos,' said Ella. 'Aside from checking these names, there are some people I have been told to see there. Can I get a bus from here?'

'Of course,' said Anna, 'I will take you to the bus station.'

They climbed back on the scooter, and drove a short distance through the town centre to the bus station, which was outside the tight maze of streets on the outside edge of the town. Anna found the bus for Ella, and saw her safely on board, waving to her as the bus pulled out.

The bus wound its way through country roads, populated mainly by olive trees and goats, with the occasional goat that had climbed up into the tree, to get to the higher tastier leaves. Ella smiled; it always amused her to see goats standing in the higher branches of trees, like some sort of surreal Christmas decoration. For a long time she had thought that the shepherds must have got drunk at night, and put them up in the trees as a joke on the tourists; but finally she saw a goat one day, climbing up into the tree. It seemed to have no trouble at all with tree climbing. She had always known they were sure footed on the mountain paths, but had never guessed about the trees. The descent was rather more ungainly, however, more of a slide and jump.

Every now and then they drove past a house, or a house in the process of being built; just a concrete shell with holes where the doors and windows were going to go. Gradually it became more urban, as they approached the outskirts of Kefalos. The road signs had been counting down the kilometres to Kefalos for some time now, and it was clearly beginning. Countryside gave way to vineyards and fields of vegetables. They passed a castle that had brown archaeological signs naming it as The Castle of Saint George. A huge spreading tree, with bright yellow blossoms, grew outside the castle, and it had been supported with poles. On the roadside, a local vendor was selling rose water ice cream, from a cart with a sun shade. The bus stopped to let people off and on at the castle.

Then the shops and town proper, began. Finally the bus drove around the edge of a Venetian wall. Kefalos had clearly been fortified at some point in history. They drove along the harbour's edge for a minute or two, then turned into a big bus parking area. The driver called out 'Kefalos.' Everyone started gathering their bags and packages, and getting off. Ella joined the throng.

She made her way over to the tourist information booth, carefully dodging the people from the tour companies, who were trying to lure people to their time share holidays with scratch cards that declared you had won something, but had to come to such and such a place to collect the prize. And immigrants trying to tie jewellery onto her, and then try to get money for it. Inside the booth they immediately greeted her in English.

'Could you tell me the way to Demeter's bar, restaurant and bed and breakfast, please?' asked Ella.

'Yes,' said a woman, 'I know the place. Just walk along the harbour front for about five minutes that way, (she pointed,) until you come to Despina's Square. It has a dolphin fountain in the middle. Turn inland there, and Demeter's is about halfway along the street behind the fountain.'

Ella thanked her and headed out. She walked along the harbour's edge, but her view of the water was soon obscured by stalls that had been set up all along the edge of the road. Some were selling leather handbags and belts, others, toys. But mostly they were selling street food. The smells were assaulting Ella, and she soon couldn't resist making some purchases. She bought Loukoumades (small cinnamon and honey donuts) from one stall and Kourabiedes (almond cookies, white with dusting sugar) from another. Finally she bought a couple of sticks of souvlaki (barbequed skewered pork) and ate them as she walked along. Street souvlaki was always so much tastier than restaurant souvlaki. The portions were smaller, but the flavours seemed more concentrated. Soon Ella had arrived at Despina's Square with its dolphin fountain. She sat on a bench to watch the water and eat her loukoumades and kourabiedes. They were very good too. When she had finished, she rinsed her hands in the water and shook them dry. Ella headed down the street going inland, and could see the sign for Demeter's about halfway along. When she arrived she took a seat outside. A waiter came over straight away and greeted her.

'Yassass, Tha eethala ena Hellenikas gaffez, gleekez, parakalo, kay ena tentura.' (Hello, I'd like a sweet Greek coffee please, and a Tentura- a cinnamon flavoured liqueur from Patras,) said Ella.

'amaysuss,' (right away,) said the waiter.

He returned quickly with the coffee, the shot of liqueur, and a large glass of water. 'teepotta na farnay?' (anything to eat?)

'okhi efharisto,' (no thanks.)

The waiter left and Ella took a sip of the Tentura, which was thick and sweet and loaded with cinnamon flavour. She finished that and moved onto the coffee which was thick and sweet, and flavoured with cardamom. Finally, her taste buds assaulted and satisfied, she drank the iced water.

The waiter came back after a while with the bill in a little shot glass. It was four Euros. Ella put five in the glass and took it indoors. At the bar a woman was writing something down beside the till. Ella handed her the shot glass and said,

'Athena Michaelides apo ton Agios Spiridos yia Aegos, mou eepay na airtho etho,' (Athena Michaelides from Agios Spiridos on Aegos, told me to come here,) 'eckettay enna thomateeo yia apopse?' (do you have a room for tonight?)

'Yes, of course,' replied the woman, coming out from behind the bar. 'Come with me,' she led Ella through a door and up some stairs. They went into a small room which overlooked the street, and Ella could see down to the harbour past the fountain, from the little balcony.

'How is my old friend Athena?' asked the woman.

'She is very well,' replied Ella. 'I went to church with her yesterday, then she cooked lunch afterwards for Nikki and I.'

'She was always a very good cook. And Nikki, I haven't seen her in years, is she well too?'

'Yes, she seems very well. She works at the bank.'

'Like her father, God rest his soul, so sad. She was always the clever one in that family, not like her bad brother,' the woman turned to one side and did a pretend spit into the air.

'How much is the room?' asked Ella.

'Twenty Euros for you, as you are a friend of Athena,' replied the woman. 'I am Ireni, and you will meet my husband Allessandro tonight, as he is out buying fish at the moment.'

Ella handed Ireni a twenty euro note, and Ireni handed her the room key. 'I have some things to do here this afternoon, but I will come back for dinner this evening.'

Ireni nodded and left.

The room was simple, a bed and small table with a chair, a little wooden balcony on which you could stand, but not sit, and a small bathroom with a toilet and shower. The only mirror was a small one, on the wall by the bed. It was about as basic as it could be, just hooks to hang clothes on, but it would serve her purpose for one night. Ella stretched out on the bed and relaxed for a few minutes, letting the tension seep out of her spine.

After about fifteen minutes of semi relaxing, semi dozing, Ella had a quick shower, and put on her other top, a lighter blouse than the t-shirt and jacket she had been wearing, as it was much hotter now. There was less wind on Kios, than on Aegos, so it felt a lot hotter. She plaited her hair while it was still wet, so it would be curly when she let it down later. She hung her new blue dress on one of the hooks, so it would not be crumpled when she wore it this evening. Ella put on her alternate pair of sandals, and put her purse and the piece of paper with the three names on it, in her culottes' pocket. She left the room and put the key in her other pocket. Ella went down the stairs, and once again stopped at the bar to talk with Ireni. 'I want to find these three addresses,' she said showing Ireni the piece of paper, 'I wonder if you could give me directions please?'

'Two of these addresses are in Kefalos town, and I can draw a map of how to get to them for you. The third is in a village outside the town. You would need to take a taxi to get there.' Ireni got a piece of paper and a pen and started drawing a map of the streets in Kefalos. She marked two places with crosses. She put Demeter's bar on the map, and the harbour, and the museum. 'I have put the museum, because it is very big, and will help you find the other streets if you go wrong. Everyone knows where the museum is, it is so big. If you get lost coming back, go to the sea and walk along the harbour wall, that is the easiest way.'

'Thank you,' said Ella, 'You have been very helpful. I will see you later.'

She set off through the back streets, looking at the map every time the road came to a junction. Town houses lined the roads, their tiny gardens filled with fragrant blooms. Cats sat on garden walls, and watched her pass them, with very little interest. Some did not even bother to look up. There was not much shade on the streets, and Ella was getting quite hot. It was not long before she reached the first address.

She rang the bell, and a young woman came to the door. 'Psackno yia Adonis Zacharoulis oh opeeoss eetan filoss tou Panicou Papadopoulou yia Aegos peeso sto dekaennaya exintha enna.' (I am looking for Adonis Zacharoulis who was a friend of Panicos Papadopoulous on Aegos back in 1961,) said Ella. The woman looked a bit puzzled and Ella thought she had probably said some things wrong in Greek. 'O Andrass mou eenay Adonis Zacharoulis, alla aftoss eenay eekossee efta kronon.' (my husband is Adonis Zacharoulis, but he is 27 years old.)

'O pappous tou esos?' (his grandfather, perhaps?) asked Ella.

'Ockee, aftoss eenay o treetoss geeoss, signomee.' (No, he is the third son, sorry.)

Ella thanked her for her help, and apologised for wasting her time, and left.

She walked on for a bit, looking at the map for guidance, then passed a café, and decided to sit in the shade for a bit, and drink a frappe, and cool off. It was very cooling and refreshing, and she soon felt a bit more collected. Okay so strike one, she thought to herself, but she still had two more leads, no need to get despondent yet. She reminded herself about all the new friends, and the Uncle she had already found. A little sparrow hopped about fearlessly by her feet picking up crumbs that had fallen to the floor. After Ella had finished her drink and paid for it, she started off again, following the map, which was very good. It tended to ignore all the small roads, but all main junctions were marked, and it was not long before she arrived at the next address. She had to open a big metal gate to get to the front door, and when she rang the bell, a big dog started barking and did not stop. An elderly man opened the door holding onto the dog's collar. Ella went through her little speech again, rather more nervously this time, somewhat wary of the dog.

The man said he was sorry, but no Adonis Zacharoulis lived there, he was Achilles Zacharoulis. Ella apologised and left. Strike two, she thought. The village trip would have to wait until the next day, it was too late now.

She looked at the map once again. The museum was very nearby. Ella decided to go and see what times it was open, she needed to distract herself and not dwell on thoughts that she might never find Adonis after all.

The museum was indeed huge, and the booth by the front gates said it was open until seven o'clock. It was four thirty now so Ella decided to buy a ticket and go inside as there was still plenty of time.

All around the big, imposing museum building, were carefully manicured gardens. A path led up the steps to the museum itself, which somehow reminded Ella of Versailles Palace. Grand main doors led into an entrance hallway, which was lined with paintings and statues. Then Ella looked up, and almost let out a gasp, as the whole ceiling was painted with a scene from nature, depicting angels in different seasons, amongst the plants and animals of the countryside. It really was very beautiful. Rooms led off from the main hallway to other rooms, in which furniture, armour and pottery were exhibited. Another area displayed weapons, and another books and textiles. Ella read some of the little tags describing the items, when something particularly caught her interest, but mainly just wandered round soaking up the atmosphere and history. When she had been through all the rooms of the house, she went out through some more grand doors into a courtyard. The whole courtyard was edged with statues and columns

depicting Greek philosophers and artists. In the centre of the courtyard was a fountain with a centrepiece of a boy playing with a dolphin. Beyond the courtyard were the splendid gardens. Ella could only imagine the amount of water it took to keep them looking so lush and green. Palm trees and statues of sportsmen and warriors in bronze and marble, were positioned on the edges of lawned areas, with borders planted up with pretty flowers and herbs. She sat down on a bench in the shade of a palm tree, to take it all in and enjoy the aromas of the gardens. Set into some stone paving slabs just in front of her, was an image of Medusa, snakes whirling about her head. Ella found the gardens entrancing, and a little mesmerising, or perhaps that was just the effect that sitting looking at Medusa was having on her. Whatever the reason, she decided it was time to get up and move about a bit. She finished exploring the gardens, and went back to the house to the little shop, where she bought some postcards of various places she had found especially attractive; the ceiling painting, and several scenes from the garden, with one of Medusa of course.
Ella left the museum, and decided to walk back by the sea, regardless of whether or not she was lost, though she didn't think she was. The road from the museum wound downhill towards the sea. Ella was not aware she had been walking uphill during the day, but apparently she had. Obviously she had been paying too much attention to the map to notice. The road was signposted in the direction of the harbour, though she had already figured that out because of it being downhill. It was a fairly obvious assumption, that if there was a hill, and the sea was nearby, it would be at the bottom of the hill. It wasn't rocket science.

Soon Ella arrived once more at the harbour wall. The stallholders had packed up their wares and gone home now, and the frames of the empty stalls looked a little bleak against the sea wall. It wasn't long before Ella reached Despina's Square and the dolphin fountain, and then arrived at Demeter's bar. She nodded a hello to Ireni and then went up to her room to change into her dress for dinner.

Ella put aside her negativity and disappointment from her failed day, with ten minutes of relaxation and meditation, which included the intention to bring good, positive events into her life. She slipped into her new blue dress, which looked nice with the white sandals, and took her hair out of its plait, which left it cascading in waves around her face. She was quite pleased and uplifted by the end result. She was not normally one who got excited by clothes and looks, but on this occasion, she felt quite proud of herself. Ella went downstairs to the bar area, where Ireni said hello to her, and the waiter stared at her for a moment. Ella grinned to herself. It was nice to make an impression sometimes.

'You look very beautiful tonight,' said Ireni.

'Thank you,' said Ella. 'And thank you for the map you drew. I did not get lost once, and I very much enjoyed the museum.'

Ireni leaned through the door into the kitchen, and called out to someone, and a rather large man emerged, cleaning his hands on his apron. Ireni introduced him to Ella, as her husband Allessandro. They exchanged some rapid fire Greek, and then Allessandro said he was very pleased to meet Ella, in English.

'I hear you were out buying fish today?' said Ella. 'So you can recommend what will be nicest for my dinner.'

'But of course, if you are eating with us, I will serve you only the very best. Come through the kitchen, the restaurant is in the garden. Most people go down the side path, but you shall come through the kitchen and see the fish.'

Allessandro showed Ella all the fish and other delicacies, laid out in the kitchen. She commented on how nice the parrot fish and barracuda looked, and peered curiously at a white dip that looked like hummus, but clearly wasn't. Allessandro told her that it was a tahini and garlic dip, which he was perhaps a little famous for locally, as he refused to give his recipe to anyone else, since his grandmother had entrusted him with its secret. Ella pointed to a ceramic garlic bulb hanging over the back door to the garden. 'That is very unusual,' she said.

'It is to keep the vrikolakas, vampires, away,' said Allessandro, perfectly seriously.

Ella nodded, not sure what to say. The blue and white eye, in glass or ceramic, to ward off evil, she was used to. She even had it as her key ring at home; but she had not heard people talking specifically about warding off vampires before. Allessandro took Ella through to the garden, which for a tiny, town restaurant, was surprisingly beautiful. A dozen tables were arranged in the paved, walled garden. At the back of the garden, a waterfall cascaded down the wall into a small pond, lit with green and blue lights. Plants climbed the remaining walls, and wooden columns were placed around the walls, and draped with white swathes of fabric. In the far corner was a full sized statue of Demeter, holding a flaming staff in her right hand, and a sheaf of corn in her left. Her headdress was made of woven corn too. In front of the restaurant wall, was a small raised plinth area that was currently unoccupied. Ella had her choice of tables, as the restaurant had not got any customers yet, it being only half past seven.

'There will be Greek music there later,' said Allessandro, pointing at the empty plinth stage. 'We will be busy, and all the tables will be full. Why don't you sit here by the stage so you can watch the musicians. Best seat in the house.'

Ella sat where he directed her.

'Do you like red wine or white?' asked Allessandro.

'I like both, but I prefer red,' said Ella.

'Do you like the Greek wines too? Mavro Daphne and Retsina?'

'Yes, I think they are both very nice,' Ella smiled.

'I will send Ireni out with a drink for you.'

A couple of minutes later, Ireni appeared with a jug of sweet red wine and two glasses, and a bowl of purple olives. She took a seat beside Ella saying, 'Do you mind if I join you for a while?'

'That would be lovely,' replied Ella.

'I have brought you some wine, on the house, and thought we could perhaps get to know each other a little bit while Allessandro cooks your fish.'

'That is very kind,' said Ella.

'I grew up on Aegos, and went to school with Athena Michaelides. We were best friends for many years. Later on I met Allessandro, who lived with his family here on Kios, in this very restaurant. I moved here when we married, and hardly see anyone from Aegos now. We had four sons, you will see two of them tonight, playing the music. Mikhali, the eldest, plays bouzouki and Yermanos, who is second eldest, plays the guitar. My two youngest, Soterios and Ptolemy, are at university in Athens.'

Ella once more told her story, filling in all the details she had discovered since she arrived on Aegos.

'But you know, I think I may have met Elizabett once,' said Ireni. 'Athena and I were in town, Vathy, hanging out in a café, when Elizabett and the crowd she used to go with, came in. Athena called them over, and introduced me, and we had a lovely afternoon chatting. I remember practising my English with Elizabett. She glowed somehow, and seemed to make everyone around her happy.'

Ella smiled. Everywhere she went she seemed to meet someone who had known Liz, albeit briefly, and moreover, remembered her. Her mother must have really made an impression on people, she thought.

'So what did you find today?' asked Ireni, sipping her wine, and pouring some more into Ella's glass.

'Nothing at all,' said Ella. 'One of the addresses was a young man with the right name, but it was not a family name, so nothing there. The other was not even Adonis, but Achilles. It just said A. Zacharoulis in the registry. So I will take a taxi to the village tomorrow, and try the last one, I suppose. I don't have anything else to go on. After that, I don't know.' Ella shrugged.

'I will get Allessandro to drive you there, rather than messing about in a taxi,' said Ireni, eating an olive, rolling it deftly around her mouth, before popping the stone out clean, into the ashtray.

'No, no, a taxi will be fine,' said Ella, 'I don't want to put you to any trouble.'

'It isn't any trouble at all,' said Ireni. 'He has to go out that way to the farms anyway, and buy vegetables. He will enjoy having the company, and I'm sure you will enjoy seeing the countryside. Also he will be there to speak to the person in Greek, which might be useful.'

'That would make things easier,' Ella agreed, 'and I would love to see the countryside and the farms, it sounds lovely.'

'Then it is settled.'

Allessandro came out with a bread basket, and a plate, and cutlery. Ireni rapidly told him in Greek what she had arranged, and he beamed, clearly looking forward to the company on his buying trip.

Ireni said she would leave Ella to enjoy her food, as she had some things to get on with, but would come back later.

Allessandro reappeared with a small plate containing a filleted parrot fish, decorated with tomatoes and green peppers, and a second small plate of the white dip. He wished her kallee orexee and dived back into the kitchen.

Ella tried the fish, it was very good, fresh and tasty, not overly strong in flavour, but nice. Then she tried the dip. The garlic flavour was actually more subtle than she had been expecting, and the tahini flavour came through strongly. It really was very good. Ella had not realised quite how hungry she was, and soon demolished everything; all the dip, along with all the bread, the fish, peppers, tomatoes, and all the rest of the olives. She drank some more of the wine too.

Allessandro returned to clear the plates, and smiled to see them all empty.

'It really was very good,' Ella told him.

'Are you ready for the barracuda,' he asked.

Ella said she was, half grinning to herself, because it seemed like he was asking if she was ready for a dance of some sort. Somehow barracuda sounded more like a dance than a meal.

He returned with a huge platter, in the centre of which was a large slab of battered barracuda fish. It was surrounded by chips, rice, salad, lemon wedges, pickled samphire, tzatziki, and black olives. One look was enough to convince Ella that she would not be feeling hungry much longer, this plate full would surely fill her up. The restaurant was starting to fill up too now, several of the other tables were occupied, and the level of hustle and bustle activity had increased.

Two young men came out and started to set up stools, microphones and instruments on the plinth. They both smiled and nodded at her. She smiled back.

The barracuda was moist and tasty, and very fresh. It still tasted like the sea somehow, and was especially delicious with the pickled samphire. Everything was very good. Ella pressed on, she wanted to have finished eating before the music started, so she could give it her full attention.

Finally, Ella cleaned the plate and sat back satisfied. Ireni came out to clear the table, and with her came a little girl in a white dress.

'This is my niece, Nansia,' said Ireni, 'she would like to sit and talk with you for a while, is that okay?'

'Of course,' said Ella, smiling at the little girl as she climbed onto the chair.

'My cousin Mikhali and my cousin Yermanos are playing Greek music soon,' said Nansia, in slightly hesitant English.

'Do you watch them play music often?' asked Ella, as slowly and clearly as she could.

'Whenever I am allowed,' answered Nansia. 'Do you want to see my stones?'

'Yes please,' answered Ella, wondering what she was going to be shown.

Nansia pulled four flat stones out of her pockets, and laid them out on the table. Each one had a little painting on one side. One was a dolphin porpoising out of the sea, leaving a plume of white sea foam behind it, another was a little house on a mountain, another a goat standing beside an olive tree, and the final one was a woman in Greek costume. They really were exceptionally good, and Ella told Nansia so.

Nansia shrugged, 'I make lots of them, and sit in the square, and sell them to the tourists.'

'How long does it take you to paint a stone?' asked Ella.

'About three or four hours,' said Nansia.

'How much do you sell them for?'

'I say two Euros, but will sell them for one euro, if people are not wanting to pay so much.'

'I think they are worth more, they are very good. Can I buy these ones, or are they your special favourites?'

'You can have them,' said Nansia, knowing it was the right thing to say, but also looking at them, as if thinking about the hours that lay ahead to make the next lot of pocket money.

'That is not good business sense,' said Ella, pulling a ten euro note out of her purse, and putting it into Nansia's hand. 'Now put this away in your pocket, before someone comes and tells you, you are not allowed to take it.'

Nansia grinned, folded the note up small, and pushed it deep into her pocket, saying, 'thank you very much, pretty lady.'

Just then Mikhali and Yermanos came back out onto the plinth and began to play. They started off with the old fashioned Greek song, 'Never on a Sunday.'

They were very good, and both Ella and Nansia watched them, fully absorbed in the music.

They barely noticed Ireni bringing out three plates of galaktobooreeko (a filo custard pie with lemon syrup drizzled over it) and sitting down to join them. Nansia squealed with pleasure and began to eat her dessert immediately, but Ella paused to thank Ireni, and inform her that this was her favourite Greek dessert, before she dived in. The three of them ate contentedly, while the men played several Greek songs; The Sea is Deep, Ferryman, Athens, Love that Becomes, and what sounded to Ella like My Cretan Lemons. Of course it was entirely possible that she was mistranslating, but the music was beautiful and haunting, whatever they were singing about, lemons or not.

At the end of every song they clapped, and Ireni shouted 'bravo' and Nansia called 'oppa' and jumped about, getting quite excited. The men clearly loved it. Most of the customers at the other tables had finished eating by now, and were just ordering drinks and coffees, which the waiter could easily handle by himself, and Allessandro came out to join them, with a tray of coffees, a jug of water, a can of fizzy orange for Nansia, and three shots of tsipouro for the adults. Ireni got up and took the microphone, and sang a slow sad song, while the men accompanied her. Then Allessandro sang the next song, which was rather more boisterous. Ireni grabbed Ella and Nansia, and they linked shoulders and began to dance between the tables, picking up willing customers as they went. Soon a whole train of them were step kicking and bobbing, in a line joined at the shoulders, knocking into chair legs as the pace picked up. At the end, everyone collapsed back into their seats with many shouts of 'oppa' and much clapping. The men took a break to have a cold drink, and some of the customers left, thinking the entertainment had ended. Allessandro and the waiter pushed the unoccupied tables back against the wall, making some space in the middle of the floor. After about half an hour, the men came back on, and tantalisingly played the first few bars of Zorbas, then stopped again, and gestured at the remaining people. Everyone laughed, and they repeated the process. Allessandro and Ireni got everyone up, and linked, arms over each other's shoulders; Allessandro and Ireni at each end, with their free arms stretched out. This time the notes of Zorbas started and did not stop. The dancers carefully picked out their steps, following the slow rhythm, and getting used to the repetition of the steps, and when to bob down. Gradually, Mikhali and Yermanos began to pick up the pace, the dancers following it easily. The dance got faster and faster, but still the line of people managed to follow it, until finally it ended, and everyone flopped into their seats exhausted, cheering, clapping, and shouting 'bravo' and 'oppa.' The men played a couple of slow melodies, and brave little Nansia, stood up and did a magic trick with a spoon and a napkin, making the spoon 'disappear' up her sleeve. Everyone cheered. The waiter refilled the jugs of wine.

Ireni got up to sing another song, and the waiter came and did a sort of dance in front of her on the floor, that looked a bit like Cossack dancing, somehow mixed with slow Greek dancing. He would touch his foot to his hand and jump into the air, then come crashing down to the floor in a crouch. It was very impressive.

Then Alessandro sang a song, and Ireni danced, a beautiful slow, whirling dance that was like a painting of the music. Nansia and the waiter tore paper napkins into little shreds and threw them over Ireni like confetti, and Ella joined them. The throwing of flower petals, and torn paper napkins, had replaced the plate smashing that the government had long since banned.

All too soon, it was all over. The customers paid their bills and left, and Ireni put Nansia to bed. Mikhali and Yermanos joined Allessandro, Ireni and Ella for a night cap of another tsipouro. Ella finally excused herself to retire and settled up with Ireni in the bar, before going up. Ireni would only let her pay for the two fish courses, and that only came to eleven Euros. Ella tried to give her fifteen, but Ireni was adamant she would not take more than eleven. Ella bid her a sleepy goodnight and went up to her bed, placing her four pretty stones on the little table.

Chapter Eight

Ella awoke, disorientated for a second, by the different bed and room, then quickly got her bearings. She showered, and put on some clothes, packing the rest of her things into her backpack, including the pretty little stones. Then she went down to the bar and said good morning to Ireni, who was already up, and busying about. Ella gave her the room key, and Ireni brought Ella a coffee and an orange juice. A few moments later she reappeared with a bowl of Greek yoghurt, with walnuts and honey sprinkled liberally on top, and a little bowl with spoon sweets (like a cross between runny jam and sweet preserved fruit), that might have been apricots or greengages, it was hard to tell, and a roll. Ireni wished her kallee orexee, and left her to it.

It was a very good breakfast, and Ella felt certain she would be full until lunchtime on it. Ireni came out and cleared the things, and asked Ella how she was today. Ella replied that she was fine, and added that she had had a wonderful time the previous night. Ireni poured Ella another coffee, and told her Allessandro would be ready to go to the farms shortly, if that was okay with her. Ella said that it absolutely was, and settled back to drink her second coffee. After Ella had a quick bathroom break, Allessandro showed Ella to his four wheel drive jeep, and they set off out of town.

Allessandro winked at Ella and said, 'it might get a bit bumpy, I'm going to cut across the mountain tracks, as it knocks nearly an hour off the journey, okay,'

'That's fine by me,' grinned Ella, 'I love seeing places I would not normally see otherwise.'

Moments later, they turned off the road onto what could barely be described as a dirt track. The jeep bounced along, and Ella felt like she was on some kind of crazy fairground ride. It was fun though, and with the open top, and the breeze blowing on her, it felt exciting and good.

Allessandro was obviously enjoying himself too, as they bumped over rocks, and drove at an alarming tilt, along the edge of the hillside. The countryside around them was deserted, apart from the occasional black snake, which they swerved to avoid. Goats watched them from a safe distance, with what could only be described as disdain, before resuming the chewing of whatever foliage was in front of them. Birds flew away before the jeep got near. It was an exhilarating journey, and with nothing around for miles, except more countryside, Ella felt like this was how Greece truly looked, before tourism had come along and spoilt it a little bit.

It was not long before a proper track, leading down to a farm, appeared. Ella could see poly tunnels and an orchard, as well as a large number of orange chickens pecking about in an open space.

'This is the farm, where I buy some of my vegetables,' said Allessandro.

'It looks big,' said Ella, 'what do they grow in the poly tunnels?'

'Bananas, tomatoes, aubergines, that sort of thing.'

They pulled into the yard beside some farm equipment, and parked up. They both got out of the jeep. A man came over and greeted Allessandro, and smiled at Ella, and the two men began talking rapidly in Greek.

Allessandro opened the back of the jeep, where there were several large lidded boxes. The other man went over to a shed, and reappeared with three large crates of fruit and vegetables. Allessandro loaded them into two of the boxes, and locked the lids down. These vegetables would not be rolling round the jeep during any further off road stints. The two men talked some more and then the farmer went away, and came back with three chickens, that were obviously freshly killed, as they were not yet plucked or gutted, and still had traces of fresh blood on their necks. Allessandro opened another box, which turned out to be a cold box, and put the chickens inside. He took out his wallet and paid the farmer, they chatted briefly for a bit longer and then he called Ella to get back into the jeep as he was ready to leave.

'Okay, so now we head to Aliveri village, to try and find your Adonis Zacharoulis,' said Allessandro.

'Thank you for this,' said Ella, 'I am a little bit nervous.'

'Ireni told me your story, last night. I hope we find something useful for you today. I really hope we find your father, but perhaps that is too much to hope for.'

'If it is not him, but is a relative of his, I will not tell them who I think he is to me, just that he was a friend of my mothers,' said Ella.

Allessandro nodded, 'that sounds like a good idea to me.'

They drove down the farm track, which joined up with a proper road, of sorts, and after a short while, that joined up with a slightly better road. Allessandro drove round winding mountain roadways, first upwards, and then back down again. A small village was visible below them, in the foothills.

'That is Aliveri,' said Allessandro, 'what is the actual address?'

Ella dug about in her backpack for the piece of paper from the town hall, finding it after pulling out her spare clothes, and putting them back again.

'Odos Dionyssus 26,' she said.

'When we get into the outskirts of the village, look for side streets on your side marked Dionyssus,' said

Allessandro, 'I will look out of my side. It is only a small village, all the streets likely come off of the main road through.'

They wended their way down the mountainside, the road forming hairpin bends, all with no kind of barrier to the edge, as was standard it seemed. After about another ten minutes, they reached the foothills and the outskirts of Aliveri village.

They drove slowly along the main street, until Ella saw Dionyssus Street and told Allessandro. It was a fairly narrow street, so he parked the jeep on the main road and they got out to walk. About half way along the street which was a mixture of houses and small shops with flats above, was a small pottery shop at number twenty six. Allessandro looked at Ella and shrugged, and they opened the door and went inside. A young man in his early twenties was working at a pottery wheel, but was just finishing as they walked inside. He ran a wire under the drinking goblet he had been throwing, and carefully moved the finished item to a shelf to dry. He turned to them greeting them with a 'Yassass.'

'Psackno yia Adonis Zacharoulis,' (I'm looking for Adonis Zacharoulis) began Ella.

'Eemay Adonis Zacharoulis,' (I'm Adonis Zacharoulis) he replied.

Ella felt a little despondent, and it must have shown in the way she looked, for Allessandro quickly jumped in and spoke rapidly to Adonis in Greek. They talked for a little while, as Ella looked absently at the pottery wares for sale. Some of the bowls with a metallic finish, were really beautiful. She heard Allessandro say the words grandfather and mother, but was not really trying to follow what he said in any way carefully. She felt a bit like the heart had been knocked out of her, and she was never going to find Adonis now.

After the men had been talking to each other for a while, Allessandro turned to her and said, 'He has a grandfather called Adonis Zacharoulis, for whom he is named. He does not know definitely, but the dates fit, and he thinks it may have been him that was friends with your mother back in 1961.'

Ella looked at the young man more carefully. If this was true and this Adonis was her mother's Adonis, then this young man would be her half nephew. She couldn't stare for long, but if there was any resemblance, she thought it might be wishful thinking. She asked Allessandro to ask, if his grandfather was still alive, and if so, where he lived now.

Another exchange took place in rapid Greek, and Allessandro turned to her grinning. 'His grandfather moved to Aegos five years ago. He had always said he left his heart on Aegos, and wanted to go back there to live out the rest of his days. He lives in Zanthos town now.' Allessandro talked to Adonis some more, and Adonis wrote down the address for him. Allessandro gave it to Ella, who put it away carefully in her backpack, as if it was made of gold leaf.

Ella felt quite excited again now, and also like she was on an emotional roller coaster. She selected two of the metallic bowls, which would make lovely fruit bowls, and bought them from Adonis. Adonis now looked very pleased with the outcome of the visit too. They made their way back to the jeep.

'That was a nice gesture, to buy some of his pottery,' said Allessandro.

'I think it is very beautiful,' said Ella. 'Do you think Ireni will like it? I bought one as a gift for her.'

'She will love it, I am sure,' said Allessandro.

They drove back, partly through villages, partly off road on the mountain tracks, and for the last part, along the coast road. When they arrived back at Demeter's, Allessandro went to put the produce away and Ella went into the bar to see Ireni and give her the gift of the pottery bowl.

'That is very beautiful, and it is so nice of you, thank you so much,' said Ireni. 'Did you find him?'

'I think I have found him, and I have an address, but he has moved to Aegos, so I will have to wait until tomorrow now, when I am back there.'

'I think this search is teaching you to be very patient, yes?' laughed Ireni. 'Do you have any plans for this afternoon?'

'None at all,' said Ella, 'My boat leaves at five o'clock from Samios, and that is all I have on today.'

'Good, then you can come out with Allessandro and I, on our boat?'

'Oooh I would love that thank you,' said Ella excitedly. 'I love boats.'

Ireni gave Ella a cup of coffee, and told her to wait there for a little while. Ireni busied herself phoning someone, and telling her to come into the bar to work, and gave a variety of rapid instructions to the waiter, who was obviously being left in charge. Ireni went to the kitchen to tell Allessandro what was going on, and Ella went to the bathroom, and put her bikini on underneath her shorts and t-shirt.

When she came back, Ireni was coming out of the kitchen with a cold box in one hand, and a small pile of towels in the other.

'Come,' she said to Ella, leading her back out to the jeep. They climbed into the jeep, and Allessandro soon came out, wearing a peaked cap, and carrying another cold box, which he put in the back.

They drove down to the harbour, along the main road, parking up near the boat jetties. Allessandro carried one cold box and Ireni the other, though she did let Ella carry the towels. It was only eleven o'clock, but most of the fishing boats and tourist boats had already set out for the day. The harbour was relatively quiet. They walked down some stone steps, and then along wooden jetties until they came to a boat called Demeter. It was a medium sized wooden, white painted, pleasure boat, that at some point in its past had been converted from a fishing boat.

Allessandro jumped onto it and leant over the side as Ireni passed him the cold boxes, one at a time. Then he helped Ireni up the three wooden steps on the side of the boat, and finally helped Ella on.

Allessandro leapt back off, and untied the boat from the jetty at each end, throwing the ropes onto the deck. Then he jumped back onto the boat again, before it started to drift away from the jetty. He went into the little wheel house, and started the engines, while Ireni and Ella sat down on the padded wooden seats on deck. Soon Allessandro was manoeuvring the boat towards the harbour exit.

'Do you have all your things with you?' Ireni asked Ella.

'Yes, I have everything in my backpack,' replied Ella.

'Good, because we will sail up the coast, and end up at Samios harbour, in time for you to catch your ferry.'

'That would be great, thank you,' said Ella.

They chugged along, through a route marked out with buoys floating in the water, until they reached the harbour entrance. They turned starboard, out into the open sea, which was as calm as a pond.

At first, they sailed along a little way out from the coast, but still having a clear view of the town, and all the buildings. Later on, the castle could be seen from the sea, it looked much more of a defensive fortification, from out there on the water. Ella could see how, in its prime, it might have deterred some invaders.

As they sailed on past the outskirts of the town, the coastline became more rugged, and Allessandro brought the little boat in closer to the coast. The cliffs were made of stratified rock that clearly sloped downwards, towards the sea. Ella commented on how stunning they looked.

'You can see how the island came up out of the water, with all the earthquakes, with the rock sloping like that,' Allessandro told her. 'In fact, it still happens to some extent. In a little while I will go in closer still, and you will be able to see the algae that is now above the water line, since the island tipped up a bit more with the big earthquake ten years ago.'

Ella peered at the coastline, then pointed out to Ireni, a cormorant she had spotted sitting on the rocks. They sailed along quite close to the coastline and the sheer rocks, and Ella could indeed, see the sloping algae, that was now exposed and pink. She wondered how close the bottom of the boat was to the rocks. She knew that the rock face was like an iceberg, with a much larger amount of it below the water, at who knew what angle or depth. Well, Allessandro obviously knew the waters, as he was sailing confidently along a route he clearly knew. Ahead of them, Ella could see an arch formed out of rock with water flowing through it. 'Are we sailing through there?' she asked.

'Yes we are,' replied Allessandro. 'Wait until you see the bay on the other side.'

'Don't worry,' said Ireni, 'he knows what he is doing, we come here all the time. The water is plenty deep enough for our little boat.'

It was a strange feeling, sailing under the huge rock arch, water lapping back and forth between the sides of the boat and the nearby rock. Then they were through and inside a beautiful bay. The sandy beach was deserted, as there was no access to it down the steep cliff, the only access being by small boat, and there were no other boats in the bay. Allessandro sailed in as close to the shore as the little boat could go, which was about fifty yards out. 'This is Sigota Bay,' he said proudly. 'The arch is the only way in or out, because there is a rocky reef preventing entry any other way. The big tourist boats can't get through the arch, so only small boats can visit this bay. If you want to visit the beach, you have to swim ashore, unless you have a dinghy.'

'We will stop here for a while, and you can have a swim if you like,' said Ireni, as Allessandro turned off the engine, and dropped anchor. 'Swim to the beach if you want, there is no hurry. I will prepare some lunch, and Allessandro might fish for a bit.'

Ella did not need telling twice, and stripped off down to her swimwear. She climbed down the little wooden steps they had used to get onto the boat, which went down to just below water level before they ended. She had never liked jumping into water. She loved to swim, but wasn't keen on being underwater.

Ella decided to swim round the boat, going past the stern first. The water was lovely and warm, and tiny little fishes swam around her. She could see clear to the bottom. It was like a swimming pool, but one with fish and sand and rocks. She could see urchins amongst the rocks way below her. She swam the length of the starboard side, then swam in front of the

bow. As she did so, she panicked and spluttered a
little water, before she regained her composure, and
quickly swam on down the port side. There was a
real sense of primal fear when swimming in front of
the bow of a boat, close enough to be in its shadow.
She had never done that before, and did not think
she would ever try it again either, it was a most
disconcerting sensation. She had no idea why it
should feel so dark and terrifying, but it did, and out
of nowhere too. She decided that she could definitely
swim much further, and struck out for the beach. In
very little time, she was able to stand up and walk the
rest of the way ashore. The sandy beach was
perfect, littered with only shells, and the occasional
piece of driftwood. She walked the length of it,
enjoying the feel of the sun drying and warming her
body. Ireni waved at her from the boat and she
waved back. She could see Ireni pottering about on
the boat, and Allessandro had dropped a fishing line
over the starboard side, and was drinking a bottle of
beer as he fished. Ella did not take long to fully
explore the tiny beach, and peer into the rock pools
at the edges of it, where it met the sea. She was not
one for laying about in the sun, so she waded out to
waist high, and then began to swim back to the boat.
She climbed up the wooden steps on the port side,
and Ireni handed her a towel as she came aboard.
Ireni put down another towel for her to sit on as she
dried off, then handed her a Mythos beer from the
cold box. It was cold, refreshing and delicious.
Ireni was preparing a Greek salad from items in the
cold box. She had put a cloth over the trunk that
stored tools and spare fuel, and was using it as a
table. She had already put out plates, and cutlery and
salt, along with chunks of bread, what looked like
revitho keftedes (little chick pea burgers) and some

sort of pie with olives in it, that almost looked like a pasty. She added the bowl of country salad to this, and pulled out a pot of tzatziki from the cold box. Then she pulled out a bowl containing stuffed tomatoes and stuffed peppers. She called Ella and Allessandro over to eat. Allessandro collected a plateful of food, and went back to tending his fishing rod. Ireni and Ella sat companionably to eat. Ella had put her shorts and t-shirt back on, as she was dry already. She somehow felt it wasn't really decent to eat in a bikini. Greeks were very reserved, and she felt she had inherited something of that reserve herself.

The little keftedes were indeed made of chick peas, and the pasty type thing turned out to be potato and olives in sesame dough, and was mouth wateringly good. The tomatoes and peppers were stuffed with rice, pine nuts, herbs, onion, raisins and a little cheese. Ella had worked up quite an appetite from her swim, and ate some of everything. Allessandro got up to get himself another beer and handed another to Ella. She felt full and content, and very lazy as she sat in the sunshine, with the little boat bobbing gently beneath her. Ireni handed her another plate of food, and gave some extra potato pie to Allessandro saying, 'It all has to be eaten up, Allessandro will need the cold box for all the fish he is catching.'

Allessandro grinned and reeled in his line, which did indeed have a fish on it. He hit the fish on the head with a lumpy stick, then put it to one side, and pulled in a small net he had had dangling over the side of the boat in the water. Four more fish were in that, and he dispatched those quickly too. He took the cold box, a knife, and the fish, forward to the bow, where he was presumably going to gut them, and put them away to take home. After a while he returned, and put the cold box away in the, now cleared off trunk, along with his fishing gear. Ireni stashed away the plates, and empty pots and beer bottles, also in the trunk, while Allessandro turned on the engine, and automatically hauled up the anchor. They left the beautiful little bay the same way they had come in, through the arch of rock.

They carried on sailing along the coast, seeing the little bay now from the sea, with its rock reef barrier. It was something of a siren to unwary sailors, lured in by its beauty and privacy, only to be caught and wrecked on the rocks. Only a small warning beacon acted as a deterrent.

Further out at sea, was a huge wooden ship, in the style of the old fashioned pirate galleons, Ireni pointed it out to Ella as a tourist cruise ship. 'They go along the coast, stop for a swim, moor up at a deserted island and cook a barbeque lunch, then cruise back in the afternoon. It is very popular with the tourists.'

The coastline they were sailing near to, now became a group of small caves, disappearing back into the rocks.

'People bring diving gear and swim over to the caves and then explore inside, but it is quite a dangerous hobby I think,' said Allessandro. 'It is easy to get lost in the caves, or get stranded by the tide. It is not safe to swim on the surface to the caves, as you could easily get dashed against the rocks by the sea. The tides and currents are strong around them, and you would have to be a very strong swimmer to swim against them. Legend has it, that one of the caves leads inland up to the mouth of the river Styx, and that if you go through the right caves, you can reach Hades itself. It is just a story though, I think.'

Ella peered into the darkness of the caves as they sailed past; they did have a rather creepy feel about them. Completely unlike the sunny, welcoming bay they had just left.

Allessandro took the boat out into deeper waters now, as the coastline became more built up with the start of Samios town. As they sailed along, a pod of dolphins played in the waters around the bow for a while, and Ella was fascinated to watch them. They stopped following as the Demeter neared the harbour wall of Samios. It was a truly huge harbour, looking even bigger coming in from the sea in a little boat like this. The pretty pastel coloured houses lined the bay like some sort of ornate, giant, cupcake. The harbour seemed to cut deep into the land, rather than being wide and stretched out like Vathy was. Allessandro sailed right up to the middle of the harbour, further inland than the ferry was able to go, and tied the boat up at an available post.

'Lets go and have a cup of coffee before your ferry comes in,' he said.

'Oh yes,' agreed Ella, 'absolutely. My treat to thank you for such a wonderful afternoon. And Baklava too.'

They all climbed off the little boat, and Allessandro led them to what was obviously a favourite café, where Ella ordered the coffees and Baklavas.

After they had finished, and Ella had paid the bill, they hugged and said goodbye. Ella said that she hoped she would see them again one day, and they said that they were sure they would. Whilst they had been having their coffees, they had sat and watched the ferry pulling into the harbour, so now Ella made her way round to it to embark.

When Ella reached the ferry, she was surprised to see Anna waiting there.

'Hello,' she said, 'I didn't expect to see you again so soon.'

'I was hoping to catch you before you left,' said Anna. 'I went to the bus station, but when you weren't on the bus, I thought you might have come on an earlier bus, and been shopping, so I came to wait here instead.'

'I came in by boat,' Ella replied. 'Some friends brought me; we had a lovely afternoon on their boat.'

'Did you find your father?'

'Not yet,' said Ella, 'but I think he has moved to Aegos now. Anyway, I have an address, and am very hopeful for tomorrow.'

'That is good. I will light a candle for your success,' said Anna. 'I wonder if you would give this bag to Dimitris please?' Anna held up a green canvas bag.

'Of course,' said Ella, 'I would be delighted.'

'My daughter, Soula, wanted to write and thank him for the gifts. Then she wanted to put in some drawings she had done, and a little gift she had made out of shells. Then my husband Panayiotis wrote him a letter too, and sent some cigars. So I baked a cake he used to like, when we were younger. I hope you don't mind, carrying all this extra stuff?'

'Of course not, it's a pleasure. I'm sure Dimitris will be very happy. I will go and see him tonight.'

Ella and Anna said goodbye, and Ella got her ticket out, and walked onto the ferry. She wandered up to the top deck, where she could wave to Anna, and look for Ireni and Allessandro on the Demeter. She could see the little boat, but they did not seem to be on it, then she saw them walking down the street carrying bags and boxes; they had obviously been shopping for supplies. She watched them climb back onto the little boat, and load it up with their packages.

It was almost five o'clock, and the ferry had finished loading up cars and other vehicles, and the ramp that formed the doors when pulled up, was being hoisted into its closed position, ready for setting sail. The engines which had been idling for some time now, began to pick up speed, and it was clear the ferry was getting ready to leave. Ella could see that the Demeter was sailing out into the harbour too. In fact, it was soon close enough for Ella to see Ireni and Allessandro waving up at her. She waved back, and to Anna who was standing on the harbour side too. Then the ferry began to turn, and she couldn't see any of them properly anymore. By the time the big boat had turned enough for her to look over the opposite side, Anna was just a faint dot, who had stopped waving and was now walking away. The Demeter was nowhere to be seen. Ella stood on deck until the ferry was out of the harbour, then went below to the little café. She ordered herself an ice cream frappe, and bought a packet of thin, cinnamon biscuits. Hands full with her drink and bags, she half walked, half lurched to an empty seat by the window. The ferry was rolling a little bit, it did feel as if the wind had picked up a little when she was standing on deck, but it wasn't enough to trip over, or spill her frappe. Ella did not get sea sick, even when it was very rough, she felt as if she had been born with sea legs. But this was certainly not rough, just a gentle side to side, rolling motion. Really quite relaxing. Ella was glad of the frappe with its caffeine, or she might have been falling asleep by now. She was aware that the day was far from over; she still had to get back to Agios Spiridos and see Dimitris, and Carolina at the very least. She actually felt like she could sleep for about a week; this last week had been so packed full

of people and activities, it had been quite intense.
And to think, it might all be at an end tomorrow.
The hours crossing passed in no time, and Ella didn't
bother going back up on deck, she was just glad to
sit and relax. When the announcement came for foot
passengers to disembark, she gathered up her
backpack, and the bag for Dimitris, and plodded
down the steps to the off ramp.
Stepping ashore, she saw Panicos grinning and
waiting for her. He hugged her hello. 'Well anipseea
mou, did you find him?' he asked.
'Not yet,' said Ella. Panicos raised his eyebrows
questioningly. 'I found someone who I think was his
grandson, and his grandfather sounded like the right
person, but he moved back here to Aegos some
years ago. I have an address in Zanthos, I will go
tomorrow.'
Panicos groaned, 'So you had a wasted trip, little
one, he was here on the island all along.'
'Not wasted,' said Ella. 'I found Anna, and she was
happy to hear from Dimitris. In fact I have a parcel
from her, to give to him tonight. I made some new
friends too, and went on a lovely boat trip with them
today.'
'Everywhere you go, you make friends, anipseea
mou,' laughed Panicos. 'Do you have time to have
dinner with me here in Vathy? I know Nikos would
love to join us, he is waiting just over there,' Panicos
pointed, and Nikos waved at them. 'I will, of course,
drive you back to Agios Spiridos after dinner.'
'So long as I see Dimitris tonight, that will be fine,'
said Ella.
'Say hello to Nikos, and I will put your things in my
car,' said Panicos.

'Be careful though,' warned Ella, 'there are breakable things in the bags.' Panicos nodded acknowledgement.

Ella walked over and said hello to Nikos, who asked the same questions Panicos had, and got the same answers.

'Thank you for bringing my friend Panicos back to me,' Nikos said, 'It was lovely to see him again yesterday morning. We talked for a couple of hours until he had to go to work. I felt like all the years since I last saw him just melted away.'

'I am glad that worked out, friends should stay in touch. That is what friends are for, being there for each other.'

Panicos came back over to them. 'I have rung work and got the day off tomorrow, so if you like, I can drive you over to Zanthos?'

'If it's not too much trouble, I would love that,' said Ella.

'Of course it's not too much trouble, I love spending time with my niece,' said Panicos, squeezing Ella's arm. 'Now for dinner. Nikos has suggested a fish restaurant, which he says is the best in town, because it sells the fish he caught.'

They walked along the harbour a little way, turning into the town, then a couple of streets in, on the left, was a little fish restaurant called Andreas Tyrimos. It was very bare, and there were no outside tables, and no tourists inside, which was always a good sign. A couple of tables were taken up by local Greeks, a very good sign.

They sat down at a table by the window. A fish tank of exotic fish was against the wall behind them. The other walls were painted with boats, nets, mermaids and dolphins. A large net hung from the ceiling, making a kind of false ceiling. Paper fish and seashells were caught within it. It was very charismatic, but not in the least commercial, or in any way posh. Just a simple, sea themed place. Did what it said on the tin, thought Ella, a place to eat fish.

A waiter came over, and Panicos and Nikos talked rapidly to him in Greek. Nikos turned to Ella and said, 'He says the octopus is very good indeed tonight, and the swordfish is very fresh. I know this is true, because I caught it this morning. Shall I order that for us?'

There was no sign of any menu, and Ella was happy to go along with whatever Nikos suggested, and told him so. She heard Panicos order a litre of kokkino krassee, (red wine), and then, as soon as it had begun, the ordering was completed.

They all chatted happily, making a start on the wine as soon as it arrived. Nikos and Panicos talked about the old days, and about Liz. Ella told them all about her short trip, her visit to the museum, the Greek music and dancing, and the boat trip to Sigota bay and swimming. It was as if they hadn't seen each other for months, they had so much to talk about.

The octopus arrived; a huge platter of tentacles, grilled to perfection, then chopped into inch long pieces and served, drizzled with a little olive oil, and red wine vinegar. There was also a huge basket of sesame bread, and a small bowl of pickled samphire, and another of skordalia (a garlic, potato and olive oil dip, predominantly garlic flavoured) and that was it. They helped themselves to the octopus, which was perfectly cooked, tender, yet crispy on the outside, with a fantastic flavour. Suddenly Ella remembered something, 'I need to find a shop to buy a fish for Bob,' she said to Panicos. 'Is it too late? I promised him.'

Nikos looked puzzled, and Panicos explained about Bob the cat, to him in Greek. Nikos laughed.

'I will see what can be arranged,' said Panicos, and they all went back to the job of devouring the octopus.

When the waiter came back to clear the dishes, Panicos spoke to him in Greek. As usual it was too fast for Ella to catch the whole conversation, but she did pick up psaree (fish) and gattoss (male cat) so she had an idea what they were talking about.

'He says it is no problem,' said Panicos, 'They have some small fish, and some heads and tails in the kitchen, they will wrap up for you to take with you, at no charge.'

Ella thanked him. Then the main course arrived. They each had a swordfish steak, with chips and salad on the side. The fish had been marinated and then cooked in sweet lemons, and was absolutely delicious. By the time they had finished, Ella was absolutely stuffed, and beginning to feel a bit sleepy again. Luckily they did not bring out any cake, just three shots of lemon liqueur, and the bill, which Nikos and Panicos insisted on paying between them. Ella was too tired to join in with that argument. The waiter brought out a neatly packaged assortment of fish, and presented it to Ella. She nearly giggled, but instead thanked him.

They strolled back down to the fishing harbour car park, where Panicos was parked, and said goodnight to Nikos, who wished Ella every success for the next day. They got into Panicos' car and headed off to Agios Spiridos.

In the car, Panicos was making conversation, but Ella was trying really hard not to doze. It had been a very long day, and swimming in the sea, and lazing in the sunshine was always tiring, even when you weren't doing very much else.

'Do you mind if we go to the hotel first, so I can put my bags down, and have a shower and get changed? I feel very tired and grubby, and I am carrying around this fish for Bob.'

'Of course, no problem,' said Panicos. 'I will go to the bar and have a beer and a chat with Christos.'

'Oh please tell him my news, then that will save me a little time, as I already have to see Dimitris and then Carolina.'

'Of course I will talk about you,' laughed Panicos. Shortly, Panicos pulled into the parking area in front of the Zeus hotel, and got Ella's bags out of the car for her. Ella ran in to reception and got her key.

'I will carry your things upstairs for you,' Panicos said. As they arrived outside Ella's room, Bob appeared, as if out of nowhere.

'Hello Bob,' said Ella. 'Have you missed me?' Bob rubbed against Ella's ankles, as if to confirm that indeed he had. He let Ella stroke and fuss him, and even let Panicos fuss him too. Bob made little chirruping sounds. Ella put down the foil package, which Bob could clearly smell, as he was jumping up for it, and opened it out, to form a sort of makeshift dish for the fish. Bob was all over it as soon as he could get to it, pushing Ella's hand out of the way. Panicos went down to the bar, and Ella let herself into the room with her packages. The maid had sorted out her washing, and washed the dishes she had left in the sink, and the room was pristine. She took her blue dress out of her backpack and shook the creases out of it, putting it on a hanger ready for after her shower. She also took out the letter and photo from Anna, and added them to the green bag, which she left by the door. Then she put away the rest of her things, leaving the pretty stones out on the table, and went for a quick and invigorating shower. Ella brushed her hair as dry as she could, leaving it loose, to finish drying, then dressed in her blue dress and new gold sandals. She picked up her purse and keys, as well as the bag for Dimitris, and opened the door.

Outside, on the porch, Bob had disappeared without finishing the food. He had obviously taken the biggest fish away to eat and enjoy, somewhere private. Ella folded up the rest of the fish and put the package into the fridge, so some other cat or creature didn't eat it in the night. Bob could have it for breakfast.

Ella went down to the bar, and as she walked in, Christos gave her a little whistle. 'You look very Greek tonight,' he said.

Panicos told her she looked very nice and asked if she was ready to go right away, or if she wanted to stop, and have a drink first. Ella said that she still felt quite tired, so they should probably go straight over to Dimitris. Christos said that was a big shame as she was making the bar look pretty, and he was sure it would soon fill up with people if she stayed. Ella giggled, and Panicos gave Christos a little frown, like a protective father might.

Panicos said he would drive to Manolis' bar, which would save Ella getting even more tired, and they set out. Even though it was just up the road, Ella had to admit, it was further than she felt like walking.

The bar was fairly busy, but Dimitris had two staff working the bar, and was himself, just hovering between bar and office, in a rather managerial capacity. When he saw Ella come in, he came rushing over to her as if he had been waiting for her, which he probably had.

'You look very beautiful tonight,' he told her.

She thanked him.

'How was your trip?' he asked.

Ella told him her news in brief, while Panicos hovered nearby. Dimitris was clearly very keen to find out how things had gone with Anna. He ushered them to a quiet table, bringing with him a bottle of Metaxa, and three glasses. He poured them each a shot.

'So, did you find Anna?' he asked eagerly.

'Yes, I did,' said Ella. 'She was very happy to receive your parcel, and sat down and wrote this letter straight back to you.' Ella handed him Anna's letter. Panicos and Ella talked quietly amongst themselves, whilst Dimitris read the letter. His face went through a roller coaster of emotions, ending with a tear which he wiped hurriedly away.

'Poor Anna,' he said. 'It was probably just as well I didn't know about Panayiotis though. At the time, I might have killed him. At least she is happy now. They all are.'

Ella pulled the photograph out of the bag and handed it to Dimitris. Dimitris was too choked up to speak, and looked at it for a long time. Panicos and Ella made small talk, while Dimitris collected his emotions. He finished his Metaxa, and poured them all another shot.

'Then today,' began Ella, 'when I was coming home, Anna was waiting for me at the ferry, and gave me this bag to give to you.'

Dimitris looked in the bag and pulled out the two letters, reading the one from Panayiotis first. Then he read Soula's letter, and had to excuse himself, going to his office for a few minutes.

'This is a very emotional thing for him,' said Panicos.

'Yes,' said Ella, 'when he comes back, I think we should make our excuses, and leave him to his thoughts for tonight.'

'I agree that is a good idea.'

So when Dimitris had collected himself and returned, Ella explained that she had had a very long day and was very tired, and suggested they catch up properly another time. Dimitris took both her hands in his, and thanked her most profusely for what she had done; his voice catching, and eyes welling up, once again. Ella gave him a big hug, then left with Panicos.

They drove down the road, and parked up outside Aphrodite's. Even though the restaurant was still quite busy, most of the customers had finished the main part of their meals and were just drinking, or struggling through their free desserts. As soon as Carolina saw them, she came rushing over to greet them. Andreas waved from the bar.

'Come and have a drink, and tell me how it went,' urged Carolina.

Andreas whistled appreciatively as Ella came up to the bar, and patted the bar stool next to him. 'You look stunning tonight,' he said. 'A real Greek Goddess.'

Carolina put two plates of Ravani, drizzled with honey and ice cream, in front of Panicos and Ella, and after protestations from Andreas, went back for one for him too. Carolina poured shots of kumquat liqueur for them all. Ella reached for her purse, but Carolina insisted it was on the house.

'So, did you find him? Are we celebrating?' asked Carolina.

'Not yet,' said Ella. 'But, I think I found his grandson. It sounds like his grandfather is the same man who was seeing my mother.'

'So his grandson would be your nephew, or half nephew then?' added Andreas.

'Yes, but I did not mention any of that to him. I want to find the man first, and make sure he is my father, before claiming any more relatives,' Ella smiled and winked at Panicos, who gave her a broad grin in return.

'So where is the real Adonis then?' asked Carolina, eagerly.

'It turns out he moved back to Aegos five years ago. Apparently, he said his heart was on Aegos, and he wanted to grow old and die here.'

'That sounds like the right man,' said Panicos. 'Adonis would say something like that.'

'So you have been on a, how you say, wild duck hunt?' said Carolina.

'Not really,' said Ella. 'I got an address for him in Zanthos, and Panicos is taking me there tomorrow. Also, I had a lovely time on Kios. I made some new friends, and listened and danced to Greek music. I went to a wonderful museum, and had a lovely boat trip to a little hidden bay where I swam and had a fabulous lunch. I really did have a great time.'

'Was that Sigota Bay?' asked Andreas.

'Yes, have you been there?' asked Ella.

'Many a time. It is a lovely peaceful, unspoilt place, that only small boats can visit. And the fishing is very good there, because the big boats can't get into the bay. I go there now and again to swim and fish.'

I swam to the beach and then back, after I had explored a bit. Allessandro fished off the boat, and caught four or five fish. Ireni made us a lovely lunch, that we ate on the boat, in the bay.'

'Sounds heavenly,' said Carolina.

'It was,' agreed Ella. 'Perhaps we can all go one day, if you will take us in your boat, Andreas?'

'I would be honoured,' said Andreas.

'Would you mind telling me the names and addresses of the people you met during your search?' asked Carolina. 'I know it is a strange request, but I am making a list of all the people you have been to, trying to find your father. It is very interesting. I will make it pretty, and present it to you when you have finished.'

'That is a lovely idea,' said Ella, leaning over the bar to give Carolina all the details, as she wrote them down on a little pad. She did not include Anna and her family, as she did not want word to travel back through the grapevine to Dimitris' mother, and make things difficult for Dimitris and Anna. Better some things stayed secret for now. Panicos and Andreas chatted away to each other as if they had been friends forever.

Eventually, Ella said that it was getting very late, and she had a big day the next day, so she really did have to be getting herself to bed. Panicos got up to take her home.

'You can stay for a while if you want, the hotel is right next door, I'll be fine,' said Ella.

'Nonsense, I'm not letting you walk back on your own,' said Panicos, and also made his farewells to Carolina and Andreas.

He drove Ella round the corner to the hotel. 'Shall I pick you up at ten in the morning?' he asked. 'That way you can sleep in a bit, and recover from today. We will still arrive in plenty of time.'

'That sounds great,' agreed Ella, sleepily, 'I'll see you at ten, my wonderful uncle.'

Panicos beamed, and said goodnight, watching her climb the stairs to her porch before driving off, back to Agios Nikolaus.

Ella let herself in to her room, and changed into her night slip. She brushed her teeth and hair, and hung up her dress, and put the new gold sandals away carefully in their box. She stood on the balcony for a moment, breathing in the cool night air, and drinking a glass of water to offset all the alcohol she had drunk. She did not feel in the least drunk, but the last thing she wanted to be tomorrow, was hung over. She looked at the dark lizard shape in the rock, and at the empty pool sparkling in the moonlight, before climbing under the cool white sheet and falling instantly asleep.

Chapter Nine

Ella awoke at half past seven to a gentle tap tapping on her door. She lay there a moment in bed, listening and grinning. Bob had arrived for his breakfast. Between taps, the tip of his little white paw poked under the door. Ella went to the loo, and quickly pulled on her swimsuit, and grabbed a towel and her keys, getting the foil packet of fish out of the fridge. Bob's tapping had become more insistent now, and was accompanied by moderately loud meowing, just to make the point.

He practically fell into the room when Ella opened the door, but soon regained his balance and composure, and trotted onto the porch beside her. Ella put down the package, opening it out for him. 'Enjoy your breakfast Bob, I'm going for a swim. Kallee orexee.' She climbed down the steps into the cool water of the swimming pool, and began swimming lengths up and down, in a lazy breast stroke. At first, she was just swimming on auto pilot, but gradually she came fully awake, and swam with more enthusiasm. Finally, when her arms and legs started to ache, and she was getting a little bit out of breath, she climbed out of the pool and wrapped herself in the towel. As soon as she had stopped dripping, she padded back up to her room.

Bob was still working his way through the last of the fish, but paused to look up at her, and chirrup. Ella put down a bowl of water for him.

Ella went inside and collected up her washing from her trip, which included her bikini, and took it into the shower with her. She half trod, half hand washed the clothes including her swimsuit, then got out and dried off, putting on a long skirt, sandals and a peasant blouse. She plaited her hair, then made herself a black coffee. Ella took all the washing and towels out to the balcony and hung it on the line, then came back in for her coffee and the rest of the bag of rusk bread. She took this out to the balcony to breakfast on. She gave the pool guy a wave, and then settled down to nibble the crispy bread, drink her coffee, and watch the lizard rock, which today had several goats clambering on it.

After clearing up Bob's debris, and washing up the bits and pieces, Ella put her purse, keys, sunglasses and the address for Adonis in her bag, and headed down to sit on the wall outside reception in the sun, and wait for Panicos. It was not long before he pulled up.

They greeted each other happily.

'Are you ready for your big day?' asked Panicos.

'I am a little bit nervous, but we don't even know if he will be in, let alone want to see me.'

'It will take us about an hour and a half to get to Zanthos, if we take the main road across the island, and don't stop anywhere on the way. Okay?'

'Fine,' said Ella. 'I'm ready.'

They set off on the drive. 'Did Bob finish his fish?' asked Panicos.

'He finished it for breakfast this morning. He seemed very pleased with it, purring away happily. He woke me up knocking on the door at half past seven this morning.'

'And you were happy with that?' laughed Panicos.

'Well, it's nice to wake up smiling,' said Ella, 'and it meant I had time for a nice long swim.'

The drive across the island was not the most scenic journey, but the main road got them there quickly. To have gone by bus, through all the villages, would have taken about two and a half hours, at least.

As they neared the outskirts of Zanthos, Panicos asked for the address. Ella read it out to him, 'Odos Krittee 6, Parossa, Zanthos.'

'Oh I know Parossa,' said Panicos, 'it is a little village just outside Zanthos town. I drive through it when I am driving the bus to Zanthos.'

Panicos turned off the main road, and drove down some side roads until he came out on a country road. 'The village is just up ahead now.'

They found Krittee Street with no trouble at all, it really was a very small village, and Panicos parked outside number six, which was a small house with a neat little garden, growing an array of vegetables and fruit trees.

'This is very nice,' said Ella.

They knocked on the door, but there was no reply and no sound of movement from within. A woman came out from the house next door saying, 'aftoss eenay exo, tha epistrepsee se peripou theo.' (he is out and will be back around two.)

'Efharristo polly,' said Panicos and Ella in unison, to the woman. They went back to the car.

'So what do we do now?' said Ella, 'wait about in the car, or a coffee shop?'

'Well we could do that,' said Panicos, 'but it's only half past eleven, that's a long wait. I know a lovely place very near here, a beauty spot. Why don't I show you that? It will pass the time more pleasantly.'

'That sounds ideal, thank you,' said Ella.

Panicos drove for about five minutes into the countryside, and then parked up just off road, in a little unmarked parking area.

'This is the Akales Valley, a protected area. It is very beautiful to walk through.'

They began to walk along a little path, that soon led them in amongst the cypress trees. A stream ran alongside them. Occasionally they had to cross the stream across stepping stones, or little rough log paths, raised just enough from the water to form an open bridge. It was the kind of walk that needed concentration. It was not difficult, but if you didn't pay attention it would be easy to slip and fall. Under the tree canopy, there was a strong smell of pine resin. Whenever they passed into a patch of sunshine, lizards could be glimpsed sunning themselves on the rocks, before darting away out of sight. They walked along the narrow ledge that ran along the side of the hill for a few metres. Once again Ella thought about how the Greeks did not pay any attention whatsoever to health and safety issues. One had to rely on common sense and personal responsibility, which Ella found very refreshing.

Then the path opened out, and the river below was bordered by big grey rocks, and the water, which was considerably deeper here, swirled around in a whirlpool. Finally the path wended back into woodland, and came to an end at a shallow pool.

'You can wade through that pool a little further, but then it becomes a sheer rock face and a waterfall,' said Panicos. 'The water comes up to your waist at the deepest point, and is quite cold.'

Ella said that she thought she would give it a miss on this occasion. She looked up, and saw a huge rock, shaped like a distorted skull, blocking the two sides of the cliff, as if it had rolled down the hill at some time, and got stuck there. Perhaps it had. It gave the little pool an air of dark, brooding mystery. She gave an involuntary shiver.

Panicos noticed the shiver and said, 'Let's get back. There is a beautiful little monastery I want to show you too.'

They traced the path back the way they had come, but just before they reached the car parking spot, there was a path off to the left, that Ella had not noticed before. They walked along it a little way until they came to some trees, then, just under the canopy of the trees, some wooden steps climbed up the hillside. There were no sign posts or indications that anything was here. Even the path was pretty well hidden.

'The monastery is open to the public, but it is so tucked away that practically no one knows it is here,' said Panicos as they climbed the steps. 'It is fully funded by the church, and does not need the extra income from visitors, like some of the monasteries do, so it puts up no signs, and stays mostly private. You will love it, it is a very beautiful and peaceful place.'

They walked up the steps. There were a lot of them and Ella was beginning to get out of breath when they came to the top, and a clearing in the trees. Ahead of them was a gate in the arch of a thick stone wall, that ran to both sides as far as they could see. Panicos pulled a bell pull beside the gate, and after a short time a monk came over and opened the gate, standing aside to let them enter. He silently held out a thin scarf to Ella, who put it over her head. The monk led them through into a courtyard, where herbs and vegetables grew in terracotta pots in the sunshine. Some wooden steps led up to a terrace, where more potted herbs grew. The view from the terrace was terrific, Ella could see the countryside for miles around. She could also see the top of the waterfall in the distance. At the far end of the terrace, the monk led them through a big heavy, wooden door. Inside was a church. Ella crossed herself and lit three candles, while Panicos lit two. The monk faded discretely into the shadows, as they walked around the church kissing the icons.

'This is my final prayer for a successful outcome,' whispered Ella.

'I lit a candle for that too,' said Panicos.

They walked around silently and respectfully, taking in the beauty of the little church, so often used by the monks. It felt really lived in and loved, unlike some churches which felt cold and empty. When they reached the collection box by the door they both put notes into it. The monk reappeared and took them back outside. There was no gift shop here; no nod of any kind to tourism. God was the point of this place. The monk walked them out, and closed the gates behind them, disappearing immediately. They walked back down the steps to the car, lost in thought.

'Thank you for taking me there,' said Ella, 'it really was lovely. I can see how the monks feel close to God in a place like that.'

'And now we have time for a quick lunch,' said Panicos, driving back to the village and stopping at a deserted taverna.

He ordered Stifado, a kind of rabbit stew, with lots of small onions, tomatoes and wine. Ella ordered the same. They did not bother with starters, as they only had about three quarters of an hour for lunch. Panicos ordered them a bottle of Alpha beer each. The Stifado arrived with a basket of bread to dip in the sauce. It was a very nice meal, that went well with the beer and the countryside. Ella found she was picking at it rather aimlessly, and not noticing it as much as she usually did Greek food, despite the fact that it was delicious. She was distracted by what was to come next. Panicos noticed this, and did not make aimless conversation, allowing her to collect her thoughts. The waitress came over and asked in

Greek if everything was alright, and Panicos replied that it was all perfect. He also asked for the bill. The waitress brought the bill, with a small plate of watermelon, which they both found very refreshing. Panicos paid the bill, which Ella was still too distracted to even notice, and they left.

They drove back into the village, arriving at number six Krittee Street at ten past two. Panicos gave Ella a reassuring squeeze on the arm, telling her he was sure it would be alright, and they walked up to the door and knocked.

After a moment or two, a tall, thinnish man opened the door. Panicos recognised him immediately, and greeted him in rapid Greek. Ella caught, my old friend, but not much else. She stood quietly, absorbing the fact that this was probably her father, standing before her, letting it seem as if Panicos was the one who had sought him out, and she had just come along for the ride. Although they had not discussed it, Panicos seemed to be going with this plan of action too. Adonis looked generally, very moved, to see Panicos again after so many years, and hugged him firmly. Panicos spoke in English.

'This is Ella, my niece from England.'

Adonis smiled at Ella, 'Come in both of you, come in.' They followed Adonis through into a room, shaded from the sun, and furnished with dark wood, and old fashioned furniture.

'Sit down, I will bring us some drinks,' said Adonis, disappearing into another room.

'How are you feeling?' Panicos whispered to Ella.

'I'm just a bit numb I think. You should go on talking to him as you have for a bit, then I will introduce myself properly when I feel more collected, or as things develop.'

Adonis reappeared with a tray. There were three tall glasses, and three small glasses, a big jug of iced water, and a bottle of ouzo. He poured some ouzo for them, and told them to help themselves to water. Ella took a sip of her ouzo and water, and felt immediately, a lot more confident.

'Panicos, I looked for you, but they told me you'd moved away to Athens. Where are you living now?'

'I live in Agios Nikolaus. I have an apartment by the sea. I drive a bus, sometimes to Zanthos. I must have passed you many times over the years.'

'I only moved here from Kios about five years ago. I missed Aegos, but I couldn't quite face living in Agios Spiridos.' Adonis looked a little sad and wistful. 'But how is it that you have a niece, tell me? You don't have any brothers or sisters.'

'Ella is the daughter of a good friend. You know how you call people Uncle or Aunt, because they are close, like family?'

'So Ella,' began Adonis, 'tell me about yourself, where are you from, what do you do?'

Ella took a deep breath, and another large sip of her ouzo, and began. 'I was born in England, but my mother sadly died in a car accident when I was only about four and a half. I didn't have any other relatives nearby, so I was brought up in a children's home by Nuns. I work in a travel agents, and Greece is my favourite place to travel to. Years ago, I was baptised Greek Orthodox, and I take Greek classes at evening school. Millaoh leego Ellenika.' (I speak a little Greek.)

'Where was your father, when all this happened?'

Ella put down her glass, and reached over and put her hand on Adonis' arm. 'My father was on Aegos. My mother was Elizabeth Hudson. I was born in May 1962.'

She stopped speaking to let Adonis process the bombshell she had just delivered. Adonis went white. 'Panaigeea mou.' (Holy Mother.) 'So you are my daughter?'

'Yes, I think, no I'm sure, that is true,' said Ella. Adonis finished his drink in one big gulp, and poured another.

'And Elizabett, poor Elizabett, died in 1966?'

'Yes, I'm sorry, that is true too.'

'All those years,' said Adonis, drifting off. 'All those years. I didn't even know she was pregnant.'

'What happened between you?' asked Ella. 'Why did she run home, after you had asked her to marry you, and she had said yes? Please, even if you don't want to see me again, I need to know what happened?'

'Oh, ee koree mou, (my daughter) of course I want to see you, to know you, to have you in my life. You are my flesh and blood. I have only known you existed for five minutes, but now I know you are mine, I will never let you go.'

Ella couldn't control herself; tears streamed down her face. This was so much more than she had hoped for. Panicos reached across and held her hand, and Adonis stood up and put his arm around her shoulders, as she sobbed with relief. Years of searching, and pent up feelings, were flowing out of her, and for the moment at least, there was absolutely nothing she could do about it.

Panicos poured them all more ouzo, and added a little water to the glasses. Then for good measure, he poured out glasses of water too. He handed Ella the ouzo, and she sipped it gratefully. She was calming down now, her emotions returning to her control. Adonis sat back down, and sipped his own drink.

'You look like Elizabett, but darker skinned, more Greek coloured,' he said. 'Okay, let me tell you my side of the story. It's true, I did ask Elizabett to marry me, one night, in Zefiros' restaurant. And she said yes, she would. We were going to go to Kios for that Christmas, and tell my parents then. We had arranged it all, we were going to tell the family, and then marry early in the New Year. I wanted to wait until the spring which is more traditional, and the weather is nicer for dancing in the streets, but Elizabett wanted New Year. She was very insistent, I didn't understand why. I see now that it was because she was already pregnant with you, and by spring it would have been too late, she would have been too big.' Adonis paused for a moment as if he was mentally kicking himself.

'I went back to Kios quickly, in October, just to get my post, and some things from home. I was spending most of my time on Aegos by then, with Elizabett. There was a letter from the government. I had been called to do my national service, starting in November. It has been shortened now, to only nine months, and you can get lots of leave for all kinds of things —it would be very different now. But back then, it was for a year and a half, with hardly any leave, and no pay. There was no way to get out of it. My heart fell into my boots when I saw it. I knew Elizabett and I would not be at my family's home for Christmas, and we would not be able to marry at New Year, as we had planned. I knew I had to go back and tell her, and ask her to wait for me. When I told her, and showed her the papers, she was so upset, she cried and cried. I mean, I knew it was bad, but she had a job and a flat, I thought she would be able to wait, and carry on here with her friends. She would not speak of it any more. When the time came for me to go away, she held me and cried so much, but I still did not know she was pregnant. If she had only told me, when she first knew, we could have married straight away. She could have lived with my family on Kios, while I did my national service. You would have been born on Kios, born a Greek. Maybe Elizabett would still be alive now.' Adonis wept.

Ella knelt in front of him and held his hands in hers.

'When I came home on my first leave in the late spring, she was gone. She had not left an address, no-one knew where she was. Heleni was gone too, and Nikos, and you Panicos. Everyone was gone away. When I came out of national service, I asked Manolis if he had heard from her at all, if she had said she was coming back, but he didn't know. He had no address. Yiorgios didn't know anything either. I waited for five years, wondering if my Elizabett would ever come back to me. Then I met Hariklia. I never loved her the way I loved Elizabett, but she was a good Greek girl, and our families wanted us to marry, so I did. We had a son Stavros, but Hariklia died soon after the birth, from some kind of infection. My family helped me bring Stavros up. They brought him up really I suppose. I felt a bit empty. I have spent my whole life missing Elizabett, and wondering how things might have been if we had married that summer. Stavros married young, and had a son, Adonis. He lives on Kios now, and Stavros and his wife moved away to Thessaloniki, where her family are from.'

'I met Adonis, and bought some pottery from him, when I was looking for you,' said Ella. 'I have been everywhere looking for you, and talked to so many people about Liz and the old days, I almost feel I have got to know my mother, as well as finding my father.'

'Adonis is your nephew, I suppose,' said Adonis.

'I did not tell him why I was looking for you, just that you had been friends with my mother a long time ago.'

'Elizabett left the island right after you went into national service,' said Panicos. 'Of course none of us knew where either of you were, you just both disappeared without saying anything. Nikos was broken hearted that all his friends had gone away, and moved to Vathy to be a fisherman. He is still there now. Because of Ella, I have met him again, in fact we all had dinner together just last night. Poor Yiorgios died of a heart attack ten years ago now. Heleni married and moved out to Limonaki, and had two daughters. Manolis died five years ago. I moved away to Athens, but came back to Aegos some time ago. There are a lot more stories to tell about all of that, but maybe they are for later.'

'Elizabett must have gone back to England to have me, because she could get free healthcare there, and it would be slightly easier for her. Though being a single parent, an unmarried mother, was still tough in those days, even in England. It must have been very hard for her.'

Adonis sighed. 'And you Ella, you never married?'

'No, I suppose I never found the right person. I have always felt like I was searching for my roots, I never really felt like I could settle.'

'But you should see the way some of them look at her,' said Panicos. 'Manolis' son Dimitris has a soft spot for her, I can tell. So does Christos. He is the son of Yiorgos, who owns the Zeus hotel. Andreas, Christos' cousin, he likes her too, I think.'

Ella blushed. 'I'm sure none of them think of me like that.'

'You clearly did not see the way they looked at you last night, when you wore that blue dress,' laughed Panicos.

'Well I don't know about that,' said Ella, 'but Aegos has won my heart, that much is certain.'

'How long have you known Ella?' Adonis asked Panicos.

'Only five days,' said Panicos, 'but she adopted me as her uncle right away. She is a very special person. Special like Elizabett was.'

'So you have been busy since you got here, meeting people and searching for me?' Adonis said to Ella.

'Yes, very busy. I even went to Kios. But it has been wonderful and exciting, and I met some lovely people. The end of the story is happier than I had hoped and dreamed of.'

'Well,' said Adonis, 'let's go out into the garden, and sit in the sun, and I will make us some coffee.'

They sat in the sun and talked, until afternoon became evening, all filling in the details of tales that had only been briefly touched upon. Panicos told his sad story. Ella told Adonis of her quest, and all the stories of the people she had met. Adonis told them about his life, and how he now had a little greengrocers shop in Zanthos.

As evening crept on, and they all became aware of the growing darkness, Adonis said, 'Can I buy you both dinner, at a little place I know in Zanthos?'

Ella and Panicos agreed that would be lovely.

'I will drive, as I have to drive back tonight anyway, so I probably shouldn't drink any more,' said Panicos.

They all piled into Panicos' car, Ella getting in the back, and Adonis sitting in front to give directions. They soon arrived in Zanthos town, Adonis pointing out his greengrocers shop as they drove past it. The narrow streets widened as they turned down towards the beach. They passed a deserted little ruins that had once been a church, but was now disused. Then they drove along the beach a little way, then parked in a reasonably sized, open, gravel car park.

'We can walk from here, it's not too far,' said Adonis. They got out of the car, and walked along the paved path that ran alongside the beach. The sea made slapping, drawing sounds against the pebbles of the beach. It was a very pleasant sound. In the distance, they could see the lights flickering on the nearby coast of the mainland. Soon the road began to fill with shops and tavernas on the inland side. There were more people about now, some taking their vrathee volta (evening stroll) along the main coastal promenade, others heading home after closing their shops for the evening, and still others, like themselves, heading to favourite places to dine. Some of the little tourist gift shops and mini supermarkets they passed, were still open, taking advantage of the evening tourist trade. They walked on along the promenade, chatting companionably, Adonis pointing out little things now and again, a shop, a plant, a cat, a bug, a boat out on the water. The main promenade came to an end, and the path wended on through some houses. The streets were cobbled and a gutter ran down the middle of them, to carry off rain and dirt in the wet season. A family of cats seemed to be living in a doorway they passed. The mother cat was sitting in the doorway, feeding a couple of kittens, and washing them as they fed. Three or four other kittens were exploring the street, without straying too far from Mum.

'Do you like cats?' Ella asked Adonis.

'Oh yes, of course, very much,' he replied. Ella told him all about Bob, and Panicos added the story of his little ginger three legged friend. Adonis said that a cat sometimes came by the greengrocers shop and shared his lunch. Greek cats had friends everywhere, it seemed.

They came back down through the tiny streets, to a little bay on the seafront. The whole bay seemed to be lined with restaurants, but Adonis led them to the furthest one, at the far end of the bay. The tables were positioned right on the edge of the sea wall. If you got up in too much of a hurry, or were rather drunk, it would be very easy to totter over the edge, and find yourself in the deep, dark, harbour water.

They say down at a table, looking out to sea. On the opposite coast, lights twinkled. Perhaps people there were sitting at their tables eating dinner, thinking the same things about them. It was like being on the deck of a ship, with land in sight.

The waiter came over and greeted them. Panicos ordered a peach juice, and Adonis asked Ella if she would like wine. She said she would, and he ordered a half litre of red wine. The waiter left them menus and they all set about studying them.

'What is good here?' Panicos asked Adonis.

'The fish is always good,' began Adonis. 'The pastitsio is very good, as is the moussakas, and the souvlaki is excellent. For starters I recommend a mixed meze, it is excellent. In its own right it makes a very nice lunch.'

The waiter returned with their drinks, tableware, and a basket of bread.

'Shall we have the mixed meze starter then?' asked Panicos. Everyone agreed, and that part of the order was made.

'For the main course?' asked the waiter.

'I would like the souvlaki please,' said Panicos.

'Pork or chicken?' asked the waiter.

'Pork thank you,' replied Panicos.

'I would like the pastitsio please,' said Ella.
'Make that two pastitsios,' added Adonis.
The waiter finished scribbling and went away. He soon returned with a big bowl of Greek salad, topped with the customary slab of feta cheese, and a small bowl of beetroot dip, and another of sesame dip. They all ploughed into the cold starters, dipping bread into the dips, and crunching the salad, while drinking their wine and peach juice. It was not long before the waiter returned with the cooked part of the meze. He put down a small plate of calamaries, another of courgette fritters, another of saganaki (battered fried cheese) and a final plate of gigantes, (butter beans in a red sauce,) saying kallee orexee, as he left them to their meal.

Everything was delicious, and they picked at each thing as they talked, in the Greek way.

'I have been practising my Greek cooking at home,' said Ella. 'I can make pretty much everything we have here. I'm not very good at bread and cakes yet though.'

'Well then, you can come and visit me anytime you like, anipseea mou,' laughed Panicos.

'Me too,' said Adonis. 'Seriously though, how long are you staying on Aegos? Would you like to come and stay with me for a while, so we can get to know each other?'

'I would love that,' replied Ella. 'I did not really say when I would be going back to England. I made my leave open ended, so I could stay here for as long as it took me to search for you. I did not expect to find you so quickly.'

'Then that is settled, you must come and stay with me,'

Panicos looked a little crestfallen, realising he would not see Ella so much on the other side of the island.

Adonis quickly added, 'of course, you Panicos, are welcome anytime you want, too. I have two spare rooms, and you can stay over whenever you like.' Panicos brightened, 'that would be great. I will be gaining a brother again, rather than losing a new found niece, in that case.' Everyone smiled.

They had eaten their way through the meze starters, and the waiter came out to clear the plates, and ask if everything was alright. They all exclaimed that it was excellent. He returned immediately with the main courses, which had obviously been ready for a little while. But they had been talking, and not hurrying the food at all. Greeks eat food warm or cold, the temperature is not really so important.

Ella tasted her pastitsio, 'this really is delicious,' she exclaimed.

Panicos said that the souvlaki was delicious as well.

'If you want, I can drive over and collect you on Sunday. Would that suit you?' Adonis asked Ella.

'That would be great,' said Ella. 'Would it be alright for me to bring Bob?' she asked, somewhat nervously.

'The little gatoss (boy cat)?' queried Adonis. Ella nodded. 'Of course, it will be nice to have a cat around the house again. It has been many years.'

'I don't know that he will come inside much, at least, not at first,' said Ella.

'Once he notices that the food keeps coming from there, and he is welcome, he will soon come in. He will be curled up on an armchair in no time, you'll see.'

They finished their main course, and were still chatting, Panicos and Adonis telling stories of the old days, when the waiter came and cleared their plates, and asked if there would be anything else. Panicos and Adonis ordered coffees, and Ella ordered a mint tea.

The waiter soon brought their drinks, along with three small pieces of sweet kadaifi. They all ate the sweet treats with great enjoyment, then Adonis went up to the bar and paid the bill. Panicos and Ella stood up stretching, as Adonis came back.

'It's good that the car is parked at the other end of the promenade. I could do with a walk to help digest all that food, and stretch our legs, before we sit in the car for an hour and a half,' said Panicos.

Ella agreed, and they began the gentle stroll back to the car. People were sitting outside tavernas eating, and outside bars drinking, walking the promenade like themselves, or just sitting on benches or walls, resting their feet, and taking in the night air.

As they walked parallel to the beach (ee paraleya), they saw the occasional couple walking by the water's edge, having a romantic moment away from the main throng.

Finally they came to the parked car, and all climbed back in. Panicos drove the short distance back to Adonis' house, and they all got out once again.

'Would you like to come in for a drink?' Adonis asked.

'No, unfortunately we really must be getting back. It's quite a long drive, and I have to work early in the morning,' replied Panicos.

Ella hugged Adonis, who promised to collect her at noon on Sunday, and who once again had a tear in his eye.

Panicos and Ella got back into the car and drove off, waving until Adonis was out of sight.

Ella let out a big sigh.

'Happy?' asked Panicos, himself wearing a big grin.

'Yes, of course. But it has been a very emotional day. I still feel quite odd and shaken up. I think I need to relax and do nothing for at least one whole day. I wonder if all my new friends will mind waiting to find out what happened?'

'I'm sure they will understand,' said Panicos.

They drove along in silence for a while. They had got onto the main road in no time, and there was practically no other traffic, so they were whizzing along. It was very dark in the countryside, so there was nothing to see except the road itself. Occasionally the blackness seemed a little darker where they passed mountains.

'I can't stop thinking about how different things would have been if my mother had told Adonis she was pregnant, if not as soon as she knew, then as soon as he asked her to marry him. To think I could have been born Greek, grown up on Kios, or Aegos even. Then to think that Liz might still be alive, that I might have grown up with a mother and a father, grandparents even. But then Stavros and young Adonis would not have been born. That metallic fruit bowl I have in my room would not exist. So many things would be different. Every time I think of it, my head simply swims.'

'Try not to think about it all too much for now,' said Panicos. 'Just relax and let all the new information soak into you. Let time help you to find peace with it all. I imagine Adonis is sitting in his chair now, drinking a Tsipouro, and thinking many of the same thoughts you yourself are.'

They drove on through the night, and the journey seemed to go much quicker going home. Whether it was because the roads were clear, or whether it was because the fear and anticipation had gone, was not certain, but they were soon pulling up outside the Zeus hotel.

'I'm afraid I won't be able to see you for a few days, I have to work long shifts,' said Panicos. 'I could come over to Adonis' house on Monday if you like, and we could go for that mountain walk I told you about. The peace and quiet of the mountains might be just the thing for you then?'

'That would be lovely,' said Ella. 'I will look forward to it.'

'I'll be there about half past ten or eleven then,' said Panicos. 'Goodnight little one.'

'Goodnight Uncle,' replied Ella, waving as Panicos drove off.

It was quite late, about eleven, but Ella was still feeling quite awake and wired. No way would she be able to sleep with all these thoughts running through her head. Instead of going into the hotel, she walked round the corner and along to Aphrodite's restaurant. There were not many people left in there, but they had not yet closed, as a few people were still sitting at tables drinking.

As soon as she walked through the door Carolina saw her, and called her over to the bar where she sat chatting to Andreas. Andreas gave her a big smile, and sat up straight on his bar stool, where before he had been slouched forward on the bar.

'Did you find him,' called Carolina, before Ella was even halfway across the room.

Ella nodded and grinned, and Carolina let out a whoop of joy, that had all the remaining customers staring at them. Ella hurried the remaining distance to the bar stool beside Andreas, but before she got there, he climbed down and picked her up by the waist and spun her around, before putting her down on the bar stool. Carolina poured them all tsipouros.

'Where is Panicos?' asked Carolina.

'He had to go home, to be up early for work tomorrow. He dropped me at the hotel, but I am too awake to sleep, so I came here, hoping you would still be here.'

'So, tell us all about it then. Was he pleased to see you?' asked Andreas.

Carolina scowled at him as if to say, 'don't rush her, let her tell it in her own time.'

'We both cried. He never even knew Liz was pregnant. He was filled with joy to meet me. He is coming to collect me on Sunday, and I am going to stay with him for a while, so we can get to know each other.'

'Oh how wonderful,' gasped Carolina, 'what a happy ending, I'm so pleased for you.'

They all toasted 'stin yammas,' and downed their glasses of tsipouro. Carolina poured three more.

'Why did Liz leave so suddenly?' asked Carolina. Andreas raised his eyebrows at her as if to say, 'now who's rushing her, and prying?'

'After Adonis asked her to marry him, and she said yes, they planned to spend Christmas with his family on Kios, and tell them they were getting married. Then Adonis' national service came up for the November, and he had to go away for a year and a half. He hoped Liz would wait for him, and not mind having to postpone everything, but of course he didn't know she was pregnant with me. It all seemed to fall into place for him when I told him that today. He said, with great regret, that if she had told him, they could have married quickly, and she could have stayed with his parents, while he did national service. I would have been born Greek, and Liz might still be alive.'

'Ah, but you practically are Greek, my little sister,' said Carolina, comfortingly.

'You certainly look like a Greek Goddess,' said Andreas. Ella blushed.

'Anyway, it's all going over and over in my mind, and I don't feel like I shall sleep a wink tonight.'

'Drink up, that will help,' said Carolina, pouring a third tsipouro.

'Do you have any meat or fish scraps that you are going to throw away, by the way?' asked Ella. 'I don't have anything to give Bob the cat for his breakfast.'

Carolina laughed, 'of course, I will go and wrap up some scraps for him.'

Ella turned to Andreas and said, 'I could sleep for a week, perhaps I will just lay about on the beach tomorrow. I'm not normally one for lying about in the sun, but I really need a day of doing nothing.'

'Why don't you come fishing on the boat with me?' asked Andreas. 'I don't have to leave early, I'm my own boss. I could pick you up at about nine.'

'I think that would actually be a very relaxing day,' said Ella. 'Fishing, swimming, sitting in the sun, yes, I would love to, count me in.'

'Count you in to what?' asked Carolina, emerging from the kitchen carrying a fat foil packet.

'I'm going fishing with Andreas tomorrow,' said Ella. 'It's just what I need, a quiet day relaxing on a boat in the sun.'

'That does sound like just the thing to unwind,' said Carolina. I will put together a cold box of picnic food for you both.'

'Oh please don't go to any trouble,' said Ella.

'It's no trouble at all. I will do it now, because I won't be here in the morning, and Andreas can take it with him. It will just be leftovers from the restaurant anyway.'

Andreas grinned, he had obviously had restaurant leftovers as a picnic before, and looked very pleased with the idea.

'Well I suppose I should go to bed and try to sleep. I am a little tipsy now from all that tsipouro, so I should sleep okay,' said Ella.

Carolina passed Ella a bottle of fizzy water from under the bar. 'Drink this before you go to sleep, then you won't have a fuzzy head in the morning.'

Ella thanked her and bid them both goodnight. She walked back to the hotel and up to her room, just remembering to drink the water, pop to the loo and clean her teeth before collapsing onto the bed and falling asleep in her undies.

She was awoken at seven forty five by Bob, knocking and meowing fairly insistently. She got the impression he had been at it for quite a while already. Ella threw on a dress over her undies, and went out onto the porch with the foil package and a plate. There was a good few days worth of scraps in the package, so Bob was sorted out until his big move, that he did not yet know was coming. As Ella pulled out pieces of meat and fish scraps, and put them on the plate, she talked to Bob. 'How do you feel about coming to live with me in Zanthos at my father's house?' Bob put his head on one side, uncertain what was required of him, but hearing a question. 'The food would be very good, of course, this sort of standard, all the time.' Bob heard food, and purred, rising up on his hind legs to brush against Ella's legs. 'Well, I'll bring a cat basket on Sunday, and if you want to come, you can get in it. If you don't want to come, I won't force you.' Ella put the food down for Bob.

She got herself a black coffee, and showered and dressed in shorts, sandals and t-shirt, with her bikini underneath. She plaited her hair, and put sunglasses, towels, and her cotton shawl in a bag. It was getting near to nine, so she went to wait outside. At a couple of minutes to nine, Andreas pulled up in his truck, and pushed open the passenger door for her.

'How do you feel this morning?' he asked.

'Fine actually,' she replied. 'I'm looking forward to a nice quiet, relaxing day at sea.'

'Your wish is my command,' said Andreas, laughing. They drove down to the harbour, which Ella had not yet visited. It was further round the coast than she had walked on Agios Spiridos beach. It was a small harbour, much as she would have expected from a small village. Andreas' boat was very similar to Allessandro's, but more kitted out, as the working fishing boat it was. Andreas helped her aboard, then passed her two cold boxes. He climbed aboard himself, carrying a third cold box, which was clearly heavy, and full of rattling bottles. He noted Ella's look about the quantity of cold boxes, and said, 'food, drink and bait.'

They set out to sea, and soon were the only people, and the only boat for miles around. Ella sighed in contentment. This was exactly what she needed. Andreas spotted a shoal of fish and anchored the boat. He baited a line and handed it to Ella, showing her how to let the line drop down into the water. He hooked her finger around the line, and told her to call him if the line went tight. Then he baited another rod for himself, and lowered it over the other side of the boat. Between them they caught a couple of dozen fish, of several different types, in the next couple of hours. Andreas got them a beer each out of the cold box, putting the lines to one side. He gutted the fish and washed them in a net, before putting them in the cold box that the bait had come out of.

'We can really relax now,' he said, 'we've caught enough fish for the restaurant for dinner.'

He got the boat underway again, and sailed inland to a little deserted beach.

'Shall we go for a swim before lunch?'

Ella did not need asking twice. She stripped to her bikini and climbed over the side. Despite his trying not to be obvious, she had noticed Andreas looking at her appreciatively. They swam to the beach, and lay in the sun like tourists.

'This is exactly the sort of day I had in mind,' said Ella, 'thank you.'

'Not at all,' said Andreas, 'it has been a very nice day for me too.'

Ella noticed that Andreas was looking at her, as if he was about to say something serious, so she jumped up and ran back into the sea, until it was deep enough to swim. She looked back, and Andreas was already in the water too. They climbed back onto the boat, and Ella handed Andreas a towel. She dried, and then put her shorts and t-shirt back on. She was still damp in places, but didn't want to encourage any sort of romantic activity. There was too much going on in her life right now, the time just wasn't right.

Andreas got them another drink, and handed her the cold box of food.

'See what Carolina has packed us for lunch, would you?'

Ella could not believe that everything in the box was restaurant leftovers, if it was, the restaurant would be broke in a week. There were dolmades, revitho keftedes, souvlaki, bread, hummus, salad, fava, cheese balls, pistachio nuts, olives, and ravani. It was a feast. But after the fishing, swimming and sun, Andreas and Ella made short work of it.

Later in the afternoon, they cruised back into the harbour, and Andreas dropped her off at the hotel. Friday and Saturday passed in a whirl. Ella visited Dimitris and told him everything that had happened. He was of course, overjoyed for her. She went and saw Nikki and Athena, and told them everything. She sat down with Yiorgos and Christos in the hotel bar and told them everything. They agreed it would be a great idea to take Bob, and Yiorgos said he would bring a cat basket on Sunday morning. Ella visited Bani and Haroula, and spent a long time telling them everything. They had been the first people she had met, and they were amazed at her story. She caught a bus to Vathy, and told Nikos how it had all gone, and a taxi to Limonaki to talk to Heleni, and Stavros from the cafe. She even popped into Zefiros' restaurant one night, and talked to Yiannis Zefiros. The only people she did not talk to, were those on Kios, but she was sure she would go there again soon. On Saturday afternoon Dimitris took her over to the little church to light a candle, and say thank you to Agios Spiridon. Before she knew it almost, she was going to sleep on Saturday night, her new life about to begin.

Chapter Ten

Ella awoke early on Sunday morning and went to church. Bob was not around when she went out, which she thought was a good thing as he was more likely to be around later on, when the time came for him to go into the cat basket.

After church, a lot of people said hello to Ella. Carolina met her outside.

'It's your birthday next week, isn't it?' she said to Ella.

'Yes, next Thursday,' replied Ella, surprised, 'though I don't know how you remembered that.'

'Well, I'm good at dates. I'm going to shut the restaurant on Thursday evening, and have a little party, please say that you and Adonis will come to it. Yiorgos said there will be room for you to stay in the hotel overnight, so you don't have to drive back, and can have a drink. It would mean such a lot to me if you come.'

'Of course I will,' said Ella, 'I'd love to.'

'I had to catch you today, because I probably won't see you before then, but say eight o'clock.'

'It's a date,' said Ella. 'We'll be there.'

Ella walked back through the village to the hotel and packed up all her things. She took her bags down to reception, where Yiorgos was sitting on the sofa. He got up, and gave her a cat basket. Ella took the last of the foil packed meat from her bag, and opened it into a bowl shape. She put one of her towels in the bottom of the basket, and then put the foil bowl in too. She went outside and up to her porch. Sure enough, Bob was there waiting. She put the basket down, and looked at Bob.

'Well this is it Bob. Do you want to come with me?'

Bob wandered over to the basket, and climbed inside. Ella was amazed, she had never seen a cat get into a basket under its own steam before. Bob did not head straight to the food, but instead sat down on the towel and curled up. Ella took this as a very clear sign that he did indeed want to go with her, and shut the basket lid. Bob was unfazed.

Ella carried Bob down to the foyer, alongside her luggage. He seemed perfectly happy. Yiorgos came outside. 'It looks like he wants to go with you,' he said.

'Yes, I think so,' said Ella. Yiorgos said goodbye to Ella, and that he hoped to see her soon, at the party. Ella said that she would definitely be there, and to hold the room, as they would take him up on it for sure.

Then Adonis pulled up in his car. They put Ella's bags in the boot, and carefully placed Bob on the back seat. They waved at Yiorgos, then they were on their way.

They chatted comfortably on the drive to Parossa, Ella turning every now and again, to speak to Bob, who was still sitting happily in the basket, paws crossed in front of him. He looked like he was thinking, 'it's okay, I'm totally cool with this.' Perhaps he had just been biding his time, for the day when someone would adopt him, and feed him properly all the time, and he could just kick back and enjoy his retirement.

'I phoned my grandson last night,' said Adonis, 'and explained everything to him. It was a long conversation that went on for the better part of an hour. I told him all about Elizabett, then at the end, I told him he had an aunt he had not known about. I told him it was you in the shop the other day, asking after me. He is keen to meet you properly now.'

'How lovely,' said Ella, 'I look forward to seeing him again too.'

'I also phoned my son, Stavros, on Thessaloniki. He was amazed that all these years, he had had a sister he knew nothing about. He and his wife Mia, plan to visit just as soon as they can get away.'

'It's a little overwhelming, suddenly having all this family, after having none at all for so many years,' said Ella, emotionally.

Adonis reached over and squeezed her hand, comfortingly.

It was not too long before they arrived at the little house in Parossa. Adonis carried Ella's bags into the house, and Ella carried Bob in the basket. She carried him slowly, so he wouldn't be jiggled about, and so he could see the front garden and house, he was being carried through. She opened the back door, and put the basket down on the sheltered patio. Bob stood up and stretched. Ella opened the lid and gave him a stroke. He climbed lazily out, and nuzzled her legs. Ella put the bowl of meat, which he hadn't really touched on the journey down, on the floor, and went to get a bowl of water to put beside it. When she came back Bob was eating happily. Ella left the cat basket and towel where it was for now, in case Bob wanted to nap on it. She went back into the house.

'Let me show you your room,' said Adonis, leading her upstairs. He pointed out the bathroom, his room, and the spare room, then led her into a pleasant, sunny room, where he had put her bags. The room was painted white, with a wooden floor, on which a purple rug had been placed. There were lilac curtains, a heavy wooden wardrobe and a dressing table with a chair. There was a comfortable looking bed, covered with a peach coloured, patterned throw, and a bedside table with a lamp on it. On the wall were some pictures of flowers. On the dressing table, was a glass vase filled with fresh garden flowers, filling the room with a lovely fresh scent. 'This is beautiful,' said Ella, looking out of the window into the back garden.

'I'll leave you to unpack your things, then come down and see the kitchen, and where everything is,' said Adonis. 'I'll make some coffee for us.'

'Thank you, that would be lovely.'

Left alone, Ella sighed with contentment. She began to wonder if she might stay in Greece for good. She pushed the idea around a bit in her mind, and found she liked it very much. She hung her clothes up in the wardrobe, and put her shoes in there too. She put her t-shirts, underwear and swimsuits in the dressing table drawers. She took her shampoo, toothbrush and toothpaste, to the bathroom, and unpacked her potions and lotions, hair ties and comb onto the dressing table. She put the four painted stones on the bedside table, and propped the picture of Liz, up against the bedside lamp. She put the coaster from Manolis bar, next to it. She looked up, hearing a little meep, and to her great surprise, saw Bob standing hesitantly in the doorway of the bedroom.

'Hello Bob,' she said quietly, and sat down on the bed, patting it next to her. Bob hesitated just a moment longer, then came trotting over and jumped up beside her. Ella spent a few minutes stroking Bob as he purred contentedly, then lay down and fell asleep. Ella quietly picked up the coffee, tea and other kitchen bits she had brought with her, as well as the pottery bowl made by young Adonis, and went softly downstairs.

Adonis was in the kitchen making Greek coffee in a brickee, (a small, tall pan for boiling Greek coffee on a stove.) He finished, and poured the coffee into cups, and filled two glasses with water.

Ella put the supplies down on a counter.

'I will show you where everything lives after coffee,' said Adonis.

'I bought this bowl from your grandson,' said Ella, 'I thought it would make a nice fruit bowl.'

'I think so too,' said Adonis. 'We will find some fruit to go in it shortly.'

They took their coffees and waters out onto the patio, and sat sipping the rich coffee and cardamom flavours.

'Where did Bob go?' asked Adonis.

'You'll never believe it,' said Ella, 'he's asleep on my bed.'

'I told you he would soon feel at home, I just didn't expect it to be that quickly. That cat wants to be with you, I think.'

'He is a very special little cat. I feel as if I have known him forever.'

Adonis looked at the cat basket and said, 'that will not do for a day bed for him. I have an old fruit crate in the shed, I will fetch it. If you go up to the landing, there is a big cupboard full of linen. In the bottom is a green blanket that I never use anymore, as it is rather old. But it is soft. If you go and get that, we can put it in the box and make a bed for him. I expect he will sleep on your bed quite a lot, but cats do like to be near people, so it would be good if he had a bed out here too.'

Adonis put the cat basket in the boot of his car, and Ella took the towel up to the laundry basket and fetched the blanket. Bob opened one eye and looked at her from the bed, but then shut it again, and went back to sleep.

As they stood back to look at the comfortable cat bed they had made, Adonis commented that Bob needed some proper bowls. He went into the kitchen and returned with two old tin bowls, one filled with water, the other with cat biscuits.

'I bought some supplies,' he said sheepishly. He took the now empty, foil bowl and water bowl away.

At that moment Bob appeared in the doorway to the patio, and walked over to them. He examined the cat bed, sniffed it, climbed into it, walked around in a circle for a minute, then sat down, as if to say, 'yes, that will do.' Then he got up and walked over to the biscuits and water, and tasted both, to show he also approved of them.

Adonis suggested they look around the garden for any fruit that was ripe. As they wandered round the front and back gardens, pausing to collect ripe fruit and vegetables, Bob walked nearby, checking out the territory for himself too. Adonis was growing a lot of vegetables and herbs, but also had fruit and olive trees. When they had looked everywhere, and had their hands full, they headed back to the kitchen. Bob decided to continue exploring the garden. Ella was not in the least worried that he would wander off, he seemed very much at home already, as if he had lived there for years. Ella watched, as he crouched and waggled his tail end, hunting a mouse no doubt.

In the kitchen, Adonis filled the new fruit bowl, and put it in centre position on the dining table. He showed her where everything lived, putting away Ella's supplies as he went along, nodding approvingly at the box of mountain tea. Ella noted that the cupboards and fridge were well stocked with supplies, and wondered if it was always so, or if this had also been done in preparation for her arrival. She looked forward to cooking in the homely little kitchen. Adonis showed her how to use the stove and the washing machine, and where the switch for hot water was.

'Do you stock your shop with vegetables you grow?' asked Ella.

'Sometimes, if I have a big crop of something,' replied Adonis. 'Usually I buy in from farms around the area. If you like, you can come into the shop and help some time?'

'I'd love to,' said Ella, 'how about Tuesday? Panicos is coming over tomorrow to take me on a mountain walk he promised me, but I would be happy to work in the shop the rest of the week.'

Adonis smiled, 'that would be wonderful, it will be nice to have some help.'

Ella went up to her room and fetched the picture of Liz with Adonis. Now she knew it was him, it was easy to recognise him. She also carefully picked up the dried flowers, held between tissue paper and card. She took them down to Adonis.

'This was the only picture I had, to try and find you,' she said, showing him the photograph.

'That cannot have been easy,' he said, 'with the hat and sunglasses on. I remember that day, we went out to the country together.'

'On the road to Limonaki?' asked Ella.

'Yes,' said Adonis, surprised. 'How did you know that?'

Ella carefully unwrapped the dried flowers on the table. 'I walked past that field myself, on my walk to Limonaki, and recognised the flowers. That field smells so beautiful. Then later, when I spoke to Heleni, she said Liz had told her that the two of you made love the first time, in that field, and I knew that was why she kept the flowers, to remind her of you.'

Adonis coloured slightly. 'I think you were probably conceived in that field; perhaps that is why she kept them too.'

'I think you are probably right. I felt something very powerful when I walked past that place. Anyway, I want you to have them now, and I think Liz would want that too.'

Adonis took the flowers and carefully rewrapped them, clearly very moved, 'I think Elizabett would be very happy today, to see us both together at last.'

'I think so too,' said Ella, sighing happily.

That evening Ella cooked Keftedes, with herby new potatoes and gigantes, for their dinner, giving a little of the raw meat to Bob, who ate it quickly, and fell asleep in his new bed. He seemed exhausted, but it had been a long and eventful day for everyone.

After dinner, Ella and Adonis sipped some ouzo and water, and chatted about all kinds of things. Ella was pleased when it was time to go to bed, as she had had an exhausting day herself. She fell asleep happily in her new room.

The next morning, Ella awoke at seven thirty, to the sensation of Bob tapping her softly on her face, with his paw. He was obviously a creature of firm habits, who liked to have an early breakfast. Ella pulled on shorts, a t-shirt and flip flops, and padded down to the kitchen, grabbing the packet of cat biscuits and filling Bob's bowl. She filled his water bowl too, then looked up to see Adonis grinning at her from a chair on the patio. Bob gave Adonis a look too, as if to say, 'aha, you get up earliest, perhaps I shall come down and bother you for food instead.'

Adonis poured a coffee and brought it out for Ella, who took it gratefully.

'I'm useless before coffee,' she said, 'though I really like to wake up with a swim.'

'The sea is about fifteen minutes walk through the village, and then down a short track,' said Adonis. 'Or there is a hotel in Zanthoss, called Lavris, which is happy for locals to use the pool if they want. I will introduce you, and you can swim there if you want. It is about five minutes drive though.'

'Thank you, that would be handy, I do love to swim. Apart from walking, it really is my main exercise.'

'What time is Panicos coming?' asked Adonis.

'About half past ten, or eleven,' replied Ella.

'I will be going to the shop in a few minutes, to open up. Why not invite him for dinner, then I can say hello to him too.'

'I will do that.'

Panicos arrived a little early at ten fifteen. Ella ushered him inside, and showed him around. 'I have only been here a day, but already I feel so at home,' she said.

'Your room certainly already seems to look like yours,' he replied. He smiled when he saw the little area they had made for Bob. 'Oh that reminds me,' he said reaching into his pocket and pulling out a plastic bag, 'I have something for Bob.' The bag contained a piece of fish. Panicos said he had got some for 'his' cat, then thought to get a bit extra for Bob, as he was certain Ella would not have had time to go shopping yet. Bob heard his name and got up from his box where he had been napping, stretching sleepily. He had not finished all of the biscuits, so Ella put the fish in the bowl alongside them. Bob trotted over and began to eat.

'I'm going out until this evening Bob, I'm sure you'll find plenty to do,' said Ella.

'Have you got walking boots and a sun hat?' asked Panicos. 'I have water and snacks in the car, so you shouldn't need anything else.'

Ella ran upstairs and put on her walking boots, and grabbed a sun hat. She pushed some money into her shorts pocket, along with the door key Adonis had given her the night before. They shut up the house, leaving Bob out on the patio, happy with his fish, and went out to Panicos' car.

'It's about half an hour's drive from here to the start of the walk up to Vanoliotanas mountain village,' said Panicos, as they drove off. 'Of course we could drive up to the village by adding a quarter of an hour onto that time. The walk up takes four or five hours.'

'It sounds amazing, I'm quite excited,' said Ella. 'Oh, by the way, Adonis asked if you would stay for dinner tonight.'

'I'd love to,' replied Panicos.

It wasn't long before they had finished driving through the beautiful countryside, and parked in a small parking area, near some sparse woodland, and a rough track. Panicos got a backpack out of the boot of the car, and put it on.

'Okay, we're off,' he said.

The track at first seemed to be leading to someone's farm. Then suddenly it got much smaller and rougher, and went downhill through some rough scrub bushes, to cross a dried up ditch. They walked across the ditch and walked along the opposite side for a little way. The ditch became a small stream; in the shade of the trees, with some flowing water in it. The opposite side of the stream was hedged and fenced off, someone's private land. They began to walk uphill, away from the house, and into thicker, dark green woodland. Then they had to clamber down a bank, and cross the stream via some rather uneven stepping stones. Ella was glad of her grippy walking boots. The ascent up the opposite bank was just as awkward and steep, and at one point Panicos had to offer Ella a helping hand. Then they came to a clearing where there was a little shrine. It looked like a bird box, but bigger and more open, filled with statues, pictures, candles, oil and various other strange little bits and pieces.

'There is a little church just up the hill, a short way over there,' pointed Panicos. 'This is where people leave offerings for the Saint, hoping for miracles and cures.' Ella nodded.

They walked on. The path became quite steep and narrow, as it continued up through, now thick, forest. Finally they reached what seemed like the top of the hill. The forest came to an end, and Ella could see lush, green forest beneath her in most directions. She was looking down on telegraph poles and farm houses, in occasional clearings in the trees. It felt very high up. After they had paused for a few moments, Panicos led on. They were climbing again, this time on a dry path that cut between rocks, and was lined with loose rocks, that slipped a little under foot. This part of the walk required much more concentration. After about half an hour they came out into an open flat plateau, with more, higher rocks on their right, and a vast drop on their left. If Ella had thought they were high up before, they were at least twice as high now. Panicos sat down on a flat rock, and got out two bottles of water for them. It was most welcome after all that climbing, the second half being entirely exposed, in the hot sun. It was very quiet and peaceful, with not a soul around for miles. The view was amazing, and the flat rock ridge they were on seemed to stretch on forever. Ella peered into the distance around them, but could see no signs of any mountain village. After a short break, and half a bottle of water, they got up to continue. They walked along the ridge in the baking sun for a good half hour, maybe more. Ella felt like she was in a barren desert somewhere. Finally the path became rocky again and they had to pick their way downhill, through loose rocks. They came out on something that resembled a rough road. They followed this for a while until they came to a place where a small clump of trees grew, and gave some shade. Large rocks underneath them provided seating. Once again, Panicos got out the water, but this time handed her an apple and a Danish pastry as well. 'You'll need a snack to keep your energy up,' he said. He was right, Ella did feel like eating. After they had finished the snack and the water, Ella popped behind a bush to pee, before they set off again. The road began to turn downwards at a bend, becoming more of a road; but a walk marker post, indicated that the walking trail again turned off onto a wooded path. They followed this uphill, at first gently, but soon it became more of a steep scramble. Ella was getting out of breath, this part of the walk was quite demanding. They came to a small rocky clearing, surrounded by trees. A few tenacious, purple orchids took advantage of the patch of sunlight to thrive. They sat on the rocks, and Panicos got out two more bottles of water. Ella thought it was a good job he knew this walk well, she would not have brought anywhere near enough water. They had been walking for nearly three hours now, most of the time clambering and climbing; Ella ached in places she did not know she had. She was glad of the sun hat too; without it, she might have had sunstroke by now. They carried on, yet further upwards, through woodland. Ella was breathing heavily, and running on sheer determination now. The woodland became shrubs, and the path narrowed so the shrubs were touching them on both sides. The ground was loose shale underfoot. Ella trod very carefully, this was just the sort of place she expected to find snakes. She did not want to surprise one, and get bitten. A last mad upward scramble, and the path emerged suddenly, on a country road, that led off up and downhill. Below her, Ella could see orchards and olive groves. Above her the reddish mountain rocks, looked like they could just as easily be on Mars. Panicos led them across the road to a hidden marker post. A tiny trail disappeared amongst trees and bushes. They struggled through, and the path opened out slightly, and continued uphill. It wound back and forwards on itself, in a series of hairpin bends, that sometimes came out into rocky, open sunlight, and at other times, were under the trees. Finally, they stepped up onto a paved track, with a bench. They sat down, and drank the rest of their bottles of water. Ella could hear traffic in the distance, now and again, but around them all was peaceful. The singing of the birds, was the only sound to be heard.

After a short rest, they walked along the track, slightly uphill to where it joined a main country road. At the edge of the road was a sign saying, country trail to Elonas, underneath which, someone had written in English, Boots required. Ella laughed. They walked along the road, and soon came to Vanoliotanas village. A couple of tavernas sat opportunistically on the outskirts, their major trade, probably being exhausted walkers. The houses of the little village got closer together, and the road became narrower, needing passing places for cars. Finally, there was only room to walk along the narrow streets, and they walked through the maze of houses for a few minutes, before it opened out into a taverna lined square. The village was very pretty. A black robed Priest hurried past them, and disappeared into one of the houses.

'Let's have a cup of tea,' said Ella.

'Good idea,' said Panicos. 'If you hadn't suggested it, I would have.'

Ella had tea, and Panicos had coffee, and she ordered baklavas for both of them, which were served with a refreshing dollop of vanilla ice cream. Ella insisted that it was her turn to pay. After their drinks, they walked around exploring the pretty village for a while, then came out at the main village square. There was a taxi waiting there, and Ella suggested they got a ride back down to the car. Panicos readily agreed, and they climbed in. The ride down, as Panicos had said earlier, took less than fifteen minutes, and they were soon back at his car. As they drove back to Parossa, Ella asked if he saw somewhere she could buy some fish, if he would stop, as she wanted to buy something extra for dinner. It wasn't long before Panicos spotted a place, and Ella jumped out and bought three pieces of swordfish, and some scraps for Bob, while Panicos waited in a no parking zone.

They arrived back at Krittee Street not long after that, and Ella took out her key and used it for the very first time, to let them in. She put the fish in the fridge, and then opened the patio door, and Bob came running over to say hello, rubbing furiously against Ella's legs.

'He has become a domestic cat very quickly,' laughed Panicos.

'I think he was just waiting for the right person to adopt,' said Ella, laughing and stroking Bob. She refreshed his water bowl, and gave him a few biscuits to be going on with until dinner time. 'There is fish,' she told him, 'but not until I start cooking dinner.'

Adonis had told Ella to help herself to everything, and make herself at home, so she poured herself and

Panicos, an ouzo and water each, and they sat on the patio with Bob, to relax.

Ella excused herself to have a quick shower, and change into a dress and flip flops, tying her wet hair back in a ponytail. When she came back down, it was just as Adonis was coming through the door.

'Did you have a good walk?' he asked her.

'It was exhilarating,' she replied, 'and the views were terrific.'

Adonis made himself a drink, and went out on the patio to chat with Adonis. Ella got on with making a Greek salad. She went out to the patio and asked, 'could we light some coals? I wanted to grill some souvlaki and swordfish.'

Adonis broke into a big smile, 'We'll get right on that,' he said, taking Panicos to help.

Ella took some pork chunks, she had put in herbs and spices and olive oil, to marinate the night before, out of the fridge. She carefully filled six skewers with chunks of the meat, then put them on a platter with the swordfish steaks, covered them with a cloth, and took them out to the men. Bob followed her every step of the way.

'I can't remember the last time I had souvlaki cooked at home,' said Adonis.

'Me neither,' grinned Panicos. 'My niece and your daughter, are a very good influence, I think.'

'I hope she decides to stay,' whispered Adonis, in a stage whisper.

Ella smiled and went back to get some of the fish scraps for Bob. The little chap was going crazy with anticipation. She kept some back to give him when they served the food too.

There was a folding table to the side of the patio, and Ella put that up, and brought out some dining chairs to put round it. She wiped it clean, and set it with plates, cutlery, wine and glasses, olive oil, salt and wine vinegar. Then she went back to cut a basket of bread. She made some tzatziki and some hummus, they only took five minutes each, then took the bread, dips and salad out to the table. Adonis had just finished cooking, and the evening air was filled with the wonderful smell of it. Ella refilled Bob's bowl with the remaining fish, and they all sat down to eat.

'This is wonderful,' said Adonis, and Panicos nodded his agreement.

Over the following two days, Adonis took Ella into the shop, and showed her what was what with the till, and the keys, and where he kept the extra stock in the back room. He even left her alone once, while he went out to do some errands, and Ella managed just fine, her Greek, easily able to cope with the requirements of shop interactions. Adonis encouraged her to look around the village and the town, and find out where all the shops were, so she could buy anything she needed. He introduced her to the owner of the hotel with the swimming pool, and he, of course, invited her to swim anytime she wanted. He told her that the pool was open to tourists between 7am and 7pm, but she could come by whenever she liked. Finally it was Thursday, the morning of the party, and Ella's birthday.

Bob woke Ella up, not with a tap to the cheek, but with his nose pressed against her cheek gently, like a little kiss. Ella got up and put on culottes and a t-shirt, with deck shoes, and tied her hair up. She rolled her swimsuit in a towel, she was determined to go to the sea or the pool, and swim this morning. She went downstairs to give Bob some biscuits, but found he already had a full bowl. Adonis was already up, sitting on the patio with a coffee.

'Happy Birthday, ee koree mou (my daughter)' he greeted her.

Ella smiled, 'Thank you, I thought I would go for a swim this morning.'

'Before you do,' said Adonis, 'I have a present for you. Actually it is a joint present from myself and Panicos.'

Adonis led her out to the front garden, where a tarpaulin had been thrown over something.

Ella uncovered the mystery object, and found it to be a shiny new, red motor scooter, with a red helmet on the seat.

'Oh my word, really,' she gasped. 'Thank you so much.'

'If you want to drive to Agios Spiridos or Agios Nikolaus, you can take my car, and I'll use the scooter to go to the shop, but the scooter will get you to the shops, the beach or the pool. It is registered to me for now, because you don't have residency status yet, but if you decide to stay on, that will be easy enough.'

'Since you bring it up, I have been thinking about it a lot, and I have decided I do want to come and live here.'

'But it's your birthday, and here you are giving me a gift,' laughed Adonis, clearly overjoyed.

'I have to go back and get my personal things, arrange the sale of my flat and car, and close accounts, obviously. That will take a few weeks, but I can open a bank account here, and arrange to get the funds from the sale of the property sent here.'

'I will arrange the paperwork, so you can get a birth certificate with me named as your father,' said Adonis. 'I think you will be able to take the name Zacharoulis, if you want?'

'I would love that,' said Ella, 'we will put things in motion as soon as possible.'

'Have you ridden a scooter before?' asked Adonis.

'Many times,' said Ella. 'I often hire one on holiday.' After an emotional hug, Ella drove the scooter off on its inaugural journey to the hotel swimming pool.

After her swim, which was a real joy after so many days without, Ella went back to the house, and made herself breakfast, and made sure Bob had all he needed for the day, then took the scooter in to the shop. She spent the day helping Adonis, who made a point of telling all the regulars, that it was his daughter's birthday, and that she was moving to the island for good. He seemed very happy.

At lunchtime, he phoned his solicitor, and put the paperwork into motion for all that they had discussed. They shut the shop early, and went home to get ready for the party.

Ella went to find Bob, and talk to him. He was asleep on her bed. 'I will be staying out tonight, so don't worry that no one is here. I will leave you two bowls of food and plenty of water, and I'll be back tomorrow morning. I'm sure I will have a treat with me.' Bob purred and went back to sleep, taking advantage of the bed while he had access to it.

Ella showered and then dressed, in her new long white Greek Goddess dress. She put on the gold sandals, and the lace shawl, then plaited her hair, so that when she let it down later, it would be full and curly. She put together a bag with a skirt, sandals and a blouse, as well as her toothbrush and comb, for the next day. She walked downstairs to see if Adonis was ready. He fell backwards into the seat which luckily, was behind him, when he saw her. She rushed over to him, concerned. 'Are you alright o Pateros mou?'

'Yes, I'm fine,' he replied, 'just you looked so much like Elizabett when you walked in, I was shocked for a moment. You look truly beautiful this evening.' Adonis was ready in his suit, so they locked up, leaving Bob on the sheltered patio, and got into Adonis' car for the drive to Agios Spiridos.

'Are you sure you're alright now? Do you want me to drive?' asked Ella.

'No I'm fine now, don't worry, just relax.'

When they arrived in the village it was nearly eight o'clock, so they went straight to Aphrodite's restaurant, leaving their overnight things in the car. Ella let her hair down and it cascaded into curls on her shoulders. The door to the restaurant was shut, and there was a sign on the door in English, 'Closed for a Private Function.' All the blinds were closed over the windows, but light could be seen inside, and there was a low hum of voices. Adonis knocked loudly on the door. Moments later, Carolina opened it and they were ushered inside. The room was full of faces that Ella recognised, but before she had time to note them individually, they all called out, 'na ta eckatosteesetay Ella, Happy Birthday Ella.'

She felt momentarily overwhelmed. She was so accustomed to birthdays with one or two friends, and no family, this seemed somehow alien. Everyone here felt like family in some way. Ella felt a little disembodied, as if she had transported into someone else's life. Then some music started up, Carolina handed her a glass of wine, and everyone started talking to each other, and allowing her to settle in. Carolina whispered to Ella that she looked very beautiful, as she handed her the wine. Carolina also handed her a little box, saying it was just a little gift. Ella looked inside. It contained the prettiest little jewellery set of peach coloured shells, comprising a necklace, bracelet and ear-rings. Realising she had not worn any jewellery, Ella put it all on straight away. 'It looks lovely on you,' said Carolina. 'You look like Aphrodite, who has just risen out of the sea.' Ella thanked her and gave the box to Adonis to put in his pocket for her.

Just then, Panicos came over, hugging her, and telling her Happy Birthday, and how beautiful she looked.

'Thank you so much for buying the scooter with Adonis,' she told him. 'It is such a wonderful gift. The very first thing I did, was drive to the swimming pool this morning. By the way,' she whispered, 'I think Adonis would probably like to announce it later, but I will tell just you now, I have decided to stay on; to come and live on the island.' Panicos gave her a big hug and beamed at her, 'I am so pleased, anipseea mou, you have no idea how pleased.'

Adonis came and steered her away, 'I want you to meet someone,' he said, leading her across the room, to the one man and woman she did not recognise. 'This is Stavros, my son, your brother, and his wife Mia.'

Ella was lost for a moment, and could not quite find any words to say, but Stavros and Mia gave her a hug, which stopped the need for immediate speech. She collected herself.

'How wonderful to meet you. I thought you were in Thessaloniki?' she said.

'We were, but Father telephoned and told us everything, and so we came over to stay for a day or two. Obviously we had to meet you. To find a sister I never knew I had, it's amazing.'

Mia handed her a gift. 'There is no name day for Ella, but your birthday is on the name day for Magos/Maya and also Hermias. Magos was a pagan who was converted to Christianity by Hermias, and later was martyred with him, both becoming saints. Maya was one of the seven sisters or the Pleiades, the mother of Hermes. She was an idealistic, strong woman, who made her dreams come true.' The gift was a statue of Hermes, the winged messenger. Ella listened, and thought it all very appropriate to her own situation. 'Thank you so much, such a thoughtful gift.'

The young Adonis came over and stood beside his mother and father. 'You have met my son already, I think?' asked Stavros.

'Yes, but he didn't know who I was then,' said Ella.

'It is wonderful to have an aunt suddenly,' said Adonis, giving her a strange pottery cup. 'I made this, it is called a Justice Cup. Thikia Koupa. It spills the liquid if you over fill it, beyond the line, so you can only drink a fair amount. It stopped people from being greedy at meetings where the cup was shared. It is also sometimes known as the Pythagorean Cup or the Tantalus Cup. Karoovmeena yenethlia.' (Happy Birthday)

'Thank you so much, it's lovely, you are very talented.'

Carolina took Ella over to a table by the door, 'You can put your gifts on here, to keep them safe.'

Ella carefully put down the statue and the pottery cup. Alongside the table, was a strange lumpy object, with a sheet thrown over it. Yiorgos and Christos hurried over to Ella. 'We made you this,' they said. 'Well really, it's for Bob,' they uncovered a large cat scratch post with sleeping areas, and dangly toys. The toys were pine cones on string, and sharks purse and cuttlefish dangling and fixed in places.

'Oh how wonderful,' said Ella, 'he'll love that. He really is very happy and domesticated now. I hope you are not missing him too much?'

'Oh don't worry about that,' said Yiorgos, 'by the end of the summer, there will be a new 'hotel' cat, there always is. No position goes unfilled for long.'

They laughed.

'You look wonderful tonight,' said Christos, 'May I have a dance with you later on?'

'Of course,' said Ella, 'it would be my pleasure. Though Adonis and Panicos will be first I expect.' Just then Allessandro and Ireni came over and greeted her. 'Carolina got in touch with us, and told us you had found your father. We are so pleased. Of course we couldn't miss your birthday, so we brought the boat over. Mikhali and Yermanos came too, they will play some music for you later. Nansia made these for you.' Ireni handed Ella two beautifully painted stones. One depicted Demeter's restaurant with its beautiful garden, and the other depicted Despinas Square with the dolphin fountain.

'Oh thank you, they are so lovely. She really is very talented.' Ella displayed the stones on the gift table where everyone could see them. Mikhali and Yermanos came over to say hello. 'We have written a song for you, but you will have to wait until a bit later on to hear it.'

People took turns coming over to Ella with gifts and congratulations, each expressing their pleasure that she had successfully completed her quest. The gifts were all very thoughtful, and personal.

Nikos had brought one of his drawings of Liz, which he had framed. Adonis was very pleased to see Nikos and Heleni again too. Heleni had copied out a book of the poetry she had written that summer, back in '61. Nikki and Athena had brought a little icon of

Saint Spiridon. Dimitris had made a montage of photos of Liz and her friends, and put them in a large frame. Panicos had burnt a CD of himself playing the flute, like he used to in the old days. Bani and Haroula had brought a bottle of their special tsipouro. Andreas had brought a little model of a fishing boat in a bottle. Stavros from the Limonaki café, had brought a pink conch seashell. Yiannis Zefiros had brought a pretty little handcrafted, silver ring.

After everyone had had a chance to greet Ella personally, and Adonis had had some time to catch up with old friends, Carolina went over to an area by the bar, where Mikhali and Yermanos had set up their microphones. She took a microphone and said, 'In a few minutes there will be meze and you can all help yourselves, but first I think Ella wants to speak to you.'

Ella went up to the microphone; everyone clapped and yelled 'oppa.' Oppa is a word Greeks call in celebration of life, exuberance, and contentment of having enough, and the general joy of living.

'I want to thank you all for this wonderful party, especially Carolina for hosting and organising it,' she began, pausing as everyone shouted 'bravo.'

'I would also like to thank each and every one of you, for your help in finding my father. You have been amazing, and I treasure you all. And thank you for all the lovely gifts. And now, just before we eat and dance, I think Adonis wants to say a few words.'

Ella moved away from the microphone, and Adonis took her place.

'I want to thank you all for helping my Ella to find me. Just over a week ago, I didn't even know I had a daughter, I thought I only had my wonderful son, Stavros. But now I find I have a wonderful daughter too, and it has made me so happy. Of course I am sad for the way things turned out with Elizabett, and it would have been wonderful if it had been different, but life has a way of playing out the way God wants it to, and God, in his wisdom, has decided to bring Ella to me now. And one more thing I want to share with you; Ella, in her wisdom, has decided to stay here on the island, to come and live on Aegos, and to be called Ella Zacharoulis.' Everyone cheered, for quite a long time. Ella wiped away a tear and hugged Adonis.

Meanwhile, waiters had been filling several tables with meze, and as soon as the noise died down, Carolina called, 'As fannay, let's eat.'

People gathered plates of meze, and sat at tables round the edge of the room, as Greek music played on the stereo. Drinks were served at the bar.

After most people had done eating, for the time being at least, Mikhali and Yermanos went up to the microphones, and got out their bouzouki and guitar. 'This is a song we wrote for Ella,' they said beginning to play and sing. Ella did not catch all the words, but the chorus consisted of repeated lines of 'Ela Ella,' 'Come here Ella,' a pun on her name. They beckoned her up to dance, and Adonis and Panicos went with her, linking arms at the shoulders to dance in unison. At the next chorus, lots of others joined them, and the dancing continued into the night. When Mikhali and Yermanos had played for long enough, they stopped for a break, and Carolina put a CD on, once more. Although it was Greek Euro pop, it had lots of slow songs, and Ella danced first with Christos, then Andreas. As soon as they had finished Dimitris asked her to dance, and he was followed by Mikhali and then Yermanos. Finally she got a chance to sit down for five minutes. Carolina brought her over a tsipouro, and a glass of iced water. Both were just what she needed.

'I think you have quite a collection of suitors,' said Carolina, smiling.

Ella blushed. 'They are all very nice men,' she said.

'I know Andreas has quite the soft spot for you,' said Carolina.

'When I have tied up my affairs in England, and return here for good, perhaps it will be time for me to start dating,' said Ella. 'I mean, obviously I dated plenty of people in England, but I never found one who was right for me.'

'You were waiting for your Greek husband,' laughed Carolina.

When the night was finally over, and Ella fell happily onto her bed at the Zeus hotel, she thought about Carolina's words. She really did feel ready to start looking for her Mr Right, and here on Aegos, would surely be the place to find him. She also thought that when she had finished up in England, and moved herself back here permanently, her next quest would be to find Panicos' daughter, and somehow reunite them. It was the very least she could do for her wonderful Uncle. She fell asleep, blissfully happy, and peaceful.

Follow Ella's journey further, in the second in the 'Sun' series, 'Return to Aegos,' coming soon.

I have been asked where Aegos and Kios are in Greece. They are imaginary Greek islands, but based on real places, which can be found in Corfu, Kos, Rhodes (The cover picture is Monolithos on Rhodes), Crete, Samos and Cyprus.

If you are interested in specific sites and their locations, perhaps with a view to visiting them, you can contact me via my website at www.mayjpanayi.wix.com/books via the top tab 'Bio' and the drop down 'Contact.' I will answer e-mails.